MW00619754

THE CASTLE

ROBERT BROOMALL

Copyright ©2022 by Robert Broomall
All Rights Reserved

A Bluestone Media Publication

ISBN 978-1-7326275-9-8

Cover design by bespokebookcovers.com

This is a work of fiction. Any resemblance to actual persons, living or dead, is purely coincidental.

Books by Robert Broomall

A Case of Murdrum
California Kingdoms
Texas Kingdoms
The Lawmen
The Bank Robber
Dead Man's Crossing (Jake Moran 1)
Dead Man's Town (Jake Moran 2)
Dead Man's Canyon (Jake Moran 3)
Death's Head, A Soldier with Richard the Lionheart
The Red King, A Soldier with Richard the Lionheart, II
Death and Glory, A Soldier with Richard the Lionheart, III
K Company (K Company 1)
Conroy's First Command (K Company 2)
The Dispatch Rider (K Company 3)
Murder in the Seventh Cavalry
Scalp Hunters (Cole Taggart 1)
Paradise Mountain (Cole Taggart 2)
Wild Bill and the Dinosaur Hunters

For James, Heather, Diane,

Claire and David

Chapter 1

TRENTSHIRE, ENGLAND

1106 A.D.

"What's that?"

Wada pointed off to his right, where the Upper Eal ran grey in the chill autumn drizzle.

Miles peered in the direction that Wada was pointing. He saw a distant village. Near the village was a hill, and on the hill was a squarish stone building under construction. At the bottom of the hill were buildings surrounded by a wooden palisade. Miles frowned. "Looks like someone's building a castle."

He turned to Lady Blanche. "I didn't know there were any castles in this part of Trentshire."

Blanche's gaze was directed toward the buidling as well. "There aren't supposed to be."

"Do you think it's illegal?" he asked her.

Blanche shrugged. “It could be the king has granted someone a charter to build, and we haven’t heard about it. It could even be a royal castle. Either way, they’re our neighbors, more or less, so I expect we’ll find out soon enough.”

They rode on, huddled in their cloaks: Miles Edwulfson, Lady Blanche, Blanche’s maid Millicent, and Wada, leading a trio of sumpter horses carrying the party’s belongings.

Blanche was tall and olive complexioned. She had been born in Normandy, but looked Spanish. She rode astride her favorite white palfrey. She wore a red dress with a blue bliaut and a heavy white cloak and hood. Miles was a big man with a shock of blond hair. At his belt was a short sword, or scramasax. On his saddle was a war axe. His horse and saddle, as well as his clothing, had belonged to his former lord, Geoffrey of Ravenswell. Geoffrey had been executed for killing his father, the earl of Trent, and Ravenswell’s steward had given Miles some of Geoffrey’s things—all of Miles’s possessions having been lost when his neighbors burned his house.

Blanche, the earl of Trent’s widow, was on her way to take possession of two manors bestowed upon her by her late husband as a marriage gift. Miles was to be her steward. Blanche had petitioned King Henry to be allowed to take up the manors without remarrying, the petition accompanied by a large sum of money. The king and his chief nobles were in Normandy, and it had been early October before permission had been granted, with the proviso that Blanche could not remarry without the king’s consent.

At forty, Miles was reckoned old, but he looked forward to his new life. He'd caused a lot of hard feelings in Ravenswell over the past months, and though he'd ultimately been proved correct, he'd felt it was time to be moving on from the only home he'd ever known. When Blanche had offered him the post as her steward, he'd accepted. Being steward of two manors would be a big job, a job that was new to him, but he felt confident he could handle it.

The hardest part had been leaving his dog Chieftain at Ravenswell. Miles had wanted to bring the dog, but Chieftain was getting on in years. Miles's son Garth needed a dog, and Garth's children would have been heartbroken to lose Chieftain. Miles felt like he'd left a part of himself behind, which in a sense he had. Chieftain had barked and howled when Miles rose off. He had to be tied up and nearly broke the restraints. Miles found a tear in his eye as he remembered, and he sniffed and wiped the tear away.

The party left the fields and entered a gloomy wood. Everything dripped; the path was little more than a series of puddles. "More trees," Millicent sighed, looking around. She was a few years younger than Blanche, but far more world weary. "Trees are boring. England is boring. I wish you'd brought some musicians, my lady, to entertain us while we ride."

Blanche was used to Millicent's complaints. "Anything else you'd like? Jugglers? A trained bear, perhaps?"

"Just musicians," Millicent grumped. "Jugglers are boring. So are bears."

Miles and Blanche eased ahead of the others. "Any idea how much farther to Redhill?" Miles asked her. Redhill, the larger of Blanche's two manors, would be their first stop. They would visit the second manor, Fairleigh, later.

"Baron Hugo was vague," Blanche told him. "He's never been to Redhill, thinks it's about a half-day's ride."

"We should be there soon, then."

It was a two-day journey from St. Mary's Lodge, where Blanche had been staying since her husband's death, to her new estates. The party had stayed last night at a manor belonging to a baron named Hugo, Blanche sleeping at the upper end of the hall, Miles and the others at the lower end with the servants. Blanche said, "Hugo warned us to be on the lookout for robbers. Apparently they're active in this area."

Miles nodded and stretched in the saddle. He was getting used to riding. It would be necessary if he was to oversee the two manors, which were some distance apart. He looked at the trees, their remaining leaves forlorn in the rain. "You know nothing about either manor?"

"All I know is that Redhill is valued at two knights' fees, and Fairleigh at one." This meant that Redhill was required to provide two fully equipped knights, as well as the requisite number of footmen and hangers on, when requested to do so by its suzerain, the earl. Blanche went on. "Thibault was always in need of soldiers, and he couldn't wait for them to come from England, and when they did come they could only stay for forty days, so he had the manors send money for him to hire mercenaries instead. Redhill's steward is named Richalm, and he's supposed to be quite good. Fairleigh's steward is named Evrard, I believe."

Miles smirked. "Both French, of course?"

Blanche arched her brow in that imperious way she had. "Of course."

"Do you wish Earl Thibault had given you estates in France instead of England?"

"No," she said. "Normandy is in a constant state of anarchy. Every noble is at war with his neighbors there. I just want to be left in peace and quiet."

She looked back to make sure the others weren't listening. Millicent was consumed in rainy misery, and Wada, with the sumpter horses, was too far back to hear. Blanche lowered her voice. "Would you have come with me if the estates were in Normandy?"

"Do you even have to ask that question?" Miles said.

She gave him an impish grin that went unnoticed by Wada and Millicent. "I just wanted to make certain."

He gave her his own grin in return. "It might have been fun, though. You know I like exploring."

"I know you like exploring my body," she said. "You've found places I didn't even know I had."

"Just doing my duty, my lady."

"You'll keep doing it, too, if you know what's good for you."

"Aye, my lady. Duty can be most rewarding."

Miles and Blanche had first made love on the way back from Thor's Seat, after Lord Geoffrey had been revealed as the earl's killer, and they'd been at it ever since, whenever they could get off by themselves. Miles had loved his wife,

Alice, but this kind of love was different. This was all-encompassing, a vortex of emotion and sexual pleasure that Miles had never dreamed possible. It was also dangerous. Both he and Blanche could pay a high price for what they were doing. Miles with his head, because commoners were forbidden to have sexual relations with nobles, and Blanche with the loss of her new-found freedom.

The path ran along a steep hill. Mist obscured the trees. A prickly feeling ran up Miles's back, and he remembered Baron Hugo's warning about robbers. He raised a hand and the party halted.

Miles listened intently, turning his head slowly and watching the trees, especially on the uphill side, from whence any attack was likely to come.

At last he motioned the party forward again. They rounded a bend and came upon a young woman. The woman wore a much-patched cloak and hood. She was tall, attractive, and sturdily built. Red hair peeked from beneath her hood. She looked askance at the party and reached under her cloak, presumably for a dagger.

Miles turned to Wada. "Keep a lookout."

Wada nodded, his eyes searching the wet forest. Wada was a huge fellow, with straw-like hair and beard. He had befriended Miles's son Aelred in prison, and his face bore scars from a near-fatal beating he had received because of that, a beating from which Blanche had saved him at some danger to herself.

"What are you doing out here by yourself?" Miles asked the young woman.

"Lookin' for strayed pigs," she said. There was a note of insolence in her voice, and her eyes darted from one rider to another. "Ain't seen none, have you?"

"No," Miles said, "we haven't. Aren't you worried about robbers? We've been told they're numerous hereabouts."

"Robbers ain't like to harm me, are they? What good would I be to them? Next penny I see'll be me first." She tapped the hilt of her dagger beneath her cloak. " 'Sides, I'm handy with this."

Blanche spoke up. "Do you know the manor of Redhill?"

The woman lowered her eyes, as was proper for someone of her status when talking to a noblewoman. "I do, my lady."

"Are we close to it?"

"Aye, my lady, you are." She pointed behind her. "Just stay on this path."

"The boundary is marked?"

The young woman grinned, revealing white teeth. "Oh, it's marked all right. You can't miss it."

"Thank you," Blanche said.

"A pleasure, my lady." There was that hint of insolence again.

Blanche reached in her purse and gave the red-haired young woman a penny. The woman bowed in appreciation, and the party rode on.

"Did you think there was anything strange about that girl?" Miles asked Blanche.

"Like what?"

"She's out here by herself, for one thing."

Blanche shrugged. "I looked for strayed pigs often enough as a child. Did it by myself, as well, in all weathers.

You do what you must when you're poor." Blanche had been born a villein, though no one but Miles knew that.

Miles looked back at the girl, who was heading down the hill through the trees, flipping the penny in the air.

They continued riding, heads down, the damp biting through their cloaks and woolen clothes. Then they stopped.

Ahead of them, dangling from a tree branch, was the body of a man. The man might have been in his mid-30s, it was hard to say. His clothes had rotted, and most of his flesh had been stripped away by birds.

Blanche curbed her horse, which shied at the smell.

"Odd choice of boundary markers," Wada cracked. "Maybe it's some kind of local custom."

Miles said, "That girl was right when she said we couldn't miss it."

"Ooh, that's disgusting," Milli said, and she averted her eyes from the sight. "I hate this country. I hate it."

Blanche was furious. "Who dares to hang men on my land?" She lashed her riding crop across her horse's flank and galloped ahead. The others followed.

Chapter 2

They rode down the path, Blanche in the lead, Wada and the pack horses bringing up the rear. Not far past the hanged man, the woodland became a hive of activity, and Blanche impatiently slowed down because of the traffic on the path.

In one part of the woods, men knocked acorns from oak branches, and pigs fed on them in the drizzle. In another, men gathered firewood. The windfall—branches blown from trees by the wind—was long gone, so the men took branches from the trees, as was their right. Some stood on ladders to do so, balancing precariously with their sharp instruments. Other men bundled the branches into fagots and loaded them onto carts. In yet another part of the wood, a group of men sawed long branches from alders and elms, to be used as poles for building.

The woods ended, and they picked up their pace again, crossing a meadow dotted with sheep, watched over by a herdsman and his dog. Past the meadow, they came to the fields. Redhill was a large manor, with three fields. One field lay fallow. In another, men sowed winter wheat and rye, followed by boys trying to drive off the pigeons and crows that swarmed around them and feasted on the seed. The boys in turn were followed by men and women with horse-drawn harrows, spreading dirt to cover the precious seed. Cattle grazed on stubble in the third field, which had been harvested in August. A sturdy blonde girl watered the cattle using buckets suspended from a yoke on her shoulders.

The village and mill lay near a stream, with the palisaded manor house beyond. Heads turned as the party rode past. They slowed again as they clattered across the bridge and entered the village. Hearth smoke rose from the houses in the damp chill, the smoke darker and thicker from a few homes that must be burning coal. Stray pigs and a few geese wandered the street.

"Look out," Miles called, though they could all see the giant pothole in the street. They skirted it, Wada being careful with the sumpter horses.

"Why hasn't this been fixed?" Miles said.

Wada said, "Cart gets its wheels in that, it's going to tip over. Somebody could get killed."

"Or someone could fall in and break a leg," Miles added. "Maybe even drown in there, if he was drunk and he fell in face first."

Water-logged ditches lined the street. Miles shook his head. "These ditches need to be drained. Much more rain, and the street will flood."

A group of boys was vaulting one of the ditches, using a pole to propel themselves across it. With a start, Miles realized that one of the boys was actually a girl, lithe and blonde. She stopped to watch the party as they rode by.

"Never had girls doin' that in my day," Wada muttered.

"Modern times, my friend," Miles said. "Modern times."

Millicent harrumphed with disapproval.

Normally, a noblewoman and her retinue would have attracted a crowd—cheeky boys shouting questions, beggars seeking coin, curious men and women. Not now. Just stares. Some of the houses were in disrepair. Chunks were missing from walls. Gates hung askew. Fences wanted mending.

"Look," Blanche said.

Set back from the street, one house leaned perilously forward, kept from falling over only by a log propped against its wall.

Miles said, "This estate doesn't seem to be very well run. I thought you said this Richalm was a good steward."

"That's what I was told," Blanche replied.

"I think he'll need a talking to."

In the tofts, men who were too old to be in the woods or the fields mended harness and other equipment. A blacksmith's metallic hammering could be heard; so could the endless grind of the water mill. The horses' hooves squelched in the mud and puddles.

Ahead of them a small crowd gathered round a cottage. The cottage door was open, with two hulking baliffs standing guard beside it. Inside, a man whacked a stoop-shouldered old woman across the shoulders with a steward's white rod of office. "Two coppers, *grand-mère*," the man said with a French accent.

The old woman said, "You can't—"

"Yes, I can. I know you have the money. Now give it over and be thankful the baron and I don't ask for more."

White-haired and frail, the woman cringed. As she did, a grey-bearded man who might have been her son stepped from the crowd. “Leave her alone!”

The steward turned, pointing the white rod. “Stay out of this, Oli, or I’ll come to your house next.”

The bailiffs moved toward the man, who edged back. The other villagers watched sullenly, like this was something they saw far too often.

The steward turned back to the old woman. “Now give us the—”

“I told you, I don’t have anything,” she cried. “If my husband was still alive—”

“If your husband was still alive, I’d hang him.” The steward snarled and shoved the old woman aside. She fell hard against the table and cried out. To the bailiffs, the steward said, “Search the house. Tear it down if you have to.”

“No!” The old woman was in tears.

Blanche forced her white horse through the crowd, followed by Miles. “What’s going on here?” Blanche said.

The steward turned. He was a beefy fellow, his sandy hair cut short. He had a flat face, toad like, with small, close-set eyes, and an arrogant jut to his chin. Pock marks dotted his cheeks and forehead. Tapping the white rod in his hand, he looked Blanche up and down, noting her expensive clothes and saddle harness. “Begging your pardon, my lady, but what business is that of yours?”

Blanche’s dark, almond-shaped eyes widened. She drew herself up. “It is my business, sirrah, because I am Blanche of Trent, and this is my manor.”

"Your manor?" The steward raised his brows in amusement. "*Your* manor? You're a woman."

"How astute of you. Now what has this woman done?"

The steward held up a hand. "See here. Anybody can ride up and say they're lord of the manor. That don't make 'em—"

"I have the charters. I'd show them to you, but I doubt you can read. Are you the steward?"

"That's right."

Blanche spoke slowly. "You will address me as 'my lady,' or I'll have that tongue cut out of your head. Do you understand?"

The man seemed taken aback by her intensity.

"Do you?" Blanche demanded.

"Yes. My lady."

"Are you Richalm?

"Richalm?" The man sneered, some of his insolence returning, and his two bailiffs laughed. "No, *my lady*. I'm Joubert."

"What happened to Richalm?" Blanche said.

"The baron deposed him, my lady. Put me here in his stead."

Blanche frowned. "Baron? What baron?"

"Why, Baron Aimerie, of course."

Blanche shared a look with Miles, then she said, "Who is this Baron Aimerie, and by what right does he replace staff on my estate?"

Joubert shrugged. "The baron does as he pleases. Richalm refused to pay the baron's levies. And he wouldn't supply men for—"

“Levies? This manor pays levy to no one save the earl of Trent. Where is Richalm now?”

Joubert smiled. “I hanged him.”

Chapter 3

Blanche stared. "You what?"

"I hanged him," Joubert said. "You might have passed him on your way in. We kept him around for a while after he was deposed, but he caused too much trouble, so . . ." He shrugged, as though hanging men was an everyday occurrence, scarcely worth mentioning.

Blanche's jaw set. "I have the right of high justice on this manor. Not you, and certainly not this Baron Whatever."

"That's as may be, my lady," said Joubert. "You'll need to take that up with Lord Aimerie." He turned back to the old woman. "Now, if you'll excuse me, I have to—"

"No, you don't. You are no longer steward here. You and your men are to vacate the manor grounds at once."

Joubert's insolent demeanor turned threatening. His two bailiffs formed behind him. "See here, you can't—"

There was a rasping sound as Miles drew his short sword from its sheath. "You heard the lady. Clear out."

Beside Miles, Wada brandished a stout iron bar.

"And who might you be?" Joubert asked Miles.

"Miles Edwulfson, Lady Blanche's steward. This is Wada, my beadle. Now do what the lady said and leave, or you'll find yourself decorating a tree next to Richalm."

Joubert snorted at Miles in derision. "You're English. What kind of lord puts an Englishman in charge of—"

Wada whacked the iron bar in the palm of his hand. "I don't think he understands what the word 'now' means." Wada had once broken a man's head with a blow from his fist; there was no telling what damage he might do with an iron bar.

Joubert's face went red. "The baron won't like this," he warned Blanche.

"I don't care what he likes," Blanche said. "Be on your way."

Joubert indicated the manor house. "We'll have to get our belongings first."

"No," Miles said. "Leave them."

Joubert protested. "We can't—"

"They'll be distributed to the poor," Blanche assured him with a smile. "Who will be most grateful, I'm certain."

Breathing hard, Joubert hesitated. Then he beckoned his men.

"Leave your rod of office, as well," Miles told him.

Joubert tossed the white rod to the ground. He and his men started up the village street, while the villagers jeered at them. Some threw rocks or chunks of mud. Over his shoulder, Joubert cried, "You've not heard the last of this."

Chapter 4

Joubert and his bailiffs disappeared down the lane, followed at a distance by a pack of village boys, hurling insults and occasional rocks.

The white-haired old woman reached out and grasped Blanche's hand in both of hers. Touching a noble was a flogging offence on many manors, but the old woman didn't seem to care. "Thank you, my lady," she said. "My name is Winchelsey, and that's the best thing that's happened around here in my lifetime, and I'm old enough to remember when a Dane sat on the throne of England."

Blanche seemed genuinely touched. "Why, thank you, Winchelsey," she said, surprising the old woman, and everyone around her, by her use of English. Most of them had never heard a lord speak English.

A barrel-chested man with wooly hair and a greying beard hurried up. "Got here as soon as I could," he said in a breathless, booming voice. "I was helping with the firewood." He took Winchelsey's hand. "Are you all right, sister? The nerve of Joubert."

"I'm fine," Winchelsey said, patting the man's hand in return.

The newcomer turned to Blanche and bowed. It was not the awkward bow of a peasant, but the practiced bow of a man who had learned manners somewhere. "I'm Father Albinus, my lady." He indicated another man, tall and thin. "This is my deacon, Tostig."

Albinus held Blanche's reins while she dismounted. Miles and the others dismounted as well. Tostig held Millicent's reins, though she didn't thank, or even acknowledge, him.

Father Albinus went on. "You'll be Lady Blanche, of course. We'd heard you'd been given the manor back when you were married. Didn't think we'd ever see you here in person."

"I've been living in Normandy," Blanche said. "I've decided to remain in England now that my husband is dead."

"Always heard good things about Earl Thibualt," said Albinus.

"He was a good man," Blanche said.

A wiry, middle-aged fellow spoke up. He had brown teeth, those that were still there, and his hands were gnarled from a lifetime of hard work. His coarse overtunic was mended and stained, and some of the scallops that decorated the edge of his blue cowl, the hood of which was pulled up against the drizzle, were missing. "Most of the estates hereabouts, their lords stay in France. Stewards run 'em. It's one of the things what makes it hard for 'em to stand up to Aimerie."

A woman held out a cup to Blanche. "Ale, my lady?"

Father Albinus said, "Now Bertha, Lady Blanche is a noble. She doesn't drink ale, she—"

"Thank you," Blanche told the woman named Bertha. She accepted the cup and sipped. "It's excellent." She turned to Miles and smiled. "Takes me back."

Bertha, who was hearty and red cheeked, and the other villagers appeared pleased. Ale was foisted on Miles and Wada, as well, and they drank gratefully. Millicent was offered a cup and she recoiled as though she were staring at a bowl of poison. "Don't you have wine?" she said.

The villagers looked at one another. "Wine?" said Father Albinus. "No. No wine here. Likely there's some up at the manor house."

Milli started to pout, but Blanche changed the subject before Milli could get on one of her rants. "Why was Joubert harrassing you?" she asked Winchelsey. She pulled over a stool from in front of the house. "Here, sit."

Aided by Blanche and Father Albinus, Winchelsey lowered herself onto the stool. "He's convinced I have money, my lady," she said. "Thinks I have pot of it hidden away somewheres. Where would I get money, I ask you? They take everything from us. You couldn't save even if you wanted to."

" 'They'?" Blanche said.

"Joubert and the baron," said the old woman.

The wiry man added, "When they're not laying some new tallage on us, they're pulling men, and women, from the fields to work on Aimerie's castle."

Blanche and Miles exchanged a look. "So that new castle belongs to this Aimerie fellow?" Blanche said.

"It does," said the wiry man. "Hard for us to get any work done here 'cause of that damned thing—pardon the language. That's why the manor looks the way it does."

"Well, there will be no more tallages, and no more work on the castle," Blanche told them.

Another man spoke up. "And Joubert, he uses our daughters and wives like they was whores. Takes 'em as he pleases. Aimerie, too, when he's around, him and his son both."

"There will be no more of that, either," Blanche said.

A tall, middle-aged woman sounded doubtful. "Richalm tried to stop it, my lady, and they hanged him."

Blanche's voice grew steely. "I'm not Richalm." She finished her ale and returned the cup to Bertha.

The excitement of Lady Blanche's arrival and Joubert's dismissal had brought most of the workers from the woods and fields. The gathering seemed to have turned into an informal hallmote, or manor court, as the French called it, so Miles decided to take advantage of the situation, despite the weather. He picked up the white rod from where Joubert had thrown it and wiped off the mud. "Who is reeve here?"

The wiry man stepped forward. "I am. Hamo, by name."

With both hands, Miles held out the white rod. "Hamo, I'm appointing you temporary steward of the manor. If you'll take the job."

Hamo's eyes widened in surprise. Becoming steward was a big promotion, even bigger for an Englishman, for there were few English stewards about.

Miles added, "Do well, and I'll make the position permanent. You'll have lodging at the manor house and a percentage of the year's profits."

If the position became permanent, Hamo would become a free man, clear of work on the lord's fields. He rubbed his grizzled chin and looked at Blanche. "I dunno. I mean, I'm grateful and all, but beggin' your pardon for bein' honest, God, He didn't mean for women to be lords. Goes again' nature, it does."

Blanche seemed unfazed by Hamo's words; it was a common enough reaction.

"It's your decision," Miles told him.

Hamo thought. "All right, I'll do it. Reckon as how somebody has to." He accepted the rod. "I'll stay here, in my own house, though, instead of up at the manor. Leastways, for now."

"That's fine." Miles went on. "I'm steward for both Redhill and Fairleigh, so I won't be here all the time."

A rangy fellow with dark, curly hair spoke up. "Fairleigh? Heard there's been some trouble there."

"Trouble?" said Blanche. "What kind of trouble?"

"Not sure, my lady. Just somethin' I heard."

Miles and Blanche shared a glance. To Hamo, Miles said, "I won't be looking over your shoulder, but I'll keep general track of what's going on. I can read a tally stick, just so you know, and I'll expect you to be honest."

"Fair enough," said Hamo.

"You can begin with that huge hole in the main street. Then the fields and ditches need draining, and there's a house falling over—"

Hamo spread his hands helplessly. "I know about all that. Told you, men here been working on that castle. Ain't had time for nothing else. You get that part took care of, and we'll do the rest."

"It's been taken care of," Miles said. "You heard Lady Blanche—there'll be no more work on the castle." He turned to the crowd. "Where's the hayward?"

A red-haired man, about a decade younger than Hamo, raised his hand. "Simon."

"Simon, you'll be reeve. All other positions on the estate will be bumped up a notch, at least until next year's elections. Hamo can see to that. I'll get with you and Hamo about what's planted, and the value, and any issues you might have soon."

Blanche spoke to the priest. "Father . . . Albinus, wasn't it? . . . forgive me for asking, but can you read?"

"I can, my lady," said Father Albinus proudly.

"When I've unpacked, I'll send you the charters giving me possession of the estate, and you can confirm them."

"Yes, my lady," Albinus said. "And I keep the manor rolls and the customals, showing what everyone owes in rent and work, plus who owns which strips in the fields. Also, Richalm didn't keep a priest at the manor house, nor did Joubert, so I guess I'm your chaplain. At least till you decide to—"

"That arrangement will be fine for now," Blanche told him.

"Thank you, my lady."

"How did the manor come by its name?" Miles asked Albinus. "Redhill?"

"Dunno," Albinus said. "Been called that forever. Comes from the Old Ones." Like many, he crossed himself at any mention of the Old Ones. "I expect there was a deed of blood done here, turned that rise where the manor house stands red. A battle maybe. Or maybe . . ."

"Maybe what?" Blanche said.

"Sacrifice of some kind? Hard to know with the Old Ones."

Miles said, "What about the recent lords?"

Albinus scratched his beard. "Tell the truth, lords have come and gone so quick in the last fifty years, it's hard to remember half of 'em. There's been English lords, and Danish lords, mixed-blood lords, then Danes again, then English. You'll think it's funny, but the best lord we had in my lifetime was Odo, the Frenchman. He took an interest in the manor, tried to build it up, not just use it to recruit soldiers or fill his purse. Stayed the longest, too. He died without issue; that's when the manor reverted to the earl."

Miles nodded. He addressed the crowd. "There's a lot to be done here, as I'm sure you know. Winter's coming on, so you'll need to work hard. As Lady Blanche said, there will be no more unnecessary taxes or levies, and no one will be drafted to work on Baron Aimerie's castle. I'll speak to all of you individually at some point, and I look forward to working with you."

Simon, the new reeve, sniffled and rubbed his nose on an already wet sleeve. "Miles Edwulfson. You're pledge for Guildford Hundred, ain't you?"

"I was," Miles said. He had been removed from that position by the hundred leadership.

"You were a soldier, too," said the dark-haired fellow. "Good one, so I heard."

"That was a long time ago. I served with Lady Blanche's husband."

Simon went on. "Your father was a thegn, wasn't he?"

"Thegn of Ravenswell," said Winchelsey from her stool, "near Badford. And his grandad was a famous hero."

Involuntarily, Miles glanced at the large, niello-inlaid ring on his finger, at the representation of a lion on its seal. Miles had no idea how accurate the representation was, because he had no idea what a lion looked like. "Like I said, it was a long time ago. I'm Lady Blanche's steward now, and that's what matters."

A woman pointed to the fields. "Beggin' your pardon, my lady, and sorry to be so direct, but what are we to do about Baron Aimerie's pigeons? He keeps a dovecote here, and the buggers eat our seed faster'n we can sow it."

Blanche smiled. "Then I should think pigeon pies are in order."

The villagers laughed and raised a cheer. Blanche raised a hand. "Save a few of the pigeons for me, if you don't mind."

"We will, my lady. And we'll bring you some o' the pies."

Blanche nodded graciously. "That would be lovely." She turned to Miles and the others. "We should get to the manor house. There will be much to do before it gets dark."

They mounted and rode up the wet street, the villagers chattering excitedly behind them. Hamo, Simon, and Father Albinus were already deep in conversation, motioning other men to join them.

Chapter 5

The dreary day faded into an even drearier dusk. Vespers hadn't rung yet, and, given the state of the light, Miles had no idea how Father Albinus would be able to determine when to ring it. Like as not, he would just guess.

As they approached the manor house, Miles squinted at the home farm and pointed to some neatly aligned rows of low, bush-like plants. "What are those?"

Blanche peered, then laughed. "Those are grapes. It's a vineyard. Sweet Mary's milk, they're trying to make wine here."

Miles frowned. "I don't know anything about grapes and wine, and as steward I'll need to—"

"They must have someone knowledgeable in charge," Blanche said. "Let him run the operation. My guess is, it's too wet for grapes here. Probably too cold, as well. Still, we'll give it a go, since they've already started."

The party rode through the palisaded gate onto the manor house grounds. "No wonder the village is in such disrepair," Blanche said. "It looks like Joubert spent all the manor's money here."

The timbered hall appeared new, or nearly so. So did a lot of the other buildings. They halted in front of the hall. Light glowed from the hall's open door through the mist. Word of their coming must have preceded them from the village, because servants and underlings were waiting. Grooms took the horses and led them to the stables. A well-dressed man with ribbons in his beard came forward, bowing elaborately. He smelled of perfume. "Lady Blanche?" he asked in a thick Norman accent.

"That's right," she said.

"I am Marcel, the chamberlain."

Blanche raised her brow in amusement. "Joubert had a chamberlain? Rather fancy for the steward of a back-country manor." Chamberlains were usually found only in the homes of great nobles.

Marcel spread his hands, which were adorned with rings. "It is the way Lord Joubert wished it."

"Joubert is no lord," Blanche corrected, "and I have no need of a chamberlain. Millicent, my lady's maid, will run the household."

Marcel looked puzzled. "Then what will I . . .?"

"You won't," Blanche told him. "You're dismissed."

"Dismissed?" Marcel said.

"Yes. You're conversant with the word, aren't you?"

"Well . . . yes, my lady."

"Excellent, because it now applies to you. All bailiffs not born on the manor are to leave as well."

"You can't—"

Blanche's dark eyes flashed. "What did you say?"

"Well, of course you can, I didn't mean that. But . . . but where are we to go?"

"That's of no concern to me. If you hurry, you may be able to reach Baron Aimerie's castle before full dark. After that, it's up to you."

Marcel drew himself up. "Begging your pardon, Lady Blanche, but I don't think you fully grasp the situation here. Without me and the bailiffs, you will have no Normans on your staff. How will you function?"

"I grasp the situation all too well," Blanche told him. "You and Joubert and Aimerie have looted this manor blind, and I want none of you around. Now, be gone before I give in to my instincts and hang you."

Marcel stared.

"Don't want to be on the road after nightfall," Miles added helpfully. "Robbers."

Marcel glared at Miles, then turned on his heel and went back into the hall, shouting. Two men who must have been bailiffs followed him. "And don't take any of the manor's horses," Miles called after them.

Blanche and Miles entered the hall. To the left of the hall's entrance door was a storeroom from which Marcel, his bailiffs, and their families were hastily gathering their belongings. For a moment Miles felt sorry for the families, then he forgot it. No one had felt sorry for the English families when the French dispossessed them forty years ago.

Next to the storeroom was a room where dishes from the kitchen were finalized before being brought out. Screened off to the right was the main hall. They entered.

The hall was small, dark, and smoky. A fire pit blazed in the center, some of the acrid smoke rising from it to a hole in the low roof, the rest spreading through the room, burning throats and eyes and obscuring vision. The only other light came from scattered wax candles on the head table and in wall holders. The timber floor was strewn with fresh rushes. Bacon and a few hams hung from the rafters. The hall was narrow, with room for two trestle tables at meal times, one to each side of the fire pit. The head table was on a dais at the far end; it might seat six at a pinch. Behind the dais was a wall with a door and a stairway that led to a room that projected above the dais. The room's end was blocked off by a half-wall.

"This *is* fancy," Blanche said, removing her wet hood. "That's one of those new solars up there—I'll have my own quarters. Milli, you'll sleep up there with me and one or two of the maids."

Blanche moved toward the fire, holding out her chilled hands and rubbing warmth into them. "Wada?"

"My lady?" Wada said, stepping forward.

"Have the solar cleaned out. I want no trace of Joubert to remain. Milli, find fresh linen for the bed and straw for the mattress. The last thing I need is to smell that disgusting fellow when I sleep."

Milli bowed. "My lady."

Blanche went on, still speaking to Milli. "First thing in the morning, get with the maids, serving girls, and cooks. Tell them what I expect of them."

"Yes, my lady." In effect, this meant telling them what Milli expected of them, and Milli would expect a lot. For all her pouting and complaining, Milli had high standards, and Miles guessed she would oversee a tightly run household.

Wada and Milli started up the stairs to the solar, Wada standing aside so that Milli could go first—and so that he could watch her shapely rear as she went up. Still rubbing her cold hands, Blanche turned to Miles. "Tomorrow, you and I will need to meet with the grooms, the kennelers, falconers, and huntsmen. We'll need to pick out horses for ourselves, as well."

A serving boy brought a plate of cold chicken and two cups of wine. "Thank you," Blanche said, surprised. She hadn't asked for anything.

Blanche took one of the cups, and the boy placed the plate on the dais table. "Is this the wine they make here?" Blanche asked him.

"It is, my lady."

She held the cup to her nose, sipped, and raised her brows in surprise. "It's good."

"Don't know much about that, my lady," the boy said. "The baron's butler, he supervises the wine making."

"Does he now?" Blanche said. "On *my* estate?"

The boy said nothing. "I'd appreciate a cup of ale if you could find me one," Miles told him.

"Aye," the boy said and started off.

Blanche went to the table and took a bite of the chicken. "Not enough seasoning. Milli will have her work cut out for her with these cooks."

Miles had some of the chicken and made a face. "Too much spice for me. Now, me, I like some real English food—pottage. You start with some meat stock, add water, then oats and peas and beans. Carrots, onion, parsley, cabbage. Bits of bacon and ham, if you have it—maybe even venison and hare. Put in bread crumbs to thicken it. Almond milk, salt. Let it simmer all day. That's some good eating. Next day, you take what's left over, add some new ingredients, and start again."

Blanche's eyes twinkled. "As steward of two manors, I'm afraid you'll have to get used to more civilized cooking."

Miles was about to reply, when Wada leaned over the solar's half-wall. "My lady? You'd best have a look at this."

Blanche and Miles climbed the stairs to the solar. The short stairway smelled of new-cut wood. A pair of candles provided dim light in the solar. Fresh rushes covered the floor, and bolts of thick wool were tacked to the wall to help insulate the room from the cold. Mice flitted in the shadows. A curtained bed dominated the room's center. On a table near the bed was a small chest. The chest's lid was up, revealing coins, bits of coins, and even some jewelry inside, glinting faintly in the weak candlelight.

"Now we know where all the fines went," Miles said.

"A busy man, our Joubert," said Blanche.

Miles said, "Perhaps you should have hanged that lot after all."

"Yes, I'm starting to have regrets about that."

Blanche picked up the chest, felt its weight. "Wada, take this to the village tomorrow and give it to Father Albinus. Have him distribute it to the residents of the manor."

Wada cleared his throat diplomatically. "Distribute it equally or in order of importance, my lady?"

Blanche hesitated, and Miles knew what she was thinking. Equal distribution would do more good to the village as a whole, and the poor would be grateful, but the inhabitants had no doubt been taxed according to their wealth, such as it was, and that roughly mirrored their order of importance, and if she gave more to the poor, this might stir up resentment among the others, which was something she didn't need right now.

"Have him return what was taxed to each individual, if it can be determined. Otherwise, in order of importance."

"Aye, my lady," Wada said. "What about Joubert's clothes? He's got some nice things here." He lifted a cloak from a wall peg. "Look at this cloak." He ruffled the grey fur. "Wolf."

Blanche turned to Miles questioningly. As steward, the clothes now belonged to him by right.

"Keep 'em for yourself," Miles told Wada. "I've got clothes." There was no sense getting rid of Lord Geoffrey's things, even though Miles hated the memory of Geoffrey, hated how he'd looked up to Geoffrey and how Geoffrey had betrayed that admiration, killing his father and using Miles to implicate others for the crime.

Wada examined the cloak doubtfully. "Bit rich for a beadle."

Miles winked at him. "The girls will love it." He went on. "Get with the remaining bailiffs tomorrow, as well. See how things are run here and if you want to make any changes."

"Aye," Wada said. As beadle, Wada would be in charge of enforcing infractions of manor law, collecting fines, and seeing that men and women were at work in the lord's fields when they were supposed to be. Miles had gotten Wada reprieved from the Badford gallows, but because Wada had killed a man in a dispute over boundary markers—even though it had been an accident—he had engendered hard feelings in his village. So when Miles had asked him to come to Redhill as his beadle, he'd accepted eagerly.

Wada left the solar. Milli was directing the maids and servants. Her English was almost as good as Blanche's; Miles suspected they practiced together. "Hurry, there. Hurry. You English are so slow." Fresh linen and straw were being rushed in for the curtained bed. "Careful you don't knock over the candles," Milli said. "Don't want to burn the house down our first night here. Make sure you put fleabane and wormwood in that bedding, too."

As the old straw was collected, one woman asked Milli, "This is still right fresh. What do you want us to do with it?"

"Use it as you wish," Milli said. "Put it in your own beds if you like."

Miles and Blanche went back down the stairs to the hall. A wooden cup filled with ale was waiting on the table, and Miles drank from it. "Quite a first day," he observed to Blanche.

"We'll have to go to Fairleigh tomorrow and see about that 'trouble' they're having," Blanche said.

Miles nodded agreement. "I'll leave you and see to my quarters," he said. "I doubt Joubert ever used them, he seems to have spent his nights in the solar." As steward, Miles had a small house for his own use.

He hesitated, and Blanche saw the look on his face. "What?" she said.

"This will be the first time in my life I ever slept in a room by myself."

Blanche gave him an impish smile. "No, it won't."

Miles realized what she meant. "Oh," he said. "But . . . what about the servants? What about—?"

"I'll handle that," she said. She gave him a gentle push toward the door. "Warm the bed."

Miles saw that the horses and pack animals had been taken care of. Then he fetched a tallow candle—not for an Englishmen like him the more expensive beeswax—and went to his quarters, a small, half-timbered house not far from the hall. He would unpack tomorrow. He placed the candle on a table near the bed and lay down. The bed was comfortable enough—better than the old bed he'd had at Ravenswell.

He waited for Blanche. He had to be careful that he didn't fall asleep with the candle lit. Many a house had been turned to ashes because a candle had burned down and fallen over. Despite his best efforts, however, his eyes closed, and he was soon fast asleep.

Some time later, the door opened. Soft footfalls crossed the room, and the candle was blown out. The bed rustled.

Chapter 6

The rain had gone. It was a perfect autumn day, the sky blue with fleecy white clouds scudding across it, the air bracing but not cold. The remaining leaves on the trees orange and gold, some of them blowing in the air.

"A good day for hawking," Blanche observed.

"I suppose Galon took all of your husband's birds when he became earl?" Miles said.

"Quick as you please," Blanche said ruefully. "He certainly wasn't about to leave them with me. The mews at Redhill looks promising, though. At least we can thank Joubert for something."

Fairleigh had come to the earl of Trent as payment for a gambling debt. Miles and Blanche rode toward it, following directions given them by Hamo. The land grew hillier, filled with woods and lush pastures. Ahead, they saw men and a few women gathered around a broken pasture fence. Some of the men were fitting the last of three new-cut poles to the fence, calling instructions to each other as they eased the heavy pole into place, while other men and one of the women used goads and shouted to keep the cattle in the pasture from breaking free.

Miles and Blanche reined in, waiting till the men were done, the new fence pole secure and the cattle safe. "Good day to you," Miles said in English. "Is this Fairleigh Manor?"

"It is," replied one who appeared to be the leader.

"We're looking for the steward."

"Then you're looking for me. Evrard." Evrard wiped his hands on his thigh-length shirt. He was short and muscular with a broad, ruddy face and trim beard. Miles already liked him for the fact that he wasn't shy about working with the commoners he supervised. He seemed very much at ease with them. He seemed like one of them.

Miles introduced himself and Blanche.

Evrard knuckled his forehead to Blanche. He was French but over the years his accent had taken on English inflections. "Honored to meet you, my lady. Been a while since we had a lord on this manor. The earl's steward, Etienne, visited from time to time, but it's not the same."

"You have my apologies for that," Blanche said. She indicated the fence. "What happened here?"

"The Viking and his men," Evrard said.

"And a woman," added one of the villagers who'd been working on the fence.

"A woman?" said Blanche.

"Aye," said the man. "Carries a bow. Good with it, too." The man might have been handsome, save that one side of his face had been burned at some point, the skin all pink and crinkled, pulling down his left eye.

"Who is the Viking?" Miles asked Evrard.

"That's what we call him," said Evrard. "Don't know his name. Big, crazy-looking fellow. Doesn't wear a shirt, hair all done up in a topknot. Has a gang of men. They took an ox, two sacks of grain, and a silver candlestick from the church. Plus, they knocked down this fence."

"It's not the first time they've come," added another of the bystanders.

Miles frowned. "You can't stop them?"

Evrard looked apologetic. "They wear mail—at least some of them do. They have swords and axes and spears. We can't go against them."

Blanche said, "Where do they come from?"

Evrard drank water from a wooden pail. "They have a camp in the forest somewhere. Like as not they're the same bunch that terrorize the roads hereabouts."

"The robbers we were warned about," Miles told Blanche.

Blanche nodded. "How often do they come?" she asked Evrard.

The steward shrugged. "Whenever it suits them. There's no real pattern."

Miles digested this, then changed the subject. "Has Baron Aimerie asked you to pay levies?"

" 'Asked' isn't the right word. 'Demanded' would be better. 'Ordered.' He says it'll make us 'safer', just like his new castle's supposed to make us safer."

"And do you pay?"

"I do not. Nor do I send men to labor on his castle. We owe allegiance only to our lord—that's your ladyship—and through her to the earl of Trent."

There were growls of assent from a few of the men gathered around, but a number of the others demurred. Miles could tell that Blanche noticed their reaction, too.

Blanche said, "Are there any other manors around here that don't pay?"

Evrard considered. "There's Lord Guillame over to Edsworth, he's the only one I can think of, my lady. Might be one other."

One of the laborers tapped the newly repaired fence. In English he said, "I don't know, Ev. Might be worth payin' if it keeps things like this from happening."

Another agreed. "Aye, when it's your ox that gets taken, or your sheep, you think twice about not payin' a few extra pennies for protection."

"Losin' that grain hurt," added the woman who had helped with the cattle, " 'specially with winter comin' on. Bread don't bake itself."

Evrard turned to them. "We've had this discussion before. Aimerie's got no right to tax us."

The woman said, "But if it makes us safer—"

"Enough!" Blanche said. "*Monsieur* Evrard is right. You'll pay no levy to Aimerie, and we'll do something about these robbers."

"Hope you're right, my lady," grumbled the woman. "Can't go on like this."

"It won't," Blanche assured her.

Evrard put on his old wool tunic and showed Blanche and Miles around the rest of the two-field manor, which, apart from the depredations of the robbers, seemed well tended. The manor house was not as large or as new as the one at Redhill. The village was not orderly like the one at Redhill, either. Some of the cottages were grouped together, like a small village; the rest were scattered willy-nilly, as though people had settled where it pleased them, and the church was off by itself on a small rise.

"There's no sense for me to move from manor to manor every few months," Blanche told Miles and Evrard when they were done. "The two estates are too close for that. I'll take up permanent residence at Redhill."

"As you wish, my lady," said Evrard.

"I'll still be around, though," she said.

"Good, my lady. It's good for people here to see you, especially with the way things are."

"I'll need to be in residence here from time to time, of course," Miles told Evrard, who nodded.

Miles and Blanche spent the night at Fairleigh, the terrified cooks worried about feeding this haughty French noblewoman, and they started back to Redhill in the morning. The weather held fair, though it was colder, the racing clouds darker. Blanche sighed as they rode. "I came here hoping for peace and quiet, and I find anything but. It's almost as bad as Normandy."

Miles agreed. "Doesn't look like Lord Tutbury's writ extends to this part of the shire." Tutbury had been made sheriff after Blanche's husband, the former sheriff, had been killed. "First thing we need to do is do is find those robbers."

"I suppose I'll have to find them for you," Blanche said. "After all, I found my husband's killer."

"*You?*" Miles said. "You didn't find him, I did. You said the killer was Ranulf."

"And you said it was Galon."

"But I was the one who eventually figured it out."

"Only because I paid that hermit. He'd never have taken us to Thor's Seat otherwise, and you'd never have made your—" she made a face and lowered her voice like a man—"Great Deduction."

"That's the most—"

She pressed on. "Admit it, you thought *I* was the killer, didn't you? At one point, anyway?"

"Well . . ."

"I knew it," she said, smacking the pommel of her saddle.

"Everybody said it was you. I had to at least consider the possibility."

She harrumphed. "You just don't want to admit that I saved you."

"*You* saved *me*? If it hadn't been for me, Galon would have . . ."

They were still arguing in this vein when they clattered across the bridge to the Redhill manor house compound and stopped.

Two richly caparisoned horses stood outside the hall, a bored-looking squire holding their reins. "We seem to have visitors," Blanche said.

Chapter 7

Miles and Blanche made their way down the narrow, low-ceilinged hall, Miles a step behind Blanche, as befitted his station. Their feet crunched the rushes on the floor. Even in the daytime, it was dim inside the hall, though a shaft of sunlight from the west window illumined dust motes in the air. Two men sat at the head table, on the dais, eating and drinking wine. Behind the table stood the former steward, Joubert, a smug look on his face. Wada was to one side of the aisle, watching the newcomers warily.

The hall was so new that smoke from the firepit hadn't properly blackened the rafters. No banners hung from the rafters, either. Blanche was no longer entitled to use the white-on-green swan of Trent, and she had chosen no symbol for herself yet. Millicent came up, indicating the men on the dais with a flick of her head. "I'm sorry, my lady, we couldn't—"

"It's all right," Blanche told her.

Miles missed a step because he suddenly recognized the two men. The last time he'd seen the one in the center chair, four years ago, the man's hair had been worn in a Norman bowl cut and he'd been clean shaven save for a moustache. Now his hair hung to his shoulders and he had a beard. The other was the man's son; he'd be . . . what? . . . eighteen now. The father was tall and well built, with cold, intelligent eyes; the son, shorter but more powerful, like a bull, and mean looking.

Blanche marched up to the table. "You're in my seat," she told the older man.

The man continued eating, sucking juice from his fingers. "The village women brought these pigeon pies. They're quite good, except I don't think Joubert, here, is happy about his pigeons being—"

"You're in my seat," Blanche said.

The man stared.

Blanche stared back.

At last the man rose from the high-backed chair. The younger man rose as well, reluctantly. The older man said, "I beg your pardon, my lady, I didn't realize. Forgive me." He bowed. "I am Aimerie, baron of Brightwood. This is my son Ernoul, who is to be knighted in three weeks. You must be Blanche, widow to the earl of Trent."

Blanche said nothing.

Aimerie's son, Ernoul, had grown since Miles had seen him last. The beginnings of a moustache and beard fuzzed his face. He gazed at Blanche with brute lust. Without taking his eyes from hers, he said, "You know, Father, I'll need a wife upon my knighting. This one would do. She'd bring me two fat manors, plus she's good looking. A fine catch. Our family's hold on this part of the shire would be strengthened."

"She's older than you," Aimerie pointed out, not caring that Blanche heard, for all the world like he and his son were discussing stock at an auction.

"She's still young enough to bear me sons," Ernoul said. "I'll wager we'd have a lot of fun conceiving them, too."

Ernoul looked like he would take Blanche right then and there if he could, and from what Miles remembered of him, that idea wasn't idle fancy.

If Ernoul scared Blanche, she didn't show it. "I'm not getting remarried," she told him, "and certainly not to a child."

Ernoul flashed with anger, but before he could say anything, Blanche addressed his father. "I assume your visit has a purpose?"

"Blunt talk," Aimerie chuckled, "I like that in a woman. We've come to introduce ourselves. I fear we may have gotten off on the wrong foot, as the saying goes." He seemed to notice Miles for the first time, and his brows came together as though he was trying to remember something. "Miles?" he said tentatively. "Miles of Ravenswell?"

Miles bowed in acknowledgement. "Lord Aimerie."

"What are you doing here?" Aimerie asked.

"I am steward for Lady Blanche's estates."

To Miles, Blanche said, "You know one another?"

"Aimerie was lord of Ravenswell," Miles said, "until he decided to rebel against the king."

Aimerie regarded Miles evenly. "Miles, the soldier. Miles the hundred pledge. Miles the 'free man.' Now you're steward to a great lady. You've come up in the world."

"As have you, baron. The last I saw you, you were landless, at least in this country."

Ernoul had resumed his seat, eating a pie, feet on the table. "How's Aelred?" he asked Miles offhandedly. "I remember beating hell out of him one time. That was fun."

"Aelred is Ravenswell's miller now. Doing well at it, too."

Ernoul frowned. "Miller? What happened to Grim? I liked him."

"He was executed," Miles said. He turned to Aimerie. "I heard you'd gone back to France."

"So I did, but, alas, I hitched my fortunes to the wrong man. Robert of Bellême is in as much disfavor in Normandy as he is in England, and I lost my lands there, as well. I couldn't even find a lord for Ernoul to squire for, so the poor lad's had to squire for me. There seemed no future for me in Normandy, so I came back to England. It was rough going for a while, but that's behind us now."

"How did you acquire Brightwood?"

Aimerie shrugged. "It was vacant, so I took it over."

"And the former lord? What happened to him?"

"He met with an accident," Aimerie said.

Blanche interrupted. "Did you come here just to exchange memories with my steward?"

"No," Aimerie said. "As I said, I believe we've gotten off on the wrong foot. Joubert wishes to apologize for his behavior, and he swears he'll never—"

"Joubert is not coming back here," Blanche said. "And you shouldn't have brought him."

The smug look on Joubert's toad-like face disappeared.

Blanche went on. "Hamo is steward here now."

Joubert snorted in derision.

"An Englishman?" Aimerie crinkled his brow. "I don't think I like that."

"I don't care what you like. This is my estate, and I'll run it as I see fit."

Aimerie held up his hands in a placating gesture. "As you will."

"Was there anything else you wanted?"

"Actually, there was. I'm imposing a levy of two silver marks on Redhill and one mark on Fairleigh. Every estate in this district has been levied, and you need to contribute your fair share."

"And by what right do you impose this levy? I'm not your vassal."

Aimerie spread his arms. "It's for your protection. For everyone's."

"Protection from whom?"

"From the robbers who infest this district. It's my men who chase them, and that costs money. I have five knights in my service, and they don't come cheap."

"Your fief supports five knights?" Miles asked in surprise.

"No, the knights are in my hire. Hence the levy." To Blanche, Aimerie said, "I also need you to contribute a score of laborers for my castle."

Blanche smirked. "Let me guess. The castle is for our protection, as well?"

"What else would it be for?" Aimerie asked.

Miles said, "It could be to protect you from us."

"Is he always this insolent?" Aimerie asked Blanche.

"Most of the time," Blanche said.

"Perhaps you should have chosen your staff more wisely." To Miles, Aimerie said, "You always did act above your station, Miles. It must be due to your so-called noble background."

Ernoul stood and put a hand to the dagger in his belt. "Let me deal with him, Father. I'll carve that insolent tongue out of his head."

Miles tensed, ready to draw his own knife. But Aimerie said, "This is a friendly visit, Ernoul, we wish no trouble. We can't have Miles attending your knighting ceremony without his tongue, now can we? People would talk."

Aimerie smiled at his joke. Ernoul kept glaring at Miles.

Blanche said, "Are you finished?"

"For the moment," Aimerie said.

"Then hear me well. I owe you no allegiance. I will pay no levy, send no men to work on your castle. And if that man—" she pointed at Joubert— "sets foot on my land again, I'll hang him."

Aimerie showed no emotion. "I hope you don't come to regret this decision, my lady."

Aimerie came round the table and stepped off the dais, followed by Ernoul and Joubert. "Good day to you," Aimerie told Blanche. He bowed to her, as did Joubert.

Ernoul bowed, as well, but he took his time, casting a last glance at Blanche, eyeing her up and down, making sure she knew he was doing it. "Child, eh?" he said. "You'll change your tune about that."

The three men left the hall, mounted, and rode off, along with Aimerie's squire.

Miles and Blanche stood at the low hall door and watched them go. Miles said, "My guess is that these 'robbers' are in Aimerie's employ, or at least render him a share of their plunder."

"My guess is, you're right," Blanche says.

Miles went on. "He uses them to keep people afraid. If you keep people afraid, you can control them. Don't give them time to realize they can fight back."

Blanche sighed. "I suppose we're in for trouble?"

"I suppose we are," Miles said. "And sooner rather than later."

Chapter 8

Aimerie and Ernoul rode back to Brightwood, with Aimerie's squire and the former steward, Joubert, following. The partly built castle became visible in the distance, dominating the late autumn landscape. The lowering sun brought falling temperatures, and Aimerie longed for the warmth of the castle's hearth. That must be a sign that he was getting old. There was a time when cold weather didn't bother him. He had first started feeling it when he and his family were living in the woods with the robbers, in an old tent reinforced with cut wood and branches. That life had taken a toll. His two youngest children had died, and his wife, Oudinette, had suffered greatly. Ernoul had seemed to thrive on life in the woods, though. His health had been largely unaffected, and he had been free to do as he pleased—fight and drink and chase the camp girls.

Aimerie turned to the boy. Silly to think of him as a boy; he was a young man, now—a big, powerful one. "Were you serious about marrying Lady Blanche?"

"I was," Ernoul said. "It's time I had a wife. Besides, you saw her. Men would pay a fortune to bed her, and I'll get it every night for free." He scratched his wispy beard. "There's something about that haughty look of hers that intrigues me. I'll fuck that smirk off her face—beat it off if I have to. I want to make her crawl to me."

Aimerie was taken aback by the boy's vehemence even though he knew Ernoul had a history of violence with women. "Do you want to marry her or kill her?" he asked.

Ernoul ignored the question. "She's like a horse that needs taming. I want her to submit to me, as a dutiful wife should. Submit in every way. And give me sons."

"Don't talk about beating her," Aimerie cautioned, "especially in front of others. You'll be a knight soon, you must be respectable."

"Respectable? We lived two years in the woods, little better than animals. Not much respectable about that."

"Those days are past. I am to be a great baron. You are my son and must act the part, because one day you will be a great baron, as well. We come from a good family, remember that." He went on. "Blanche brings only two estates. I wonder if we couldn't do better for you?"

"I'm not worried about that," Ernoul said. "I'm off to France next spring, for the tournament circuit. I'll win my share of gold there, and the endless wars over there will bring me lands."

Aimerie had no doubt that the boy was right. He trained religiously and regularly beat Aimerie's own knights in practice duels, so much so that Aimerie had to implore him not to injure them. Still, Aimerie had other things in mind for his son . . .

Ernoul frowned as if something had occurred to him. "You don't think Blanche is involved with that steward, do you?"

"Miles?" Aimerie said. "Miles is a peasant, an English peasant at that. I know Blanche from when she was Earl Thibault's wife. There were a lot of rumors about her love life back then, but she would never lower herself that far."

"They seemed much at ease with each other."

"He's her steward, he sees her every day. That doesn't make them lovers."

They reached Brightwood Manor. The village was to their left, by the river. The castle was to their right. It sat on a rise, squat and square. A ramp led to an entrance platform by the main door. Only the battlements and the roof remained to be finished. The ramp would be turned into a fortified entranceway, but that would have to wait until next year.

Masons and other workmen swarmed over both the castle and the bailey surrounding it. The weather would cause construction to shut down soon, and Aimerie wanted to get as much done as possible before winter set in. The workmen had been drafted from the nearby estates; the masons, however, had to be hired, and they did not come cheaply. Aimerie was already in debt to the Jews, and that debt was going to increase.

Stone, lumber, rope, and barrels of rubble lay everywhere, in organized confusion. The bailey wall was wooden now, but in the coming year it would be rebuilt in stone, making Brightwood the most powerful castle in Trentshire, far outclassing that old wooden heap at Badford. When the castle was finished, Aimerie would be the second most powerful lord in the shire after Earl Galon himself, and that would be just the beginning. Aimerie would use that power to gain new lands and titles, to obtain the respect he deserved and make King Henry regret slighting him. He planned on rising far, but that was for the future.

As they entered the bailey, Aimerie's wife, Oudinette, approached from the kitchen building, wiping her hands on an apron. Oudinette came from mid-level nobility in the Cotentin, not the upper, but far from the lower. She had never been a beauty, but she had been attractive enough when she was younger. More importantly, she had brought Aimerie lands, lands since lost to supporters of King Henry. She was tall and blonde with a wide, almost sloppy, mouth. She'd once been extremely fit, but had put on weight since they'd stopped living in the woods, and who could blame her. Years of rough living had etched deep lines on her face and put grey in her hair. Her cheeks were beginning to sag.

Aimerie and his party dismounted. While the squire led the horses to the stable, Aimerie patted Joubert's shoulder. "Don't worry, my friend, you'll be back at Redhill before you know it. You and Marcel both." Aimerie knew that Joubert liked having a chamberlain. It made him feel important.

"Thank you, my lord," Joubert said and headed off.

Aimerie turned and kissed Oudinette on the forehead. "How are you, my dear? You look busy."

Oudinette sighed and Aimerie smelled wine on her breath. "Have you been drinking?"

"You'd drink, too, if you had to teach these English anything," she said. "I've been trying to show the cooks the proper way to prepare food."

"At this late hour?"

"I thought this would be a good time, when they weren't under pressure to feed everyone." She shook her head in dismay. "They're hopeless. Honestly, I sometimes think we ate better when we lived in the forest."

Aimerie laughed at that. "That's quite possible. You're an excellent cook. But we weren't as comfortable back then, eh?"

"It wasn't so bad in the summer," Oudinette allowed.

"Your memory plays tricks on you, dear." Aimerie put an arm around her shoulder and waved a hand at the castle looming behind them. "No matter. I've finally given you the home you deserve."

"And I thank you for that," she said. "It's almost worth all the bad years. Except for . . ."

He squeezed her shoulder. "Except for the children, I know."

Oudinette had lost children to childbirth, to disease, to harsh conditions in the forest. She had given up a lot for Aimerie. First, leaving her beloved Normandy and her childhood friends. Then, losing their lands, becoming outcasts, living hand to mouth in the company of robbers—men who terrified Oudinette, though her husband and Ernoul took to them readily enough. Through it all, she had been stoic, comforted by her favorite, Ernoul. Now, at last, she could be happy. She could be comfortable. She seemed to have found new spirit.

Aimerie went on. "Believe me, I haven't forgotten or forgiven King Henry for what he did to us. And I only wish Lord Geoffrey hadn't been beheaded, because that's something I'd like to have done myself. The future is bright now, though. You'll be a great lady, as you were always meant to be."

She turned away and brushed something from her eye. Looking back, she said, "How did your audience with the new lord of Redhill go?"

"It turns out that the new lord of Redhill is a woman," Aimerie said.

"A woman!"

"That was my reaction, as well. It's the earl of Trent's widow."

Oudinette thought. "I remember her. Brienne . . . no, Blanche her name was. Quite beautiful."

"That she is. So beautiful that your son has fallen for with her and wants her for his wife."

"What!" Oudinette stepped back and cast shocked eyes at Ernoul. "Surely she's too old for you?"

"She's not that old," Ernoul replied.

"But you're not even knighted yet."

"I will be in three weeks."

Oudinette looked from her son to her husband and back to her son again. "This is . . . this is so sudden. I never expected . . . How do you know she'd even marry you?"

"She will, if Father allows it. She'll have no choice. We'll make her do it, if we have to."

"The Church doesn't condone forced marriage. What priest would . . . ah, you're thinking of using Father Richard."

Ernoul nodded his head with a smile. Richard was a priest Aimerie had taken under his charge when they had lived in the forest.

"Let's not get ahead of ourselves," Aimerie interrupted. "We need to think this through."

"I've already thought it through," Ernoul said.

"Don't confuse lust with duty to your family," Aimerie told him. "We know nothing of her background."

"She was good enough to be an earl's wife, I'm sure she's good enough for me. Besides, if I tire of her, I can always get rid of her."

"Don't talk that way," Oudinette said, frowning.

"Why not? It's done all the time."

Aimerie raised a cautioning hand. "All that is for the future. We must think about the present. And for the present, Blanche won't pay our levy."

"Really?" Oudinette was surprised, as though she couldn't understand why someone wouldn't want to pay her husband's tax. "What are you going to do?"

Aimerie smiled. "I think it's time for our friend Fromont to visit Redhill."

Chapter 9

After Aimerie and his son had departed, Miles and Blanche walked down to the village, accompanied by Wada. Wada was a bit self-conscious, but also proud, wearing Joubert's wolf-fur cloak for the first time. None of Joubert's other clothes fit him. Indeed, the clothes he'd brought from home barely fit him anymore; he was gaining weight after his long imprisonment in Badford Castle's goal.

They navigated the muddy village street, going around the huge pot hole. Most lords would have ridden, to avoid the mud; Blanche was not one of them. She'd walked in mud before, and she didn't see the need for turning out the stablers just so she could travel this short distance. "Did you suspect that Baron Aimerie was your old friend?" she asked Miles.

"No," Miles said, "Aimerie's a common name. And he's not my friend."

"Did Ernoul really beat your boy, like he said?"

"He did. Being the lord's son, Ernoul could do pretty much whatever he wanted. No one was going to stop him."

Blanche nodded. "I ran across that type of lord's son all too often when I was young."

"His father's the same way. Like that fellow said, he and Ernoul used the village women like the village was a brothel and the women were its whores."

"I ran across that before, as well," said Blanche.

Miles nodded. "A good part of Ravenswell's population carries their blood, sad to say."

Miles had Father Albinus ring the church bell to summon an assembly, and they waited in the churchyard as people trickled in. The late October sun cast long shadows on the ground. Winter would begin soon, and the air smelled of damp earth, fallen leaves, and smoke from the village hearths. It smelled of the dying year.

Soon, most of the village was present, the men and women in the rear crowding among the grave markers. All of the women wore headdresses of some kind. The men were bearded, with shaggy hair. Many wore coifs of linen or wool, to keep dirt out of their hair. Miles explained the situation. Beside him, Blanche kept an eye on the villagers' reaction to what he said. Hamo, the new steward, stood behind Miles, next to Wada; and Simon, the new reeve, was at the villagers' front.

Miles told the assemblage what had happened at Fairleigh. He told them about Baron Aimerie's demand that Redhill pay him taxes and contribute to the building of his castle.

Miles paused for effect, then said, "Lady Blanche refused."

There were scattered handclaps and words of approval, but most stayed quiet. They knew that Miles's words presaged trouble.

Miles went on. "Lady Blanche believes—and I agree—that the robbers who attacked Fairleigh work for Baron Aimerie."

There was muttering at that, much of it not surprised. Miles said, "We think the robbers will come here next. And soon. Aimerie will want to teach us a lesson."

More muttering. Men and women looked at each other. "Is he going to burn us out?" a man shouted.

"No," Miles said. "If they destroy us, we'll be no good to them. Aimerie means to use Redhill as a source of wealth. The robbers will steal just enough to get our attention. Aimerie reckons that, once we've been hit, we'll go running to him for help."

"And when we don't?" drawled the rangy fellow with curly black hair.

"The robbers will keep coming until we do," Miles said.

"Guess there's no chance of us paying him?" said an older woman. The old man beside her nodded hopefully.

"No," Miles said. There were groans, and Miles spoke over them. "Once this kind of thing starts, it never stops. The taxes and labor impositions will keep coming. Men like Aimerie only understand one thing, and that's force. Give into them, and you lose everything."

"What about the sheriff?" said Giles the potter. It was Giles's house that was falling over and propped up by a log. "Can't we go to him?"

Blanche answered that one in her accented English. "The sheriff is in Normandy now. We will send to him, but we do not have much time, and we cannot count on any help from that quarter, especially with winter about to turn the roads bad."

While the villagers took that in—and marveled once again at this French woman's command of their language—Miles turned to Hamo. "Aimerie said that the former lord of Brightwood met with an accident. Is that true?"

Hamo snorted. "It is—if you call an axe blade in the skull an accident. Aimerie showed up at Brightwood one day with a bunch of armed men, robbers from the forest. He killed the lord and his family and took over. Declared himself the new lord, and dared anyone to say him nay."

Miles and Blanche shared a look. "That's one way to do it, I suppose," Blanche said. "Saves writing all those dull charters."

"How long ago was this?" Miles asked Hamo.

"Two and a half years. Just after Easter."

"So what are we going to do?" red-haired Simon asked Miles.

"We're going to fight," Miles said.

Hamo was skeptical. "And who's to lead us? You?"

"Yes. I was a centenar of footmen in Wales, so I have some experience." He raised his voice. "How many of you men have done military service?"

The rangy fellow with black hair raised a hand. He had a lazy glint in his eye that some might have taken for indifference, but which Miles took for self-confidence. "What's your name?" Miles asked him.

"Name's Ulf, but everybody calls me Blackie."

"Anyone else?" Miles asked the crowd.

No one came forward.

Miles was disappointed. He had hoped for more veterans. "Anyone been with the fyrd?" he said.

Three more men came forth. They would at least have had some rudiments of military training. The fyrd were men called up to fight in time of emergencies. At one time they had been well trained and well armed—they were the men who fought at Sand Lake, the men who beat the Vikings—but they weren't used much these days, as the French lords preferred to hire mercenaries. Mercenaries could stay in service indefinitely, whereas fyrd members had to return home after forty days to tend their lands.

Miles tried again. "Any poachers?"

There was a deal of foot shuffling and head turning. "This isn't a trap," Miles said. "You won't get in trouble. We need men who are good in the forest and who can use a bow."

After a second, Blackie raised his hand again.

"You're a poacher, as well?" Miles said.

Blackie cleared his throat and looked around. "Let's just say I been accused."

There was a lot of good-natured laughter at that.

"How are you with a bow?"

"Fair," Blackie said.

More laughter. "That's not what the earl's deer say," cried a sandy-haired young man.

"Are there others here that can shoot?" Miles said.

No answer.

Blackie turned. "Sewale, Will, get up here. I ain't doing this by myself."

Two more men, one of them the sandy-haired youngster, shuffled forward. The second man was older, solid and steady.

"Where'd you do your soldiering?" Miles asked Blackie.

"Started with King Henry at the siege of Arundel, then on to Bridgenorth. When that war ended, a bunch of us went over to France with the earl of Cornwall, but that was a shambles, so we took service with a French lord. The money was good, but I didn't take to some of the things I had to do, so I come back here."

"How long have you been back?"

"Year or so," Blackie said. "Ain't really settled in yet."

"Except for the poaching," sandy-haired Will said to some laughter.

Simon changed the subject. "Besides bows, what do you plan to use for weapons in this fight?" he asked Miles.

"Whatever's to hand," Miles said. "Axes, scythes, bills, daggers. Anything sharp."

"Pruning knife?" asked someone.

"Why not?" Miles said. "I'm sure those bastards could use a little pruning."

There was more laughter, and a large fellow who must be the blacksmith said, "I have my hammer."

Miles said, "Good. God willing, we'll find someone for you to hit with it."

"What's your plan?" Father Albinus asked Miles in his gravelly voice. "Fortify the village?"

Miles had been giving that some thought. "No. We're not going to wait for them to come to us. We're going to go after them."

There was a stir in the crowd, and Miles went on. "With luck, we'll catch them off guard. If we do it right, they may not know who we are. I don't want Aimerie to send his knights here. Not yet, anyway."

Blackie raised his hand. "When I was in France, there was somethin' like that going on. Villagers rose up to fight the nobles." He turned to Blanche, "Begging your pardon, ma'am."

Blanche smiled. "That's quite all right."

"Nobles treat their people shocking bad over there. Anyway, these rebels, they all wore hoods, with eye holes and mouth openings cut out, so's nobody could tell who they were. Called themselves *Capuchins*, somethin' like that."

"Hmmm." Miles rubbed his jaw. "That's not a bad idea. What do you men think?"

The majority nodded or growled approval.

"What'll we use for hoods?" asked someone.

"Grain sacks?" Blackie suggested.

Father Albinus said, "I'll donate some. I have extras for the crops that you lot never tithe to me."

Laughter.

Blanche said, "I'll see what we have at the manor house."

Miles noted the steward, Hamo, looking doubtful. "Hamo, you have objections?"

"Aye," Hamo said. "I do. I'll be honest, I don't hold with what you're planning." He addressed the crowd. "You're going to risk all you've built here. You're going to risk your lives, your homes, your families. Over what? A tax? I dislike Aimerie as much as any man here, but I don't fancy losing my life or the lives of my family over it. You'll be giving up your safety, giving up everything you've got. Is it worth it? For a lord we don't even know, and a woman at that? Where's the sense to that? Lords come and lords go, as you well know, and the people are left to pick up the pieces of their doin's. It ain't right, I say. It's us ploughmen that run the manor, not them."

There was muttering and shuffling of feet.

Hamo turned back to Miles. "You can take my job from me, but that's the way I feel."

"I agree with Hamo," said the new reeve, Simon. "Maybe we'll get rid of Aimerie if we fight, but seems to me like we got more of a chance of getting the manor destroyed and most of us killed. What's the sense in that?"

Father Albinus said, "Sometimes you have to fight, Simon. It's the nature of things. Aimerie's not going to quit unless we stop him. If we don't fight, we'll lose everything, anyway. Better to go down with a sword in your hand than to bow your head meekly to evil."

"That what Jesus said?" Hamo asked him.

"It's what I say, and I'm speaking as one of you and not as your priest."

There was silence.

Miles looked around the crowd. "Anyone else?"

No one spoke.

Miles turned to Blanche, awaiting her decision. "My lady?"

Blanche was grim. "We fight."

Miles nodded and turned back to the crowd. “I won’t take your jobs,” he told Hamo and Simon. “And I appreciate your being honest. You and those who agree with you can stay here and look after things at the manor.” He turned. “Blackie, you’ll be in charge after me. Then Wada.” He would have liked to put Wada in charge, but Wada lacked military experience. “We’ll divide the men into squads of six. In the meantime, I want scouts sent out to watch for the robbers, to find their camp if possible. Starting tomorrow morning and every day thereafter, until this is finished. Pick your fastest boys. Tell them to keep under cover and not get caught.”

“Please,” said a girl, “can I go, too?” It was a willowy blonde—the same girl Miles had seen vaulting the ditch with the boys when he first came to the village. She looked bright and eager.

“No!” said a tall, middle-aged woman, who must be the girl’s mother. “I lost three children to sickness, I won’t lose another to some fool ideas about fighting and glory.” She looked at Miles. “She’s not dying for you.”

“No girls,” Miles agreed. “Too dangerous.”

The girl’s face fell. She turned to her father pleadingly.

The father, one of the fyrdmen, seemed to get his back up at Miles’s refusal. “Why shouldn’t she be allowed to go? Ediva’s faster’n most of the boys hereabouts. Smart, too.”

Miles shook his head. “I don’t like . . .”

Blackie spoke up. “Ailwyn’s right. Ediva’d do a good job.”

Blackie’s word seemed to carry a lot of weight with the villagers. It certainly did with Ediva, who beamed at Blackie.

Something told Miles that Blackie was a man whose judgment he could trust, and he gave in. "Very well."

"Miles—" the mother started.

"But don't you go anywhere near those robbers, if you see them" Miles told the girl. "Do you understand me?"

Ediva bobbed her head, smiling. "I understand."

The mother, whose name was Ailova, looked angry, but there was nothing she could do.

Miles said, "All right. Blackie, divide the men as you think best. Then decide—"

They all turned at the sound of horses. Two men were riding down from the manor house. One was dark-haired and bearded, a noble by his mount and by the way he carried himself. The other was also noble, but younger.

"Looks like Lord Guillame," Father Albinus said.

Chapter 10

"Guillame?" Blanche asked.

"Lord of Edsworth," Albinus explained. "Two leagues or so northwest of here."

"Ah, yes. The steward at Fairleigh, Evrard, mentioned him."

The two men rode up, the villagers crowding around and gawking. Lord Guillame was young and dashing and good looking. His squire appeared to be about thirteen or fourteen, gawky and arrogant.

Guillame picked out Blanche as the only noble in the gathering, though he was thrown for a moment by Wada's wolf-fur cloak. He leaped gracefully from his horse and bowed to her. "Good day, lady. I seek the lord of Redhill."

"That would be me," Blanche said.

Guillame was startled. "But you're a . . . a . . ."

"A woman?"

"Yes."

"Everywhere I go in this country, people tell me I'm a woman. I know I'm a woman, I've known it for quite some time. It's not something I'm likely to forget, so will everyone please stop reminding me?"

Guillame recovered and flashed a broad white smile. "Forgive me, my lady. I meant no offense. All I was told was that the lord of Redhill had come to the manor in person."

"And who told you that?"

"The villein's grapevine. It is faster than the king's best messenger. The villeins know things before anyone else, don't ask me how. My steward learned you were here through them, and he informed me." He bowed again. "Permit me to introduce myself. I am Guillame of Edsworth. This is my squire, Hugobert."

Hugobert bowed elaborately. "My lady."

Blanche inclined her head to them. "I am Blanche, widow to the earl of Trent."

"Widow?" Guillame said. "Then we have something in common. I am a widower. My wife's been gone these past two years."

"I'm sorry to hear that," Blanche said.

"Thank you. I still haven't come to terms with her loss, but there you are."

"Have you children?"

"No, my wife died in childbirth, along with the child." He paused, as though remembering her. "And you?"

Blanche's two children had been killed by her former brother-in-law. "None," she said. She indicated Miles. "This is my steward, Miles."

Miles bowed his head. "Lord Guillame."

Guillame regarded Miles with mild surprise. "You're English?"

"I have that honor, my lord."

"Interesting," Guillame said, and he turned back to Blanche.

Blanche said, "You've come late in the day, my lord. You will, of course, accept the hospitality of my house for the night."

"I'm most grateful, my lady, and I apologize for the timing of my visit, but my mission is urgent."

Blanche raised a dark brow in question.

Guillame went on. "It's Baron Aimerie—I know that your manors pay him no taxes."

"That's right," Blanche said. "Nor shall we pay."

"I don't pay, either, and I've come to propose that we join forces against him."

Blanche glanced at Miles, but Guillame didn't follow her look. Apparently Miles's opinion didn't interest him. Blanche said, "I was told by the steward at Fairleigh that there was another lord who wouldn't pay Aimerie—that must be you. There was perhaps one more, the man said?"

"That would be Haverham Manor," Guillame said. "Its lord is in Normandy, and the manor is run by his steward. Alas, he recently surrendered to Aimerie's demands. There used to be a number of us who resisted, but it's down to you and me. That's why my visit is so urgent. Without help, I fear I cannot hang on. The depredations of the robbers are taking their toll, and those who don't pay tax receive no protection from Aimerie."

"You believe these robbers work for Aimerie, then?"

"I do."

"So do Miles and I."

While Blanche and Guillame talked, Miles watched the villagers. Hamo and Simon had disappeared, taking those who wanted no part of a rebellion with them. Blackie and Wada, assisted by Ailwyn and the other two fyrdmen, organized the men of fighting age into groups of six, while the older fellows and some of the women watched and made comments. The other women watched Father Albinus as he lined up some boys and Ediva to be used as scouts, learning from their parents when they could be spared from their work in the fields.

Blanche's voice intruded on his thoughts. "Isn't that right, Miles?"

Miles's mind came back from what he had been doing. "My lady?"

"I said we would welcome an alliance with Lord Guillame, would we not?"

"We would, my lady."

"Miles has taken charge of our men," Blanche added.

"Has he?" Guillame looked at Miles closely. "Done any soldiering?"

"I was a centenar of footmen, my ord. In Wales."

Guillame didn't seem to find those credentials impressive. "Our expeditions to Wales tend to be unsuccessful."

"Mine wasn't successful, either. I learned a lot, though." He'd learned how to fight the French, a skill he had declined to use until now.

Guillame sniffed. "Well, I've campaigned almost every year since I was fifteen. I'll make a plan and we can set about going after Aimerie."

Miles said, "Begging your pardon, my lord, but what about Aimerie's knights?"

Guillame stared. "What about them?"

"He has five. If you include him and his son, that makes seven. We've naught that can stand against that many."

"I am a knight," Guillame pointed out.

"But you're only one."

"What are you saying?"

"I'm saying we should go slowly. Weaken the robbers first before taking on Aimerie directly." Miles didn't tell Guillame about the Hoods. He didn't know if he could trust him enough for that yet. "If you could organize your men, that would be a great help. We're using boys as scouts, to warn if the robbers approach. You might do the same."

Guillame bristled. "See here, are you telling me how to run this campaign?"

"Not at all, my lord. I'm just filling you in on what we've done so far."

Guillame obviously wasn't going to take suggestions from an Englishman. "I wish to get underway immediately, I've been a victim of these robbers for too long. Now that we're allies, I'm eager to take the field."

"And we're eager to support you, but we don't want to move before we're ready."

"And how long will that be?"

"I'm not sure, my lord."

Guillame didn't like that, but before he could say anything, Blanche interrupted. "It will be getting dark soon, Lord Guillame. It's best that we head for the house."

Guillame flashed that big smile again. "As you wish, Lady Blanche. Please, take my horse."

Blanche demurred. "I'll walk. It's just up the—"

"I insist. You shouldn't be walking in this mud."

Blanche sighed. She took the reins of Guillame's horse and mounted. Guillame mounted the squire's horse, and he and Blanche rode toward the manor house, Guillame chattering to Blanche like they were old friends, leaving Miles and the squire, Hugobert, to themselves.

"Go on, son," Miles told Hugobert, "follow them. I'll be along in a moment. We'll see if we can find you something to eat."

Hugobert made no acknowledgement of the peasant's words and trudged up the road.

Miles turned. "Blackie, Wada—leave the rest for the morrow. Father Albinus, send out your first group of scouts at dawn."

Miles and Wada followed the squire back to the manor house. "Well, we've got some help, eh?" Wada said.

"Aye," Miles said.

"That Guillame fellow seems decent enough, for a Frenchy."

"He does."

"Typical lord, though. Wants to be in charge."

"That's what worries me," Miles said.

* * *

At the manor house, everyone went to sleep soon after dark. Only the richest nobles and churchmen could afford candles for staying up later. The fire pit was banked, and its dying light filled the hall with deep shadows. The hall was full of sleeping men and women, including Guillame and his squire.

The fading light from below spilled over the low half-wall of the solar, where Millicent brushed Blanche's hair by the light of a single candle, stroking the horsehair brush through the lustrous black locks that had been braided all day, now and then pulling a flea from the brush and squashing it. She smiled as she worked. Her mistress would not be sneaking off to the Engishman's quarters tonight—not while Lord Guillame was here.

"I don't approve of what you're doing with Miles," she told Blanche.

"Duly noted," Blanche said.

"He's beneath you. And he's English. Why, he's practically a savage."

"Thank you, Milli, I shall keep that in mind."

"If the king found out . . ."

Blanche looked back over her shoulder. "But he won't find out, will he?"

"Not from me, but there's others that won't hesitate to tell if they learn."

Blanche sighed. "I agree. It's not a situation that can go on forever. I thought Miles and I could keep our relationship secret, but it appears I was naïve."

The brush strokes became more furious. "So what will you do?"

"I don't know," Blanche said.

"You could send Miles packing, that's what you could do. And the sooner the better."

"I won't give him up."

The brush strokes grew harder still.

"Ow!" Blanche said.

Milli said, "God help us, don't tell me you're—"

"I'm in love with him, yes."

This time, Blanche thought Milli would brush the hair right out of her head.

"There's nothing good can come of that," Milli said. "Women have lovers, but they're supposed to be noble, gallant, beautiful—otherwise, what's the point? Now, Lord Guillame—that's the kind of man you should be looking at. He's so handsome. And he's a lord, a real Norman lord. He's not good enough for you to marry, but he'd make a perfect lover."

Blanche sighed again. Milli was nobly born, but she was the seventh child—and fourth daughter—so there had been no dowry for her, no titles to inherit. Milli's eldest sister, a countess, had gotten her the position with Blanche when Blanche was still married to the earl.

Blanche said, "I told you, Milli, I'm not getting married again."

"That's impractical, my lady. It sounds good, but it will be hard to do. Let the king find someone for you. He'll do you right."

Blanche was quiet for a bit, then she said, "What about you? Have you ever been in love?"

Milli's brush strokes slowed. "There *was* a man, a knight. Handsome and brave, he was. And willing to take me without a dowry."

"What happened?"

Milli shrugged. "The crusade. He never came back. I never learned what happened to him. And now . . ."

"And now, instead of being at the earl's court in Normandy, you're stuck in this English backwater, with little prospects of ever meeting a proper man."

"Aye, my lady. That's about it."

"I'm sorry."

Milli said, "It's the Lord's will, I suppose."

"Don't give up hope. Something good will happen for you."

"Yes, my lady," Milli said, but she didn't sound convinced.

Chapter 11

"A pox upon these English roads," Gervase growled.

Joscelin, the handsome abbot of Huntley, tried to make a joke of it. "I fear you curse without reason, my friend, for there are no roads here. There is barely even a track in this English wilderness. In truth, a goat would be hard put to follow it."

Gervase, who was Huntley's cellarer, huddled in his brown cloak. "At least it's stopped raining."

"Thank the Lord for something," Joscelin said.

It was a dark, gloomy day. The two men made their way down a long incline and crossed a boggy stretch at the bottom. Dank mist swirled around them. The trees were largely bereft of leaves.

"And still three days till we see Huntley again," said Gervase. "When I get my own abbey, please God it's not in England."

"Lady Blanche's manors are around here somewhere," Joscelin said, thinking aloud. "If we knew where, exactly, we could stay there this night." *And perhaps I could finally share her bed.* Joscelin still dreamed about Blanche. He could not believe she had rejected him, still thought she'd been playing with him, was still certain that, in the end, she would be open to his advances. He sighed. "There's no time to search for them, though. I suppose we'll take refuge at that new castle of Brightwood that we heard about. Its lord, whoever he is, is certain to welcome us, and we'll be safe there. This is bad country."

"So they say," Gervase relplied, "but I've seen no sign of it. I've seen no sign of anything save mud." Gervase, slender and sharp-featured, was a distant relation of the king, and marked for big things. He turned in the saddle and shouted to the pedlar behind them. "Keep up, there! If you can't move any faster, we'll leave you."

The pedlar, whose name was Sindolf, prodded his pack-laden horse. "Doing my best, my lords."

"Well, do better!"

The pedlar had joined the two clerics for safety, and for that same reason they had accepted him. The larger the party, the better, when traveling.

Abbot Joscelin had been in Crewe, attending his family after the death of his brother Hugh, who had been gored while hunting boar. The wound had festered and Hugh had died—in agony, they said, though Joscelin and Gervase had thankfully arrived too late to witness that.

"We should not have tarried at that priory for so long," Joscelin lamented. On their way back, the two men had sheltered for a number of days at the priory of St. Edwina.

Gervase smiled. "Aye, but the nuns were so . . . hospitable."

"That they were," said Joscelin with fond memories, especially of Sister Petronille. God's breath, that one could give Blanche a run for her money.

"Now it's back to the everyday world," Gervase lamented.

"At least that Gretch creature is dead," Joscelin said. "Give Earl Galon credit for that. With Gretch and his gang gone, an enormous debt has been removed from our shoulders. Money we could never pay. The abbey has been saved from ruin. At least for the moment."

Galon had determined to rid Badford Town of the criminal Morys Gretch and his gang. He'd sent men into Gretch's stronghold to flush him out, then surrounded the town and waited for Gretch to try to escape. Gretch did, and Galon's men caught him. They hanged him, then burned Gretch's part of the town. The fire had gotten out of control, as fires tended to do, and a considerable portion of Badford had gone up in flames.

While the two clerics talked, Sindolf struggled on behind. The coming of the French had largely destroyed the once-thriving commercial trade in England. The French were interested only in war and religion; trade and commerce meant little to them. Sindolf's grandfather had been a wealthy dealer in slaves, exporting English children from Bristol to Ireland and sometimes to more exotic venues like Marseilles and even ports on the African coast. The French had outlawed the slave trade, though, and Sindolf's family, like most English trading families, had fallen into poverty, with Sindolf eking out a living as a pedlar.

The party left the marshy bottomland and started up the long rise on the other side. There was a belt of thick brush to their left. Gervase looked back at the pedlar. "God's breakfast, that fellow's slow. Shall we just go on without him?"

Joscelin was about to reply, then he stopped.

Standing in the mist at the top of the hill, as though waiting for them, was a young man. In the man's right hand was a bow, its tip resting on the ground. The man's left fist was propped on his hip, and there was a dagger with a notched handle at his belt.

"Greetings," said the figure cheerily, and, when the figure spoke, the two clerics started, because it was not a young man after all, but a woman. She was not unattractive, tall and sturdily built, reddish hair peeking from under her hood. She grinned at them. "Bit late in the year for travel, isn't it, my lords? Dangerous country, too, so I'm told."

Behind him, Joscelin heard the slow clopping of the pedlar's pack horse as it labored up the rise. "What do you want?" he asked the young woman.

Her grin broadened. "Why, your money, of course."

"We are clerics, we have no money."

"Now, now, now." She wagged a finger playfully. " 'Thou shalt not lie.' I'm sure that's one of the Commandments, can't remember the number."

Joscelin wasn't having this from a girl, armed or not. "Get out of the way before we trample you."

"Oh, I don't think that's going to happen."

She put her thumb and middle finger to her mouth and whistled. Still smiling, she inclined her chin at something behind the travelers.

They turned and saw men advancing toward them. The men's leader was tall and heavily muscled. He was bare chested in this cold weather, and his chest was covered in designs rendered in blue ink. His eyes were wild, and his long blond hair was done in a topknot. But the scariest thing about him was the way he walked—with an exaggerated swagger, almost a dance, as if he were moving to a rhythm only he could hear, bobbing his head. He carried an axe, and there was a short sword in his belt, and he looked like he wanted to hit someone in the worst way.

The pedlar Sindolf crossed himself. "The Viking."

With the Viking was a band of men, dirty and disheveled, armed with a variety of wicked-looking weapons. They must have been hiding in the brush.

The red-haired woman smiled as the Viking swaggered up to the two clerics. "Your purses," he said with a thick accent.

"See here—" Joscelin started.

The Viking grabbed Joscelin, who was not a small man, by the arm and effortlessly tossed him from his saddle to the ground. Joscelin lay stunned. When he tried to get up, the Viking kicked him in the stomach. Joscelin bent over, retching, and the Viking kicked him again, in the ribs. The Viking drew back his foot once more.

"All right! All right!" Joscelin cried, raising a hand in surrender.

The Viking turned to Gervase, who hastily scrambled from his saddle.

Two of the robbers cut the purses from the clerics' belts. Two more pulled off the clerics' heavy cloaks, felt under their robes, and found the larger purses hidden there.

The Viking grunted with satisfaction. "Those cowls look warm. Take them off."

The clerics removed their hooded cowls and handed them over. The red-haired woman took them. "Excellent cloth," she remarked, examining them. "From Bruges?"

"Yes," Joscelin said. "How did you know?"

The Viking backhanded Joscelin's face so hard that blood flowed from his nose. "Be quiet. Hold out your hands."

Joscelin and Gervase extended their hands, the fingers of which bristled with jeweled rings.

"Remove the rings," the Viking ordered.

Joscelin said, "We're not allowed to. These are—"

The Viking brandished the axe. "Place his hand on that log."

Two of the robbers grabbed Joscelin's arms and led him toward a fallen tree. They pushed him to his knees, forced his right hand onto the tree, pried open his fingers.

The Viking swaggered over and raised his axe.

"All right! All right!" Joscelin said.

He and Gervase tugged the rings from their fingers. "We're servants of God. You're committing a Mortal Sin. You'll go to Hell for this."

"You'll see Hell first if you don't go faster with those rings," the Viking told him.

When the rings had been collected, the two clerics stood in abject dismay. The Viking grabbed the large silver crucifix that hung from Joscelin's neck and made to rip it off. "No! Please," said the abbot, and now there were tears in his eyes.

The Viking considered. He turned to the girl, who shrugged. "It's the image of Our Lord," she said. "Taking it might bring us bad luck. Besides, we'd have to melt it down to sell it, and it would be a shame to destroy such beautiful handiwork."

The Viking grunted and took his hand away.

Meanwhile, other robbers had taken Sindolf's packs from his horse and spread their contents on the ground. There were cook pots, tin cups, decorated purses, a music pipe, hoods, gloves, knives, hose of different colors, bolts of cloth, and some cheap relics.

"Why are you standing there?" the Viking said to Joscelin. "Go."

Trembling in fear, Joscelin took the reins of his horse and prepared to mount.

The Viking hooked his axe blade over Joscelin's arm. "The horses stay."

"But how will we . . .?"

"Those things at the bottom of your ass are called legs. Use them."

Joscelin and Gervase exchanged glances.

The Viking started forward. "Go!"

The two clerics took off over the hill, moving as fast as they could.

* * *

Fromont watched the two clerics go, stumbling over the rough ground. Beside him, the red-haired girl, Hersent, laughed. "A fine haul," she said.

Fromont rested an arm around her shoulders. "What shall we do with the horses?" she said.

"Aimerie will buy them from us," Fromont said. "The saddles, too. We'll wait a bit before we take them to him, though. Those shave-polls might ask questions if they see their own mounts when they show up at his castle."

The robbers put the loot in a canvas sack. It would be divided up later. Fromont swaggered over to the pedlar. "Your companions did not wait for you," he observed.

Sindolf said nothing. He had been robbed before; he was just hoping to get out of this alive.

"You are English?" Fromont asked him.

"I am."

Hersent joined the men in rummaging through the goods laid out on the ground. "This is all you have in the world?" she asked the pedlar.

"Aye," he said. "The French have seen to that. I was going to sell this lot, then go home for the winter. Wait for spring and head out again."

"Where is your home?"

"Lower Wynchcombe."

Fromont looked over the goods and nodded approvingly. "We can use some of this." To his men he said,

"Pick whatever you like. We'll pay for it from what we took from those clerics."

"Thank . . . thank you," Sindolf told him.

Fromont waved him off dismissively.

The men gathered round Sindolf's goods, chatting as they took things they needed. Fromont examined the hooded cowl he'd taken from the abbot. It would be warm, protect his head and shoulders from the elements. He gave the other cowl to Hersent. They would take the monks' cloaks, as well.

There was the sound of a horse, and Fromont turned.

It was Lord Aimerie's loutish son, Ernoul. Ernoul rode up and reined in. He ran his dark eyes over Hersent, then bowed to her from the saddle. "My lady."

Hersent made no reply.

Ernoul turned to Fromont. "My father has work for us."

Chapter 12

Ediva ran barefoot through the woods, long legs pumping, blonde hair flying behind her. She had shoes but rarely wore them. Her parents were poor and the shoes had belonged to her cousin Edith, whom Ediva didn't like because she put on airs.

Ediva was ten, and she already ran faster than her older brother Stephen, faster than that stupid neighbor boy Hugh. In fact, she ran faster than just about all the boys at Redhill—and the neighboring manors, as well. There was a tri-parish race every Shrove Tuesday, and only a handful of boys her age were able to outrun her there, and none of the girls.

Ediva was glad she'd been picked as one of the village scouts. It was a lot more fun than milking the cow, or doing the wash, or spinning and weaving and mending clothes and pricking her fingers all the time, or looking after her little brother, John, who seemed to do nothing but cry and poop. Her mother said she'd have to learn to do all these things before she got married, and marriage was not that many years off, but right now it was the last thing on her mind. She was free, where she wanted to be, in the quiet of the woods.

She stopped, as she had several times before. She had been out for a long time, and she was some miles from the village, but even after all that running, she was barely breathing hard. "Stop frequently and listen," Father Albinus had told the scouts, and she had followed his instructions.

Now she stopped again. She stood with her back to an oak tree. She closed her eyes, took a deep breath, let it out slowly, and listened.

She heard the sigh of the breeze, the flutter of falling leaves. Birds. Squirrels.

An acorn dropped.

Then she heard a noise she didn't recognize. Far off. A noise that was out of place.

She tensed, ears straining.

Was it the sound of people walking? A murmur of distant voices?

She had to get closer. This time she moved light-footedly, almost tiptoeing, dodging from tree to tree toward the sound. She stopped again and listened.

It *was* people walking. A lot of them. Crunching the fallen leaves.

She eased her head around a tree. "Don't let yourself be seen. Don't get caught." Those words had been hammered into her by Blackie and Miles and Father Albinus. Talk, talk, talk. Old people.

Don't have any fun.

She s-o-o-o wanted to get even closer, to see the horrible robbers everybody talked about.

She took two steps forward and stopped.

She saw movement, coming her way through the barren trees. It was still far off, the figures indistinct even to her good eyes, but she thought one of them had a bare chest.

Suddenly she did not want to get any closer. She turned and started running, bare feet flying. She was scared and excited at the same time and proud of herself because she was the one who had found them.

She ran as fast as she could go, uphill and down, across streams, breathing hard now but not daring to stop, and then she was running up the village street, yelling. "They're coming! They're coming!"

She kept going, across the bridge that led to the manor house where Lady Blanche lived. "They're coming! The robbers are coming!"

Chapter 13

Blanche watched as Miles gathered the men in front of the small wooden church. She worried about Miles's safety, worried about all of them, but she tried not to show it because she was their lord and it was her job not to show it. She wanted to take Miles's arm, to give him support, but she couldn't do that, either. She had to act impassive and confident and above it all, when in fact she was none of those things. Most of the villagers had gathered to see the men off. Ediva stood beside Blanche, happily munching the honey cake Blanche had given her as a reward for finding the outlaws.

Hamo, the new steward, was grumpy. "No good'll come o' this, I'm telling you," he said. "Playing at soldiers when you should be—"

"That's enough," Miles told him. "You've made your feelings clear. Now stay and be quiet, or go about your business."

Hamo grumbled, but he stayed.

"Everyone got their hoods?" Miles asked the men.

There were murmurs of assent. Some of them held up the hoods. One of them was Father Albinus.

"You can't go with us, Father," Miles told him.

"And why not?" said Albinus.

"Well . . . because you're a . . . a priest."

"Of course I'm a priest," Albinus said in his big voice. " 'Smite ye Satan,' so sayeth the Lord. If anybody's going to do some smiting of Satan, it should be a priest, shouldn't it?"

Blanche smiled. "Hard to argue with that," she told Miles.

Tostig, the deacon, said, "Father Albinus was a champion wrestler in his younger days."

"Is that true, Father?" said Wada. Wada had reluctantly eschewed his wolf-fur cloak for something more practicable—and less identifiable.

"That it is," said Albinus. "Came in handy against all those French boys in cathedral school." In truth, he looked like he could still pick up a good-sized man and throw him across the yard.

Miles sighed. "Very well, Father, you can come."

The girl Ediva had said the robbers were approaching from the northeast. Miles and the ex-soldier Blackie had previously scouted locations for an ambush along all the likely access paths to the manor. Miles said, "Blackie, are your lads ready?"

"Ready as they'll ever be." Blackie was in charge of the men with bows, also the men and older boys with slings. Primitive weapons, but they could do a lot of damage.

Blanche had seen them in action in the sieges she'd endured. She'd used one herself.

To the rest of the men, Miles said, "Remember—when we attack, stay in a rough line. Don't get excited and get yourselves separated from the others. This is going to be hit and run. Don't try to be a hero. A lot of these robbers are probably ex-soldiers, trained fighters. You don't want to get in a stand-up fight with them. Hit one, preferably when he's not looking, then get out of there. You understand?"

The men nodded, though some looked disappointed that they wouldn't be doing more. Ivor, the smith, tapped his hammer thoughtfully in the palm of his hand. Miles and Blackie had practiced the men a bit, but not enough. You could never practice enough for this sort of thing, Blanche knew, and in the end practice meant little when the time came.

Blanche stepped forward and addressed the men, her men. "May God grant you success and bring you home safely to your loved ones. Father, if you would bless them, please."

The men knelt. Tostig held a chased pewter bowl of Holy Water, from which Father Albinus sprinkled the men, using an aspergillum, and made the sign of the Cross over them.

"All right," Miles said, "move out."

Men kissed wives and daughters and fell into line. Miles's eyes met Blanche's and she felt a twinge inside her. She remembered watching her first husband, Auteuil, set off for the crusade. Remembered standing there with her children, one of them a babe in arms. This wasn't the same as the crusade, of course, but the result could well be the same. Blanche had learned the hard way that nothing was given in this world.

Miles turned and led the men from the village. Blanche watched them till they were out of sight. She hoped no one saw the tears in her eyes.

Chapter 14

The outlaws moved in a loose formation through the forest, Fromont and Ernoul in the lead, Hersent behind them, dressed as a man, the others following. They were in a light-hearted mood. This was going to be fun.

Fromont walked with a regular gait, eschewing the swaggering, dancing mannerisms. He saved those to scare his victims. He knew people called him "the Viking," and he enjoyed that. He even played to it by wearing his blond hair in a topknot and going bare-chested in all weathers, though that got damned cold at times. In truth, he was not Norse at all but Flemish, born in a village called Tenhoute, from which he'd fled at age fifteen to become a soldier, fighting for any lord who would hire him. Soldiering had been a good life—better than living in Tenhoute—but the last peace had left Fromont stranded in England, with no money. He'd fallen in with a group of men like himself, ex-mercenaries, outlaws, peasants who'd fled their manors, runaway clerics, whores, girls like Hersent, fleeing poverty or abuse. They roamed the countryside, robbing and plundering.

They had joined the robbers of Alton Forest not long after Aimerie had. Aimerie was already the robbers' leader. He was a noble, and he could plan. Fromont's goal was to return to France, or Flanders, and get back to soldiering. He wasn't happy being a robber, but getting from Trentshire to France wasn't that easy.

He'd been glad when Aimerie took Brightwood. Aimerie had taken the worst of the robbers with him—the killers without remorse, the crazy men, the men without honor. Some of these men became Aimerie's "guards;" others, like Joubert. became manor functionaries. Now they could live in relative comfort and abuse peasants, a pastime that didn't appeal to Fromont, who had declined to participate in the taking of Brightwood.

The truth was, Fromont didn't like Aimerie very much. He didn't trust him. Aimerie was a noble, but not, Fromont thought, a man of honor. And he definitely didn't like Ernoul. Ernoul had been an arrogant little shit when first they met; he was worse now. Ernoul still accompanied the robbers on their forays, however. It was good exercise for the boy, Aimerie claimed, and Ernoul enjoyed himself, even though he bristled at taking orders from a commoner like Fromont. But that was Aimerie's charge to Ernoul—that he learn from Fromont. In return, Ernoul had been given more and more responsibility, until he was now effectively the group's second-in-command.

"What's the plan?" Ernoul asked Fromont. Ernoul wore an old mail shirt and a padded leather cap, and there was a sword in his belt.

"The usual. Break fences, take a cow, some sheep, throw a few sacks of grain on a cart. You and I will cover the manor house and keep the bailiffs from coming out. Don't kill anyone unless you have to. We're here for property."

"What fun is it if you can't kill someone?" Ernoul complained. He cast a sideways look at Hersent. "What about women then?" Fromont knew Ernoul liked Hersent, though he thought that was mostly because she was Fromont's woman.

Hersent had the bow slung jauntily over her shoulder. "What's wrong?" she taunted. "Rape the only way you can get a girl?"

Ernoul's brow darkened.

"No women this time, either," Fromont said. "This will be a quick job—those are your father's orders. We'll turn up the pressure on these people gradually, if they won't see reason."

Ernoul snorted. "If I had my way, we'd burn the place to the ground."

"And then what?" Fromont said. "There'd be nothing left for Lord Aimerie to tax. The manor would be of no use to him."

"Those peasants would learn to fear us, that's what use it would be."

"They already fear us," Hersent said. "Besides, I thought you wanted to marry Lady Blanche and have Redhill for your own. It'll be no good to you if it's a wasteland."

Ernoul didn't care. "Blanche can worry about that while she's rearing my children. I'll be in France by then, winning glory and wealth, not tramping around this stupid English countryside." Something occurred to him. "Once I'm a knight, I'll need a war band. I'll need foot soldiers. Maybe you and some of this lot can come with me, Fromont. Hersent can come, as well." He leered at her. "Always nice to have a pretty face around the camp."

"I think I'll stay here," Fromont said. "For a while, anyway."

Ernoul said, "What about you, Hersent?"

"I don't know what I'll be doing," she said, "but I know it won't involve being your camp follower."

Ernoul shrugged. "Your loss."

Chapter 15

"Put on your hoods," Miles ordered.

There was a rustle of coarse fabric as the men obeyed.

Miles, Wada, and the rest of the men were hunched behind a brush-shrouded embankment, near a creek. They heard the robbers approaching, heard the drone of voices. The robbers were taking no precautions, obviously thought themselves safe. On the other side of the path, Blackie waited in the trees with the archers and slingers. This was one of the positions Miles and Blackie had scouted earlier. They would have had more cover in the summer, but there was nothing they could do about that.

Miles felt himself tense as the robbers came closer. He gripped the hilt of his scramasax. He would have felt better protected if he had his old shield and helmet and his plated jack, but there was nothing he could do about that. He was tense, but somehow calm as well, ready for whatever happened. He hadn't done this in a long time, not since Wales. In Wales it had been the English who were ambushed. This would be different. It would be good not to be on the receiving end of an ambush for a change.

The outlaws came closer. Miles could distinguish individual voices. He looked up and down his line of men and motioned them to be ready. They eased themselves to the lip of the bank. The first robbers were opposite them now. Ernoul and a bare-chested man were leading them. Behind them was a red-haired lad. The boy looked familiar, and Miles tried to place—

Some fool jumped to his feet. "Christ," he yelped in terror. "It's the Viking!"

* * *

Fromont heard someone cry out from the creek bank to his right. He turned, ready for trouble, and saw a man running away through the trees.

That turn of the head possibly saved his life, because at that moment something clipped his left ear and it exploded in blood.

He grabbed his bloody ear and bent over. Hersent unslung her bow and yelled a warning. Ernoul was yelling, too.

There was a *whump*, and an arrow buried itself in someone's side. More arrows. All from the left. Cries of pain. Fromont glimpsed hooded men in the trees. Rocks flew from slings. One hit a robber in the face and he collapsed, clutching his eye. Another struck a robber in the knee, and the man hopped around in pain. Another flight of arrows. Fromont wondered about the man who had run away and if there were more men hidden on that side, but Ernoul had already pointed his sword in the direction of the bowmen. "After them!"

Chapter 16

The robbers started into the trees after Blackie's men.

"Now!" Miles hissed. "Remember—no yelling till you're right on top of them."

He heaved himself over the bank and ran forward with his men. The line of silent, hooded men rushed up on the outlaws from behind. Miles tried to get to the Viking, or to Ernoul, but somebody got in his way and Miles stabbed the man in the back, just behind the heart. He pulled the scramasax out and slashed at another man, gouging his arm. The men in hoods held their line well, and now they were yelling and screaming as they struck with axes and spears and daggers. Wada's iron bar landed on someone's head with a sickening thud. One of the robbers turned, and Ivor the smith caught him in the face with his hammer.

"Fall back!" Miles cried. "Now!"

With the robbers thrown off balance from this second attack, Miles's men turned and ran for the creek bed and the path to their fallback position. A few of them, caught up in the action, did not want to stop, and Miles pulled them away. "Run!"

He made his way through the trees. There was shouting behind him. The robbers were getting ready to start after them when another volley of arrows and rocks hit them from behind. That was enough. Despite the efforts of the Viking, Ernoul, and the red-haired fellow, the robbers broke and ran back the way they had come. Miles didn't stay to watch. He kept going. Down the embankment, across the creek and into the woods on the other side. He ran, pulling off his hood for air, until he reached the fallback position on a hill about a mile away.

Miles waited on the hill, Wada and Father Albinus beside him. Many of the men were splashed or flecked with blood. All were heaving for breath, but excited, proud of what they'd done, clapping one another on the back and bragging.

There was no sign of pursuit. "Anyone hurt?" Miles said.

There were some cuts and scrapes. One man had broken a finger going down the embankment. Other than that, everyone was fine.

"Who broke our cover?" Miles said.

"Giles the potter," said Blackie.

Wada laughed. "He's probably still running."

"Dumb bastard," somebody said, "no wonder his house is falling down.

"It's funny now," Miles said, "but he could have gotten us all killed. We were lucky." He looked them over. "We won today, but this is just the beginning. They're not done, and they're going to be mad. Now let's get out of here before they regroup and come looking for us."

Chapter 17

Hersent left Old Frida's hut, her face as grim as her mood. Frida had dyed Hersent's red hair blue and braided it with leather thongs. All eyes were on Hersent as she marched through the ramshackle camp, and she liked that. After the disaster on the way to Redhill, she needed to show that her spirit wasn't broken. They all did.

The outlaws called themselves the Brotherhood, and their camp was deep in the forest. There were semi-permanent huts and tents, and combinations of the two. Lean-tos. Ragged children played in the cold mud, women suckled babes. The air was heavy with the smells of unwashed humanity, of sewage and sickness, of choking smoke from damp fires.

Hersent was from Yorkshire, or so she'd been told, because she remembered nothing of it. Her family had been refugees, burned out by the Bastard King, William, when he laid waste to the North. Her once-prosperous parents had finally found work on a manor, as landless cottars. They couldn't afford to feed Hersent when she got older, and so planned to sell her to slave traders. Hersent didn't like that and ran away. She'd wandered from place to place and, inevitably, ended up as a prostitute. She'd been beaten by a customer, had killed him in retaliation, and run away again.

On the road, she'd pretended to be a man, for self-protection. She'd thrown in with a group of merchants who had then been robbed by Fromont and his gang. At that point, she had decided it was better to be predator than prey, so she had joined the robbers and been with them ever since. It was the best life she'd ever known.

She approached Fromont's hut, which was made of logs, the inside walls covered with animal skins. The roof comprised thickly woven branches covered with pine boughs. Fromont leaned in the hut's entrance, which was a hide drawn across the opening, his face brooding in rage, and maybe grief. His bare-chested look was not used in camp. He wore a shirt, overshirt, and cloak. A blood-stained bandage covered his mangled left ear.

He straightened as Hersent came near, and his eyes widened at the sight of her blue hair. "You look ready for war."

"I am," she said. "How do you feel?"

"It hurts," he said of his ear, "but I've been hurt before." His deep blue eyes seemed to burn. "Those were my men, my friends. Poor Reynard . . ." His voice tailed off, and Hersent knew why. The image of Reynard's face, caved in by a blacksmith's hammer, would be burned into her mind for life.

Fromont went on. "I'll find the men who did this, and I'll flay them alive."

"And I'll help you," she said. "They'll wish—"

There was a distant whistle. Followed by another, closer in. Then a third.

A man shouted, "Somebody coming. Looks like Lord Aimerie and his son."

Fromont said nothing. He waited with hooded eyes, rage eating at him.

A few minutes later, Aimerie and Ernoul appeared, followed by a squire. Their horses picked their way along what passed for the camp's street. Men, women, and children clustered around them. Aimerie reached out and shook hands with the adults, rubbed the heads of children. Not that long ago, he had been one of these people, one of the Brotherhood. He distributed coins. A few of the women held up children for him to look at, and Hersent knew that the children were either Aimerie's or Ernoul's. Ernoul was more reserved than his father, though he acknowledged some of the women he'd bedded.

Aimerie and Ernoul reached Fromont's hut and dismounted. The squire held their horses. "Place hasn't changed much," Aimerie allowed, looking around.

Fromont was terse, his words clipped. "No, my lord."

Aimerie smiled at Hersent and gestured. "I like your hair."

"Thank you, my lord. It's how the Old Ones wore their hair for war, or so I'm told."

Ernoul said, "I've never had a woman with blue hair."

"And if you ever do, it won't be me," Hersent told him.

"Oh, ho!" Aimerie laughed at that.

"We'll see," Ernoul said.

"A drink, my lord?" offered Fromont.

Hersent brought them wine, which Fromont kept on hand for these visits, and Aimerie said, "Let's get to it. What happened? I heard Ernoul's story, now for yours."

"We were ambushed," Fromont said. "It's that simple."

"How many did you lose?"

"Seven dead, thirteen wounded, with Arnault and Eudes not expected to live."

"A bad business. Ernoul says the men who did it wore hoods?"

"They did, my lord, like those peasants in Brittany a few years back. The attack was well coordinated. They had archers on one side, and when we went after them, their footmen hit us from behind. Whoever planned it knew what he was doing."

"Hmmm. Were you able to recognize any of them?"

Fromont shook his head. "No, not with the hoods over their faces."

"How could they have known where to intercept you?" Aimerie said.

"I've wondered about that, my lord, and I've no idea. We weren't on a well-traveled track."

"D'ye think there's traitors in the camp?"

"It's possible, but who would they have sold us out to? And how would they have got the word out? No one left camp before we marched, I'm certain of that."

"If we had been more alert on the march, this wouldn't have happened," Ernoul pointed out.

Fromont glared at him, and his voice grew quiet. "Are you saying it was my fault?"

"You were in charge."

"You were there, too, and I didn't notice you being very alert. You were mostly concerned with bragging about yourself."

"Watch your tongue, lest you find yourself being pulled apart by horses after I'm knighted."

Fromont's chest swelled, and Hersent knew he was ready to go after Ernoul. Aimerie must have known it, too, because he stepped between them. "All right, all right. Instead of fighting amongst ourselves, we need to find out who these people were." He thought. "One name comes to mind. Strange that Miles Edwulfson shows up, and immediately afterwards, this happens."

"Miles Edwulfson?" said Ernoul. "Who's that?"

"Blanche's steward," Aimerie told him. "You met him the other day."

"Oh. The Englishman. I paid him no attention."

Fromont was still glaring at Ernoul, and Hersent was glad that Fromont didn't have his axe to hand.

"Miles was quite the soldier in his day," Aimerie went on. "A hero. Brought his company of footmen out of Wales, along with the old earl of Trent. Everyone else in that expedition was killed. His father was English nobility, or what the English call nobility."

Ernoul snorted at the concept of English nobility. "You think this Miles fellow was involved? If he was, that means my future wife Blanche must have been involved, as well, and I don't picture Blanche leading a revolt."

Aimerie said, "Don't let Blanche fool you. She's a hard woman. Had to be, to put up with old Trent's family."

"What about Guillame of Edsworth?" Hersent suggested. "Maybe he finally decided to fight."

Fromont nodded agreement to that idea. "Aye. He was in France when the *capuchins* were active, he'd likely know about them. Maybe he decided to try something like that here. They say he's a good knight."

"Maybe," Aimerie said. "Either way, these people must be taught a lesson. Fromont, I think you and your men should pay Lord Guillame a visit. In the meanwhile, be alert. These damned English peasants might start believing in themselves, and that's the last thing we need."

Fromont said, "Aye my lord," and his eyes were so filled with a desire for revenge that they almost glowed.

Chapter 18

Wada looked over his shoulder. "Those fellows are getting closer."

Father Albinus glanced behind him, as well. "Aye, they are."

"D'ye think they're the . . .?"

"We'll find out soon enough. I'll tell you, though, after two days of this parading back and forth, I'm ready for the real thing."

The three men had been behind Albinus's party for some time and were gradually drawing nearer. Not like they were putting effort into it, more like they were just walking a bit faster than Wada and Albinus. Wada and Albinus accompanied Millicent, who wore one of Blanche's cloaks and rode sidesaddle on one of Blanche's horses.

"Wouldn't be so bad, weren't for this damned rain," Wada went on. "Wish I had that wolf-fur cloak. Nice and warm, that is."

"But you wouldn't look like a servant then, would you?" Albinus said.

Wada sighed. "Maybe I should have been a crusader like I wanted to be. If I was in the Holy Land now, I'd be warm and dry."

"You're not in the Holy Land," Albinus told him. "Nor likely to get there any time soon. And if you were in the Holy Land, your head would have long since decorated some Musselman's spear. Just be glad this isn't snow. A little bit colder, and it would be."

They plodded down the road, Albinus using a staff, Wada's hands stuffed beneath the old cloak he'd brought from home. Their breaths vaporized in the chill air. The last faded leaves dangled from tree branches, forlorn and abandoned.

Wada tried to be polite and include Milli in the conversation. "You warm enough, Milli?"

"No, I'm not," she said without looking at him. "And you'll be pleased to call me Millicent."

Wada stiffened. "No need to get all high and mighty. You're only pretending to be a lady, you know."

She looked at him this time, and her eyes blazed. "I'm as well born as any, and you're a peasant. Don't forget that."

"You've got no right to—"

"Leave her be, lad," Albinus said. "Leave her be. There's no reasoning with women, especially French women."

"And I'll thank *you* to mind your own business, as well," Milli told him, "priest or no."

Albinus laughed heartily.

Milli went on. "How did an English peasant become a priest, anyway? Taking Holy Orders requires schooling, and that requires money."

"That it does," Albinus agreed. "And you're right, I am a peasant—from our very own parish of St. Michael's."

"No," Milli said in disbelief.

"It's true. I must have showed promise because old Lord Odo, God bless his soul, paid to have me sent to cathedral school, and from there I studied for the priesthood."

"How did you end up back here?" Milli said, and there was no mistaking the sneer in her voice when she said "here". "Seems a waste of all that money and training."

"Not to me, it doesn't," said Albinus. "It was always my dream to come back here and tend the flock. I wanted to bring religion to the people, where it belongs."

Milli couldn't fathom that. "Didn't you have any better offers?"

"Depends on what you call 'better.' Oh, I could have gone to Winchester. Could have gone to France with the bishop of Salisbury, even. I could have been an administrator, maybe even ventured into the halls of power, but that kind of life wasn't for me. Putting on airs with a bunch of stuck-up Frenchies—no offence, ma'am."

"But you could have made a difference," Milli said.

"I am making a difference. I'm doing something good, seeing to the needs of my flock, instead of being a cog in the great wheel of the Church hierarchy. It's easy to get lost there, easy to forget the things that are important. Too many of our parish vicars can barely recite a *Pater Noster*."

"Typical English," Milli sniffed. "No ambition."

Albinus said, "Well, now, sucking up to archbishops and great lords, that's not my idea of being a priest. Don't see how you're going to save many souls doing that."

Milli harrumphed and shook her head.

Behind them, the squashing of feet in the mud grew closer. Albinus and Wada turned to see their three fellow travelers toiling along. The three men carried no packs, as travelers normally did, and each had a long dagger in his belt. One was a boy of about thirteen or fourteen, his hair cut very short, revealing a scar across his rain-wet scalp. There was a birthmark beside the tip of his chin.

"Good day to you," cried the lead traveler jovially. He was a dark-bearded fellow with a bunch of broken teeth, and his English had a heavy Flemish accent.

"The same to you," said Father Albinus. "Though there's little good about this weather, I fear."

"You're right there," said the dark-bearded fellow. "Where are you bound?"

"Badford Town," said Albinus.

"You mean what's left of it after the fire," said the second traveler, a heavy-set man with thick lips.

Albinus said, "I heard about that fire. Was it as bad as they say?"

"More'n half the town gone," said the man with thick lips. "Shitte Lane's totally burned, not that that's much of a loss."

Albinus shrugged. "This'll give 'em a chance to rebuild, start over."

"There was a tavern in Badford," Wada said wistfully, "the Saracen's Head. Hope it's still there. There's a serving maid there I fancy."

Ahead of them, Millicent made a disparaging noise.

"You got business in Badford?" the man with thick lips asked.

"We're escorting Lady Millicent, here, to see her sister, who lives nearby. I'm her chaplain, Albinus. This is Wada, my assistant."

"I'm Jacob," said the black-bearded man. "This is Pierre, and the boy is Etienne. Etienne the Horny, we call him—oops, sorry, my lady, guess I shouldn't have said that. See here, we're bound for Badford ourselves, then Leicester. What say we tag along with you? We could band together for protection from thieves. Be good for the lady."

"Is that all right with you, my lady?" Albinus asked Millicent.

"As long as they're not impertinent," Milli said without looking. "And they're not to address me."

"Suits us," Jacob said cheerily, as though he hadn't been offended. He raised his eyebrows to Albinus and said in a low voice, "She always like this?"

"Always," said Albinus.

Jacob made a face.

After a bit, the party came to a stream. Beyond the stream was a hill with a stand of trees. There had been a rude bridge here, but the bridge had fallen apart and never been fixed, so they had to ford. Milli went first, Wada holding her horse's reins as he led the animal across the rocky stream bed.

"How's the water?" Jacob cried.

"How d'ye think it is?" Wada said. "It's cold. I still might go to the Holy Land. Be worth getting killed just to warm up."

Jacob, Albinus, and the others laughed.

Wada got the horse across the stream. On the far side, he stamped his feet vigorously on the gravel bank, to warm them. As he did, Albinus crossed, Jacob just behind him, both of them yelling as their legs went into the icy water. Pierre and Etienne followed, with similar reactions.

As Albinus reached the far side, five men appeared from a previously unseen fold in the ground, brandishing an assortment of weapons. From behind Wada and Albinus came the sound of steel being drawn. They turned, to see their three new companions brandishing their daggers.

"Looks like we did well," said the newcomers' leader, an ex-soldier judging by the scars on his face. "Fromont will be pleased." He scrambled down the muddy stream bank to Milli. "Off the horse, your ladyship."

Milli flared. "How dare you—"

"Off the horse, or I'll drag you off."

Milli curbed her temper and jumped down.

"Search her," the leader said.

The boy Etienne pushed forward. "Let me do it," he said eagerly. "Always wanted to feel up a noblewoman."

The leader gave him an amused look. "Want to do more than that?"

Etienne's eyes widened. "Damned right, I do."

The leader grinned. "Fair enough. You can have her first, you've earned it. She seems hot tempered, maybe you can cool her off before the rest of us take her."

Etienne reached for Milli, but she pushed him away. "No!"

"Shut up." The leader went to slap her, but was stopped by an arrow thudding into his back.

He stepped sideways awkwardly, arms flailing, then fell face first into the rocky stream.

The outlaws turned and were greeted by a flight of arrows from the stand of trees. Jacob fell, so did Pierre, and another one of the new five. Albinus hit another in the head with his staff. Wada pulled the iron bar from beneath his cloak and struck Etienne in the knee with it. The boy dropped to the ground, crying in pain, his knee shattered. The rest of the outlaws dropped their weapons and held up their hands.

A party of men, their faces hidden by hoods, emerged from the trees. Miles removed his hood. "Good work," he told Albinus and his group.

"You had us worried for a bit," Albinus said, examining his staff to make sure it wasn't cracked. "Didn't know if you were there."

Milli straightened her dress and tried to regain her dignity. "Couldn't you have acted more quickly?"

"Had to make sure none of 'em got away," Miles told her.

The rest of the men removed their hoods, as well. Blackie indicated the prisoners. "What'll we do with them?"

"Hang 'em," Miles said.

"Even the boy?"

"Do it now, or do it a year from now. He knew what he was getting into."

Chapter 19

They hanged the surviving outlaws, including the wounded ones, in the stand of trees, using rope they'd brought with them for that purpose. Father Albinus heard the outlaws' confessions and gave them absolution. A couple of the outlaws cried; the rest met their end without a whimper, including the boy Etienne.

"Kid died game, I'll give him that," Blackie said.

Ivor, the smith, said, "What'll we do with the bodies?"

"Leave 'em," Miles said. "Crows have to eat, too. Same with the ones we killed in the fight. Pull 'em out of the water first. They'll make it go bad."

While a couple of the men dragged the bodies of Jacob, Pierre, and the outlaws' leader to the stream bank, Albinus said to Miles, "Well, your plan worked."

"Worked?" said Millicent. "It almost got me raped, is what it did." She was shaking, whether from fear or anger or hurt to her pride it was impossible to say.

Miles tried to mollify her. "You did well."

"You were never in any danger," Wada added.

"That's easy for you to say," Milli snapped. "Mark me, I'm going to tell her ladyship what happened."

Blackie was unimpressed by Milli's attitude. "I expect her ladyship will be pleased with the outcome," he said to her.

"I didn't ask you to speak to me," she told Blackie. To Miles, she said, "Don't expect to use me as bait for any more of your schemes."

Miles had asked around and learned that the majority of roadside robberies occurred in just a few places, places that were ideal for ambush. He'd picked one of those spots and laid an ambush of his own. He'd put Millicent, Albinus, and Wada on the road as a lure. While Albinus and his group rode up and down the road, Miles and the others had hidden in the stand of trees. They were wet and cold from lying in the mud for two days, and they'd been about to give up, when they'd spotted the five robbers taking up positions in the fold of land near the stream.

"Let's get out of here and get warm," Miles told the group. He gestured with his chin. "Ivor."

With his hammer, the blacksmith nailed a spare hood to a tree from which one of the bandits hung.

"Let 'em know who did it," Miles said.

The party made its way back to Redhill. Everyone was in a good mood, save for Milli, who seemed to feel that her noble status had slighted and refused to speak. The rain was still falling, but not as hard as it had been earlier. Outside the village, the party split up; and Miles, Millicent, and Wada crossed the bridge to the manor house in the fading light. A servant boy came to their horses.

Miles expected to find Blanche waiting. He wanted to give her word of their success. “Where is Lady Blanche?” he asked the servant, looking around.

“She’s at Edsworth,” the boy said. “Invited to dine with Lord Guillame.”

Miles stiffened, and Milli smirked at him.

Chapter 20

Guillame and Blanche stood at the main door to Edsworth Hall, under the thatched awning, watching the rain. Blanche was wrapped in her white cloak, Guillame stood behind her. It was late afternoon. They had dined earlier, and then the rain had come. The manor yard was nearly empty, people occasionally scurrying about on some mission or other. In the distance, a smith's hammer rang on an anvil. Cattle lowed. Somewhere a woman screamed at a child.

"I had hoped we could go hawking today," Guillame said, "but . . ."

"The weather," Blanche said, "yes. It's a shame. I looked forward to seeing more of your estate. It's very nice, from what I've seen of it so far."

"Yes, it is. A fitting reward for my father's service to King William, though . . ." His voice tailed off.

"Though what?" she said.

"Though there are times I wish he'd never won it."

She looked over her shoulder at him.

"I feel so alone here," he explained, "especially since my wife died. I've no one to speak to save Hugobert and Rotrou, my steward. This is an alien land. When I was a squire and then a young knight in Normandy, the people dressed like me, they talked like me. I felt at home there. I don't feel that way here, and I don't think I ever will. These English villeins . . . I know peasants always hate the lords, but it's different here. There's a sullen hostility; you feel it everywhere you go. It's like a darkness that surrounds you, and it can be quite overwhelming at times. Don't you feel the same?"

"I haven't been here that long to notice," Blanche said. "Anyway, I have nowhere else to go. I have to make the best of what I've got."

"So do I, but . . . well, it's hard sometimes. Lonely."

Blanche stared at the cold rain.

Guillame went on. "That's why I invited you here today. I thought we should get to know one another, being neighbors and now allies against Aimerie."

Blanche said nothing.

"You seem distracted," Guillame said.

She nodded. "I suppose I am. Miles and some of my men are out there somewhere, trying to trap outlaws, and I'm wishing I was a man so I could be out there with them. I'm wondering if they're all right. For all I know, they could be dead now. Milli is with them, as well."

"Milli? Your maid?"

"Yes."

"I wondered why she didn't come with you. What's she doing chasing outlaws?"

“I don’t know, but Miles said it was necessary that she go along.”

Guillame frowned. “Sounds hare-brained to me. I think you place too much trust in this Miles fellow.”

“He knows what he’s doing.”

“Are you sure? He might have been a soldier, but he was a common footman, not a knight. This is the second operation he’s led without asking my permission, and I’m getting tired of it. Can’t you control him?”

“I told him to do it,” Blanche said.

“Forgive me, but a peasant shouldn’t be leading operations against a noble like Aimerie. It’s not right. It’s disrespectful.”

“He’s not leading operations against Aimerie himself,” she said. *Not yet.* “Just the robbers.”

“All the same, I’m supposed to be in charge. How do you think I feel when I hear that Miles is making decisions without my knowledge?”

There was a pause; the only sound was the falling rain. Then Guillame took a deep breath, as though steeling himself. “See, here, Blanche—I *can* call you Blanche, can’t I? Let’s not argue. I’ve only known you a short while, but, well . . . I’m fascinated by you.”

Blanche said nothing, and Guillame went on. “You’re beautiful. You’re strong. And . . . and you would make an excellent wife.” He let out his breath. “There, I’ve said it.”

She turned and faced him fully, disbelieving. “You’re proposing marriage?”

He rushed his words, flustered. “I suppose I am. Not formally, of course. I mean, all the legalities would have to be worked out by the priests first, but, yes, I am.”

“Isn’t this a bit sudden? We barely know one another.”

Guillame blushed and looked down. “My first wife died three years ago. I know I should remarry and carry on the family line, but I’ve been . . . frankly, I’ve been scared to try. Plus, I’ve never met the right person.” He looked back up, his eyes meeting hers. “Until now. I fell in love with you the first time I saw you, Blanche. I can’t stop thinking about you.”

Blanche didn’t want to hurt him, but it was best to be blunt. “I’ve been married twice already, Guillame. I’ve no desire to do it a third time.”

“You say that, but the truth is, your wishes don’t matter. At some point you’ll have to remarry, even if it’s only for your protection.”

“So you’ve heard that Ernoul wants to marry me.”

“News carries fast. And even if you manage to put off Ernoul, he won’t be the last. Half the eligible men in England and France will be after you. You’re a rich prize as these things go. You won’t be able to hold them off forever.”

She smiled. “I’m not worried. I paid the king to let me—”

“Don’t you think there’s someone who will pay him more?”

Blanche felt like she’d been punched in the gut. The air went out of her.

Guillame went on. "I love you, Blanche, and I believe you at least like me. Maybe in time it will become something more. I'm willing to take that chance."

Blanche said nothing. Her head was spinning. What Guillame said about the king being offered more money was true. She had been so stupid. Happiness was a dream, attainable only in the afterlife. *The priests are right—we are put on earth to suffer and have our suffering redeemed after death.* She sighed.

"You won't get a better offer," Guillame pressed. "Oh, maybe from someone who's wealthier, you will, or someone who has more land. But not from someone who actually cares for you. Someone who desires your happiness."

Blanche's throat was so dry she had trouble speaking. "I . . . I told you, I have no desire to remarry. I just want to live by myself in peace and quiet."

Guillame smiled. "As do I." He took her hand gently. "If you change your mind-*when* you change it—my offer will still be there."

"I like you, Guillame, but I don't love you. I never will."

"Love is not necessary for a marriage to be successful. It is enough that—"

"I don't think you're listening to be. There won't be a marriage."

"I refuse to accept your verdict," Guillame said. "You will come to me in the end. But don't wait too long. Ernoul is to be knighted in less than three weeks."

"I won't accept his proposal," Blanche said.

"Aimerie might make you."

"How? He can't force me."

Now it was Guillame's turn to raise an eyebrow. "It happens all the time in France and Normandy, you know that."

"This isn't Normandy," Blanche said.

"Aimerie thinks it should be. So do a lot of nobles. They chafe under the king's laws. I don't like England or the English, but I don't want that kind of lawlessness coming here."

Blanche took all this in, and after a long moment said, "Thank you for being honest. You've given me a lot to think about."

He nodded. In the village, vespers rang. Behind them, candles were being lit in the hall; more wood was placed in the fire pit to ward off the chill. Guillame rubbed his hands to warm them. "There will be a light meal in a bit, and then we should discuss sleeping arrangements."

Blanche tensed. She had been waiting for this moment, dreading it. She wished Milli were here; she had taken a big chance coming here by herself, trusting Guillame. Was this where she would have to fight him off? She'd brought her dagger, just in case.

Guillame said, "You'll sleep in the solar, of course. In the bed."

She tensed again. "And you?"

"I'll sleep down here in the hall."

He grinned at her obvious relief. "What, did you think I would try to take advantage of you?"

"It had crossed my mind."

"My intentions toward you are honorable, Blanche. I would do nothing that could turn you against me."

"Thank you," she said. He was a likeable fellow; she couldn't deny it. Good-looking, too.

They dined on cold venison, second-best bread, and cheese, washed down with a light wine. Then Blanche took her leave and retired to the solar for the night.

She lay on the straw bed, which was quite comfortable and smelled of the herbs used to sweeten the straw, but she couldn't sleep. She kept thinking about Miles. About him and Millicent, Wada and the others. Wondering if they were all right. If they were still alive. Thinking about other things, too, about what Guillame had said.

She had a lot on her mind . . .

Chapter 21

Blanche rested on one elbow, eyes bright with amusement but also showing concern. “Admit it. You’re jealous, aren’t you?”

“How could I not be?” Miles replied. “I come back here, and you’re off with that Guillame fellow.”

It was night. They were in the steward’s house, in Miles’s bed. No candle. When Guillame had escorted Blanche back to Redhill that morning, Miles told them how he and his men had caught the outlaws and hanged them. Millicent kept cutting in, of course, making it all about her, the plucky heroine who cheated a fate worse than death.

“We left one of our hoods with the bodies so they’d know who did it,” Miles said when he could get a word in edgewise.

“A bit showy,” Guillame sniffed, casting a look at Blanche, “but effective in a crude way.” He went on, addressing Miles. “And you didn’t tell me you were planning this, why?”

“Guess it slipped my mind, my lord.”

"A lot seems to slip your mind. Like your ambushing those robbers—"

"The Viking and his men were on their way here," Blanche cut in. "There wasn't time to tell you. As for the other, I told you yesterday that I knew of the plan and I approved it. I am Miles's lord, and that's enough."

Guillame seemed to accept that, albeit reluctantly.

"With luck, we'll find the outlaw' camp soon," Miles told Guillame. "Though some of the villagers are already complaining that we're keeping their children from their work in the fields."

"That was to be expected, I'm afraid," Blanche said.

"We'll add some of my people to your scouts," Guillame said.

Blanche said, "And children from Fairleigh, as well."

Guillame had left after that. Relations between Miles and Blanche had been tense the rest of the day. Now the day had ended, and Blanche had come to Miles.

"You shouldn't dislike Guillame," she chided Miles. "He's very nice, actually."

When Miles made no answer, she went on. "He's our ally—our only ally. He invited me to tour his estate. I couldn't very well say no."

Miles grumbled something.

Blanche said, "Be put out then, because I'm going to make you feel even more jealous. Guillame wants to marry me."

Miles sat up straight. "What! What did you tell him?"

"I said no, of course. I can't believe you even had to ask that. It gets better, though—or worse, depending on how you look at it. Guillame says there will be men coming at me all the time, seeking my hand."

"So? You paid the king to—"

"Guillame says someone will pay him more."

Miles let that sink in. "Would the king do that?"

"Kings always need money," Blanche said.

Miles said nothing.

Blanche put a hand on his bare shoulder. "Don't worry, we'll think of something."

She pushed him onto his back and straddled him. She leaned down and slowly brushed her nipples across his chest, along with her lustrous dark hair.

"I hate it when you do that," he said.

"Very well, then, I'll stop."

"No," he said quickly, "don't stop. I mean, I hate it because when you do it, I can't think straight."

"And, yet, other things are straight," she observed.

He pulled her down and kissed her, smoothing his hands along her naked back and buttocks. "God, I love you."

* * *

Afterwards, she murmured, "So, what's next?"

Miles cupped her breast and sucked one of her taut nipples, making her moan. "I want to get a look at that castle."

Reluctantly, she pulled away and sat up. "Why?"

"In case we have to . . . you know."

"Attack it?"

"Yes."

"I'm coming with you."

"No. It's too dangerous."

She pouted. "I got you into Badford Castle. You can't do the same for me?"

"That was different. You went there as yourself and I pretended to be your confessor. You couldn't go as yourself this time—there's no reason for you to be there. They'll know me, as well. I'll have to go in disguise."

"What kind of disguise? I don't see you pretending to be a noble." She mimicked his voice, using a bad French accent. " 'Come here, good fellow.' And I'm still coming with you."

Miles thought. "I have an idea."

"What is it?"

He pulled her to him. "I'll tell you later."

"No, tell me now."

He kissed her slowly, softly. "You're sure?"

"Well, maybe a little bit later," she said, breathing hard. She added, "Do that thing with your tongue."

"Which one?"

"Try them all. I'll let you know when you get to the right one."

Chapter 22

Blanche pulled at the dirty wimple tucked under her chin. "I hate having my hair under this. And this dress has lice."

"You wanted to come," Miles reminded her.

"Yes, but not disguised as a pig sty."

"Can't have anybody recognizing those braids of yours," Miles said, "or your fancy clothes. Just be glad you don't have to pull this cart."

Miles and Blanche, along with Wada, were dressed as poor peasants, Miles and Wada pulling a two-wheeled cart piled with battered household goods. It was overcast and cold. The roads would not dry until spring, and the cart's wheels were caked with mud that splattered Miles and Wada as the wheels turned, adding to their bedraggled air. They had borrowed the cart's contents and the old clothes they wore from people in the village. Miles had rubbed dirt on his face and into his beard; so had Wada.

Blanche tugged at the wimple, scratched a fresh bite on her neck. “Tell me again why we couldn’t visit the castle as ourselves?”

“Because if we did, I’m not sure Aimerie would let us go,” Miles said, “especially me. I got on well enough with him when he was lord of Ravenswell, but I never had reason to be in conflict with him. I paid my rents, and he stayed away from my daughters. If he hadn’t . . .”

“If he hadn’t?” she prompted.

Miles shrugged. “Besides, he and his family weren't around that much. Now, though, he might be tempted to hold us here until you promise to pax his taxes, especially if he suspects that we’re involved with the Hoods.”

“He wouldn’t dare,” Blanche said.

“You don’t know Aimerie.”

The road to Brightwood Castle led along the riverbank and through the village. The castle was on a hill to the east of the village. Villagers who once lived at the foot of the hill had been turned out for the castle’s extended bailey, as evidenced by the number of hastily constructed dwellings at the village’s western outskirts.

“I wonder where they got the name Brightwood,” Blanche said.

“The Old Ones named it,” Miles said. “That’s what Father Albinus told me.”

Wada crossed himself at mention of the Old Ones.

Miles went on. “Albinus says the Old Ones had a fort on that hill. He says men working on the castle sometimes find ancient arrowheads and bits of pottery. Sometimes there’s symbols on the pottery, but no one can make out what they mean."

"Like the symbols on Thor's Seat," Blanche said. "We had the equivalent of what you call the Old Ones in Normandy. No one knows who they were or what happened to them."

They drew closer. Wada had never seen a stone castle before, and he gawped at it, open mouthed, as they approached. Miles studied the tall structure, trying to picture it when it was finished, banners flying, covered with a coat of white lime wash, its door and window decorations painted red and blue.

The castle was square in shape, and must be sixty feet high, maybe even seventy, with the beginnings of watch towers at the northwest and southeast corners. Scaffolding enclosed two sides of the building, ramps leading between the floors. Crank-turned cranes lifted rock, mortar, and rubble to the top, where shouting workmen extended parallel walls of stones and cemented them with mortar. Other men filled the space between the walls with rubble, smoothing it level with rakes. The first merlon was being fitted to a section of the top that had been completed. Still more men worked on the castle's arrow slits, which doubled as windows. Diggers deepened the castle moat, while carts hauled off the mud that was turned up, men cursing and whipping the horses to make them move faster. In times of war, sharpened stakes would be pounded into the moat, to hinder attackers.

"What do you think?" Blanche asked Miles.

As a young man, Miles had dreamed of leading a revolt to drive the French from England. He had dreamed of restoring Mercia as an independent kingdom. Now he was starting at the wreckage of those dreams. "We'll burn 'em out," he'd said back then. Now . . .

"We can burn the wooden palisade and get into the outer courtyard," he said. "But that keep . . ." He shook his head. "The only way to take it would be a siege. We don't have the equipment for a siege, and the people we have can't spend that much time away from their fields. Our only option would be a quick assault. But the only way in is up that ramp and through the door, and they'll make that a death trap."

Blanche said, "So . . ."

"So, it's a no-go, I'm afraid. Can't be done. Not by us, anyway."

"So what do we do?"

"We hope we don't have to assault the castle," Miles said.

"Brilliant strategy," Blanche said.

"It's the only one we've got. Let's get closer. Who knows, maybe we'll see something we can use."

"Is that wise? What if we're recognized?"

"We should be all right. No one knows us here save Aimerie and Ernoul, and they're not about."

Miles and Wada pulled the cart through the village and nearer to the castle. Blanche walked alongside them, resigned to a day of tramping in the cold mud. "Now I know why God invented horses," she muttered.

Just then, a tall woman with braided blue hair passed them, swinging her hips. She was dressed like a man, with a knee-length tunic, hose that matched her hair, and a notched dagger in her belt.

Wada said, "I like that blue hair."

He must have spoken louder than he thought, because the woman heard him and turned. Miles and Blanche recognized her and froze, stealthily averting their faces. The woman looked Wada up and down. "Good for you," she said in a broad Northern accent, and she continued on her way.

As Miles and Blanche let out their breaths, the woman stopped and turned again. "Have I seen you before?" she asked Wada with narrowed eyes.

"Nay," Wada said with a grin. "Wish you had, though."

She studied him, perhaps a moment longer than was strictly necessary, taking in his scars. "What happened to your face?"

Wada was still grinning at her. "Frenchy done it."

"Why?"

"I dunno. Bored, and he had time on his hands, I guess."

She smiled. "You should be more careful." Then she turned and walked away.

"That's the girl we met in the woods, on the way to Redhill," Blanche said when she was gone. "She had red hair then."

"I remember," said Miles. "Claimed to be looking for stray pigs. She was with the robbers we ambushed in the forest. Still had the red hair. I thought she was a man from the way she dressed."

"Aye," Wada said, "I remember her too. Sorry, I shouldn't have said anything. Think she recognized us?"

"Didn't seem to," Miles said. "She seems to have the run of this place, though."

"Glad she didn't get hurt in the fight," Wada said.

Miles turned to him. "Why?"

"I don't know. Wouldn't seem right somehow. Her bein' a woman and all. Nice lookin', too, she is."

Miles shook his head. "Watch the cart," he told Wada. He and Blanche followed the blue-haired woman across the bridge, through the gate, and into the bailey.

"Are you sure about this?" Blanche said in a low voice.

"Trust me," Miles told her.

"That's the part that worries me."

Piles of stones, covered by straw and tarps, rested near the bailey's wooden wall, which they would replace in the coming year. Men sawed lumber and planed it smooth for the castle roof, some of them singing in groups as they worked, to establish a rhythm. Lead shingles were piled near the lumber. They would go on top of the conical roof. Rain would run off the roof and flow into a cistern where water was collected for cooking and for use in time of siege.

"Look," Blanche said.

Ahead of them, the blue-haired woman had joined a fellow with a blond topknot who swaggered through the crowd in the bailey, scattering people in his wake.

"The Viking," Miles said. "What's he doing here?"

As they watched, the Viking and the blue-haired woman were met near the castle moat by Ernoul. Ernoul and the Viking engaged in an animated discussion, during which Ernoul seemed to reprimand the outlaw chief, who pointedly sneered at the younger man. Then the woman and the two men mounted the ramp to the castle hill.

If anything, the castle was even more imposing close up. Miles stared at it, searching for, and not finding, any sign of vulnerability.

"Here! You!" cried a harsh voice. "What are you up to?"

Chapter 23

Miles and Blanche turned. Two men approached. The men wore conical helmets and carried spears and round shields. They also had mail shirts, which meant they were Aimerie's regular guards, not locals called up for the duty.

"I told you we shouldn't come here," Blanche said to Miles in a low voice.

"No one allowed in the bailey without permission," the first guard barked with a heavy Flemish accent. He was a greasy, rat-faced fellow, with dark hair cut short.

The second guard grabbed Miles's arm. He had long hair and was more solidly built, with a round, doughy visage. "What say, Macaire? Let's take them to Lord Aimerie." He spoke with the same Flemish accent as the first man. "Might be, they're some of those Hoods, come here as spies."

He started leading Miles away. Miles slumped his shoulders and affected a groveling tone. "Beg pardon, yer honor, but we just come ter take a look at yer castle. Wonder of the World, they say 'tis. Never seen nothin' like it."

Rat Face Macaire regarded Miles with a suspicious look. "Who are you, and what's your business in these parts?"

"Just passin' through," Miles said, "me and me wife." He pointed to the bailey gate. "That's me son out there, with the cart."

Macaire inclined his head toward Blanche. "This one don't look old enough to be his mother."

"Why, bless you, sir," Miles said, "she ain't. He's by way of me first marriage."

"What's in the cart?" the long-haired guard demanded.

"Household goods," Miles said. "Them what the lord let us keep, after he turned us off our land."

"And what lord might that be?" asked the long-haired guard, still holding Miles's arm in a firm grip.

"Guillame," Miles said, and he saw Blanche shift in surprise. "Lord of Edsworth."

Macaire snorted, as though in contempt of Guillame. As he spoke to Miles, he eyed Blanche up and down. "Why'd he turn you off your land?"

"Make room for a horse pasture, so's he said."

Macaire moved around Blanche, appraising her from various angles. "You know, your wife, here, might be a looker, you cleaned her up. Don't you agree, Baldwin?"

"She might be at that," said the long-haired guard. "Take a lot of soap, though." Then he noticed something. "Hold out your hand," he told Miles.

Miles did.

Baldwin indicated Miles's niello-inlaid ring. "Where'd you get that ring?"

Both guards tensed. A peasant shouldn't have a ring like that.

Miles decided it was best to tell the truth. "Belongs in the family, from way back. Handed down, like."

"It's worth a lot," Baldwin said suspiciously. "Why didn't you sell it?"

Before Miles could think of an answer, Blanche cut in. "Because he's too stupid. Bad as we need money, too. I been telling him forever. Jews'd pay handsome for a ring like that. Just 'cuz two hundred years back, his somethin'-or-other was Duke of the Dung Heap, he thinks he has to keep it. Maybe now we lost our land, the fool'll listen to reason."

Baldwin laughed and let go of Miles's arm. To his companion, he said, "Maybe this peasant's lucky for once. I hear Lord Guillame's in for a surprise."

"What kind o' surprise?" Miles asked innocently.

Rat Face Macaire guard cast a sharp look at his partner. "We can't say."

Baldwin seemed to show some compassion for Miles. "If you're looking for work, maybe Fromont could use you. You're a big fellow, so's your son. Always needs good men, Fromont does."

"Aye," said Macaire. He leaned his spear against a stack of sawed lumber and ran his hand down Blanche's arm. "Good women, too. I bet you *are* good, aren't you?"

Blanche jerked her arm away.

Trying to head off trouble, Miles said, "Who's this Fromont?"

Long-haired Baldwin replied. “The fellow who just went up the ramp with Lord Ernoul. The Viking, you English call him.”

“The Viking? I heard o’ him.”

“He’s lost men recently, to some group called the Hoods, so he’ll be looking for help.”

Macaire cocked his head suspiciously. “Say, you wouldn’t know anything about that, would you? The Hoods?”

Miles shook his head. “Never heard o’ no Hoods.”

Macaire put his hand on Blanche’s rear and fondled it. “What about you, girl? You know anything about Hoods?”

“I know I’d have to put one over your face if I fucked you,” Blanche told him.

Miles reacted in shock at her language. Baldwin burst out laughing, but Macaire didn’t find it funny. “Better tell your wife to watch her mouth,” he warned Miles.

“Oh, I tell her, yer honor,” Miles said, “tell her all the time. Beat her twenty times with a stick, I do, when she talks back at me. But it’s no use. Comes back mouthy as ever.”

“Maybe you should beat her thirty times,” Macaire suggested. “A bath might help, as well.”

Blanche, who was livid from being fondled, started to say something, but with difficulty bit it back.

Miles said, “You know, yer right. Maybe I’ll throw her in the river. Might be as the cold’ll bring ‘er to ‘er senses.”

“Interested in selling her?” Macaire asked him. “I’ll give you a good price. More’n she’s worth.”

“No, yer honor,” Miles said. “Reckon I’ll keep her. She’s useful, in her way.”

Macaire leaned in close. His eyes were bright, and his hot, fetid breath wafted over Miles. "You know, I could just take her. I could slit your throat, too. What do you say, English?"

Baldwin pulled his companion back. "Come on, Macaire. Let's not start trouble."

Macaire gave Blanche a last look, as though trying to make up his mind, then he put his hand on her rear again, squeezed it, and pushed her toward the gate. "Be on your way, you two. You've seen enough here."

Miles and Blanche left the bailey, Blanche's nostrils flaring with anger. "I could have ripped that man's throat out."

"I was afraid you'd try," Miles said.

"How dare he? I warned you about going into the bailey." She rounded on Miles. "And why did you have to pick Guillame as your lord?"

"Who was I supposed to pick? I don't know any other lords hereabouts."

"You could have made up a name."

"Why are you so defensive about Guillame?"

"I told you. He's our ally. Our friend."

"He's not my friend. He barely knows I exist."

"If he did, he wouldn't go making fun of you."

"Why? 'Cause he's got no sense of humor?"

"Because he's a Christian gentleman," she snapped.

They rejoined Wada at the cart. "Did you learn anything?" Wada asked.

Miles said, "We learned that Lady Blanche has a foul mouth."

By now, Blanche had calmed down. “I was supposed to be a peasant,” she said. “Besides, it was fun.”

As Miles and Wada laboriously turned the cart around and started away from the castle, Blanche said, “We need to warn Guillame that he’s about to be attacked.” She looked at Miles. “If that’s all right with you?”

“He’s our friend and ally,” Miles said. “Warn away.”

Chapter 24

Miles and Wada pulled the heavy cart away from Brightwood village. Blanche trailed them, still mad about what had happened to her with the guard named Macaire. She felt humiliated, violated. Miles glanced over his shoulder to make sure she was all right.

"Look," he said.

They followed his gaze and saw Fromont and Ernoul, along with the blue-haired girl, exiting the bailey gate. Ernoul rode; the other two walked.

"They're headed west," said Wada. "For Alton Forest, it looks like."

"They're going to the outlaw camp," Miles guessed. "They must plan to strike Guillame soon."

"We have to hurry and warn him," Blanche said, forgetting about Macaire.

Miles said, "Wada, Lady Blanche and I will go on to Edsworth. You get back to Redhill. Bring Blackie and the rest of the Hoods."

"What about the cart?" Wada asked him.

"Hide it and leave it."

"But it belongs to Ivor. And the contents belong to—"

"I'll replace everything if it gets stolen," Blanche told him. "Now, go. Hurry."

They split up—Miles and Blanche keeping to the river road, Wada going overland to Redhill. "Aimerie must want to get this over with once and for all," Miles told Blanche as they hurried along. "If he can knock Guillame out of our alliance, there's only you left, and he reckons you'll see the light and give in. He reckons you won't have any choice."

"Then he reckons wrong," Blanche said.

* * *

Afternoon.

Fromont led a group of robbers through the woods on a little-used path. Ernoul and Hersent accompanied him, with some two-score men behind. Fromont was bare chested and had an axe and short sword in his belt. A chill wind blew from the northwest, and he was glad of this stretch of thick pine forest to block it somewhat.

Ernoul huddled deep in his cloak. He wished Fromont would have let him bring his horse. He *would* bring it, when he commanded the Brotherhood. "Father's given you an ultimatum," he reminded Fromont.

"I know," Fromont said wearily. "We've had two setbacks. One more, and leadership of the Brothers goes to you. You're probably hoping this goes bad."

"Not at all," Ernoul said, and it was true. "I'll be in charge soon enough. I'll be knighted in two weeks. Command of the Brotherhood is to be one of my gifts. At least till I'm off to France." He smirked knowingly at Hersent. "I can wait two weeks." To Fromont, he said, "Until then, we do what you say."

* * *

It was late afternoon when Miles and Blanche reached Edsworth. They found the steward, Rotrou, walking back to the manor house from the village, cold and tired. Blanche accosted him. "I need to see Guillame right away," she said.

Rotrou, a heavily moustached man with a leather cap, looked her up and down, clearly unimpressed by her bedraggled appearance. "That would be 'Lord Guillame' to you, Princess. And he doesn't hold truck with villeins, so you can—"

"I am Blanche of Redhill," she announced. "Widow to the earl of Trent."

Rotrou sniffed. "Aethelgifu of the knocking house more likely." Rotrou was said to be the bastard son of the old lord, making him Guillame's half-brother, and he acted like it.

"I was here the other day, as Guillame's guest," Blanche said.

"I wouldn't know, I was away on business. But Lord Guillame doesn't bring your sort to the manor house."

Miles cut in. "Watch your tongue, *monsieur*. You're speaking to a lady."

Rotrou rounded on him. "I can have you whipped for that kind of talk."

"You can try," Miles told him.

Rotrou's eyes widened, but before he could say anything, there was the sound of horses.

They turned to see Guillame riding from the other direction with his squire. Blanche started for them. Rotrou grabbed her arm and held her in place. For that, Miles fetched Rotrou a blow to the temple that laid him on his back in the mud.

"Touch my mistress again, and I'll break your arm," Miles told him.

Guillame saw what had happened and angrily reined in his horse. "What's going on here?" he demanded of Miles. "Why did you—?

Blanche shook her freed arm. "Guillame," she said.

Guillame stared. "Blanche? Is that you? Why are you dirty and dressed like that?"

Rotrou stumbled to his feet, rubbing his jaw. "You mean she's really . . .?"

"Yes, you fool," Blanche told him.

Guillame pointed at Miles. "That doesn't give your man the right to strike my steward."

"He threatened to break my arm," Rotrou told Guillame.

Guillame's brow darkened. "Did he now?"

"Your steward laid a hand on me," Blanche said.

"That still doesn't give Miles the right to—"

"Miles is *my* steward," she reminded him. "They're social equals."

"No, they're not. Rotrou is Norman, and your man is—"

"And I own more land than you," Blanche said, "and am of higher rank."

Guillame stewed in anger, then conceded with a curt nod of his head. He looked pointedly at Rotrou.

Rotrou took the hint. To Blanche, he said, "My . . . my apologies, your ladyship. I didn't—"

"Fetch her food and wine and clothes that don't look like they're riddled with leprosy," Guillame told him.

"Very well," Rotrou said. Still rubbing his jaw, he glared at Miles and started off.

"Wait," Miles told him. "We'll need you."

Guillame rounded on Miles. "How dare you countermand—"

"Stop it," Blanche told Guillame. "We—Miles and I—were at Brightwood Castle. You're going to be attacked."

"Attacked?" Guillame said. "Attacked by whom?"

"By the Viking and his men. We heard it from one of the guards. You need to prepare."

"We've got our Hoods coming from Redhill," Miles said, "but they might not get here in time. Who do you have that can fight?"

Guillame said, "I do not recall addressing you."

"I said, stop it, Guillame," Blanche told him. "Listen to Miles."

Miles said, "You'll need to get some men ready, my lord."

Guillame looked put out at being given instructions by Miles, but he said, "There's me, of course. And my squire, and Rotrou. I don't know much about the villagers—they're English—but I assume some of them can fight. Or attempt to." He turned to Rotrou. "Make the necessary arrangements. But first, we must see to Lady Blanche's safety."

"Don't worry about me," Blanche said.

"But I must," Guillame said, bowing. "It is my duty as a knight. I'll lend you a fast horse, so you can get away from here. Your fellow will go as escort."

"I'm staying," Blanche said. "And so is Miles."

"I insist," said Guillame.

"I said, I'm staying."

Guillame turned to Miles for support, but Miles held out his hands helplessly and shrugged. "She does as she pleases, my lord."

* * *

Wada didn't think he had enough time to go all the way to Redhill and get men, so he disobeyed orders and went to Fairleigh instead. Fairleigh was closer to Edsworth. He found the steward, Evrard, and told him what was happening.

The big, bluff steward looked pleased. "So we're going to get our own back, eh? *Bien*. About time."

Wada said, "Have your men find grain sacks and make hoods out of them."

"I've already done that, *mon ami*," Evrard said. "Been waiting on a call to join your group. There's jacks on the other manors that want to help, as well. You *capuchins* are getting famous. I don't suppose you know when these outlaws will show up, do you?"

"No," Wada said, "but it won't be long. We saw Ernoul and the Viking leave for the forest earlier today."

"Ernoul? He's part of this?"

"Aye," said Wada. "He's one of the outlaws."

Evrard rubbed his hands together with delight. "Can't stand that bastard. I'll gather up some of my fellows that are handy in a fight, and then it's rig-a-jig-jig, as you English say."

He pronounced it *reeg-a-jeeg-jeeg*, and Wada grinned at him.

* * *

Fromont led his band west, then south, and into the woods just east of Edsworth. The hour was late and it was getting colder. A lot colder. Fromont had done some campaigning in southern France, and he wished he was there now. Damn England. He threw a cloak over his bare chest as a concession to the weather. "We'll stay here for the night," he announced.

"Here?" Ernoul said. "Why? It's freezing. Let's kill some people, go home, and get warm."

Fromont ignored the suggestion. "I want to hit them at dawn, when they're most vulnerable. We're near the water mill, and that's where we'll strike. Burn Guillame's mill, and that'll put the bastard on notice, proper. Be a long winter without a mill for grinding grain. We'll take what else we want and be gone before they even know we're here."

Chapter 25

Foggy dawn, late October. Frost rimed the ground and trees, turning the world monochromatic in the grey light.

Three points of fire appeared in the mist. Three men emerged from the woods, carrying lit torches. Wraith-like, a line of armed men followed them. The men's' bare-chested leader walked with a rhythmic swagger, almost like he was dancing. The men waded the icy stream by the water mill.

With his axe, Fromont pointed to the mill. "Burn it."

As the men with torches started toward the house, loud barking erupted from a nearby pasture.

A black-and-white dog stood there, hackles up, barking furiously at the men. Behind the dog, sheep lumbered away from the noise, and the shepherd boy, who had decided to get an early start on the day, ran.

"So much for surprise," Fromont said. "They'll know we're here now."

"Shut that dog up," Ernoul snapped.

Hersent nocked an arrow and raised her bow. She aimed at the barking dog, but couldn't let the arrow go.

Ernoul grabbed the bow from her. He stepped forward and let loose.

The dog squealed and was quiet. The shepherd ran for the village, yelling for help. The sheep scattered.

With a scowl, Ernoul thrust the bow back to Hersent.

Alerted by the barking, the miller burst from his house, followed by the rest of his family. The miller saw the men with torches and cried, "What—?"

That was as far as he got because Ernoul strode forward and cut him down with his sword. The man's wife raised her hands and screamed, and the children ran away in terror, dragging their mother with them. The miller's oldest son remained, crouching over the body. "Bastards," he shouted, tears on his cheeks.

Ernoul raised his sword again, but this time Fromont grabbed his arm. "No killing, remember?" Fromont said.

Enoul's eyes were alight. "Too late for that now."

Holding Ernoul back, Fromont motioned to the miller's son. "Get out of here."

The young man came to his senses and ran.

The first rays of the sun burned through the mist and tinted the frost orange and red. In the village, the church bell rang without stop. The men set fire to the miller's house. The cold air smelled of smoke.

"Take anything of value in there," Fromont told his men. "Be quick about it." He sent another group of men to the pasture. "Take the five best sheep. We'll feast tonight."

The men hurried off to get the sheep. Smoke and flames rose from the house and mill. The wood was old and it burned well. The smoke could probably be seen for miles already. "All right," Fromont said, "We've done what we came for. Let's get out of here."

Ernoul waved his bloody sword toward a nearby clump of houses. "We'll loot those first."

"No," Fromont said. "We need to go before—"

"Come on," Ernoul cried, and a bunch of the men followed him toward the houses.

Fromont shared a look with Hersent.

"Leave him," Hersent said.

Fromont wanted to do just that. But he knew what Lord Aimerie's reaction would be should anything happen to his son. He swore and started after Ernoul, followed by the rest of his men.

Ernoul and his men ran toward the group of houses, eager for plunder. Frightened faces appeared at the house doors. The inhabitants fled, one of the women screaming, the children crying with fear.

As the outlaws neared the houses, there was the sound of horses, followed by a shout. Ernoul and his men turned to see Lord Guillame and his squire, Hugobert, riding toward them, steel caps on their heads, swords drawn. Behind them came Miles and Rotrou and a handful of men, running and carrying weapons.

"Christ," Fromont swore as he came up beside Ernoul. In the open like this, the outlaws would be helpless against the two horsemen. The horsemen picked up speed, swords raised.

A worn, narrow lane led from the houses to the mill. "Quick!" Fromont shouted. "To the other side of that lane!"

Ernoul didn't understand what Fromont intended, so Fromont grabbed him by the back of his mail shirt and pulled him across the lane. The outlaws formed a line—not a line, more like a hasty scattering of men, weapons raised.

* * *

Guillame and Hugobert were getting too far ahead.

"Hold back!" Miles yelled to them, but they didn't hear, or chose not to.

Guillame's horse hit the sunken lane. There was a loud snap as the animal's right leg broke, and the horse catapulted forward, screaming and throwing Guillame. Hugobert's horse jumped the lane but stumbled badly on landing, and Hugobert fell off.

Led by Ernoul, the outlaws, who had been on the defensive and ready to run, now sensed an opportunity and went after Guillame and his squire. The Viking attempted to call them back, but to no avail. Their blood lust was up.

Miles ran forward as Guillame stumbled to his feet, dazed, his steel cap gone. Ernoul rushed in on Guillame, but Hugobert threw a glancing shoulder into Ernoul that knocked him off his stride. As Ernoul recovered, the still-dazed Guillame found his sword, and weakly fended off a blow from Ernoul.

Hugobert tried to help again, but Ernoul tossed the boy aside and swung his sword at Guillame. He was shorter than Guillame, but stronger. Miles ran in and went to plunge his short sword into Ernoul's side, but Ernoul saw him coming and avoided the blow. He backhanded Miles with the hilt of his sword, and Miles fell back, blood running down his face. The steward Rotrou took Miles's place, but was felled by an arrow. Miles saw the blue-haired girl with her bow. All of Guillame's men were here now, but they were outnumbered by the outlaws.

"Fall back!" Miles yelled. "Quickly!" He grabbed Guillame's arm. "Run!" Nearby was an old fence. "Behind that fence!"

Guillame's men ran across the field, making a mess of the newly sewn winter wheat. They climbed the fence, with the outlaws right behind. The fence wasn't much of a barrier, but it was enough. The first outlaw who tried to climb over was stabbed in the neck by Miles, and the rest stopped.

The two sides fought hesitantly through and over the fence, thrusting with swords and knives to little effect. One of Guillame's men had a pitchfork, and the pitchfork's long reach kept the outlaws at bay.

The outlaws spread out and began climbing the fence to either side. Miles and his men were going to be surrounded. "Fall back!" Miles cried again. "Make for the manor house!"

Still unsteady on his legs, Guillame protested. "I don't run from—"

Miles pushed him. "Do it!" He threw a rock at an outlaw on the other side of the fence and started running.

* * *

The robbers climbed the fence and chased Guillame and his small group of men, yelling like demons. Fromont couldn't hold them back. This had gotten out of hand; it wasn't what Lord Aimerie wanted. Even Hersent got caught up in the madness. She loosed an arrow that caught Guillame's squire in the upper back. The squire stumbled and fell. Miles and Guillame picked him up by the shoulders and hurried on.

* * *

The wounded Hugobert was slowing them down. Miles and his men were going to be caught before they made the safety of the manor house palisade. "Stop," Miles told Guillame. "We'll have to make a stand."

The two men laid Hugobert down and turned. Three more men stopped with them, the others kept running. Miles saw Ernoul come closer, met his beady eyes . . .

If the outlaws had any brains, they would let that girl stand off and kill them all with her bow, but Miles hoped their thirst for blood would overcome their good sense. He hoped his side could take a few with them before they died.

More shouts. From the outlaws, this time. Worried.

A line of men was running from the wasteland at the manor's edge, hoods over their heads. Miles recognized Wada's big form in the lead.

Even as the outlaws turned to meet this new threat, a horn sounded, and Blanche, on horseback and waving a sword, led a party of the villagers who had not joined the fight till now. They were armed with bills and pitchforks, axes and cleavers—any weapon that came to hand.

"Clear out!" the Viking yelled at his men. "Run!"

* * *

Wada and Evrard led the Hoods. Wada had an axe he'd borrowed at Fairleigh. He swung the axe two-handed at one of the outlaws, took a chunk out of the man's shoulder, spraying blood. The man fell, screaming. Beside Wada, Evrard yelled with delight as he swung his old sword.

The fighting was scattered all over the field. Men, or groups of men, slashing at each other and backing off. Slashing again or running. The outlaws were better fighters, but there were more of the Hoods and villagers, and they used the numbers to their advantage, forcing two-on-one or three-on-two fights, with someone always attacking from the rear. The outlaws took their leader's advice and began running away.

It was hard to breathe with the hood on. Wada threw it off and ran after the retreating outlaws.

He stopped, found himself facing the girl with blue hair.

The girl's bow was drawn, the arrow aimed at Wada.

She seemed to recognize him. Hesitated.

She lowered the bow, turned, and ran.

There was shouting all around as the outlaws fled. Evrard bent over a fallen man, finished him off, and kept running. The outlaws were cut down, and any who were not killed outright were killed where they lay. Blood splashed the churned-up frost.

* * *

Guillame was still hobbled from his fall. Miles lent him an arm, but the young lord shook it off. "I'm all right."

Wada approached the two men, joined by Evrard. Blood from Ernoul's blow was running into Miles's eye. He tried to wipe it away, succeeded only in smearing it over his face. "You got here just in time," he told Wada and Evrard.

The two men paid no attention to Guillame, to Guillame's visible annoyance. "I went to Fairleigh instead of Wolf Hill," Wada told Miles. "Not enough time for the other."

"You did well," Miles said. He took Evrard's hand. "My thanks, Evrard."

"Ha!" Evrard barked, slightly out of breath. " 'Tis you who have *my* thanks. Haven't had that much fun in a long time."

Wada elbowed Evrard's arm. "Rig-a-jig-jig, eh?"

The two men laughed heartily.

Wada and Evrard went to help with the wounded. Blanche was at the miller's house, on her horse, directing men to fight the fire. There wasn't much left of the house.

The mill wheel had collapsed into the stream. There would be no grinding of grain for a while, but the village could rebuild.

Miles turned back to Guillame, but he had started off.

Chapter 26

Guillame had gone to check on his squire, Hugobert.

The thirteen-year-old boy lay on his stomach in the mud, with Guillame's chaplain, Jean, tending him. Jean could read and write, so he had been given the manor's medical duties.

"The arrow embedded itself in the boy's muscle," Jean told Guillame. "No vital organs were hit. I'll cut out the arrowhead and sew the wound when we carry him back to the hall."

Guillame knelt beside the boy. "You'll be all right, son. You did well out there. If it wasn't for that sunken lane, we'd have routed the bastards by ourselves. You and me."

"Yes, my lord," Hugobert muttered. "Thank you, my lord."

"Now get some rest."

Guillame patted the boy's shoulder and went to see to his horse, Durendal—named after Roland's sword.

The animal thrashed weakly, the broken leg hideous. Rotrou's son, Chretien, was there, holding a farrier's axe—

an axe with a long spike on one end. The spike was used to dispatch crippled animals. “He’ll have to be put down, my lord,” Chretien said.

Guillame nodded, a tear in his eye.

Chretien was a youth who didn’t shirk responsibility. “I’ll do it.”

“No, I will,” Guillame said.

“Are you sure, my lord? I can—”

“I’m sure,” Guillame said. “He’s my horse, I’ll put him down. Hand me the axe.”

When the deed was done, Guillame rejoined Miles. Wada and Evrard were back, as well. Miles relayed their report to Guillame. “The Viking got away, my lord. So did Ernoul and that girl with the blue hair.”

“Damn shame,” said Fairleigh’s steward, Evrard, “I’d like to have done for that bastard Ernoul.”

“You’re talking about a member of the nobility,” Guillame reminded him.

“He’d be a dead member of the nobility if I had my way,” Evrard said.

Guillame drew himself up. “I’ll pretend I didn’t hear that, *Monsieur* Evrard. Peasants aren’t allowed to kill nobles. You, of all people, should know that. You’re Norman.”

Evrard looked chastened. “Yes, my lord.”

Wada tapped Evrard’s shoulder. “Come on, Ev, we have work to do.” To Guillame, he said, “With your permission, my lord?”

“Granted,” Guillame said.

The two men, and Miles, bowed to Guillame and started off.

Guillame called after them. "Miles. A word."

* * *

Miles wiped more blood from his eye and face. Ernoul's sword hilt had struck him on the temple, and it hurt like the Devil. He would probably need to have the cut sewn. "Yes, my lord?"

Around them, men attended to the wounded and dead. There was a scream as one of the injured outlaws was killed. At the miller's house, the flames were dying, but smoke still rose in a grey column. Ragged clouds from the west blotted out the morning's brief sunlight.

Guillame inclined his head politely. "It appears I owe you my life," he told Miles.

Miles grinned. "I think we both owe that dog, my lord. Hadn't been for him, the Viking and his men would have gotten clean away."

"Mmm." The look on Guillame's face said that might not have been a bad outcome. Abruptly, he changed the subject. "I suppose you know that I have proposed marriage to Lady Blanche?"

Miles hadn't expected this. "We don't discuss her personal life, my lord," he lied.

"As is proper. Well, I have. When she accepts, as I have every reason to believe she shall, her lands will, by law, become mine."

Where is he going with this? "Yes, my lord?"

"I intend to appoint my own steward for them."

Miles's stomach went cold, but he showed no outward reaction. "That is your privilege, my lord."

"You seem to do a good job, and people like you, but you're altogether too familiar with your betters. You're too overbearing—giving me orders back there. That sort of thing is not done, and a proper steward would know that."

Miles said nothing. Did Blanche and Guillame have an understanding? No, Blanche had sworn that she wasn't getting remarried.

Guillame went on. "Plus, you're not Norman. Frankly, you should never have had this job in the first place."

With difficulty, Miles held his temper. "Lady Blanche—"

"Forgive me for being blunt, but Lady Blanche has no experience administering an estate. It is not a job for a woman. I would feel uneasy about employing an Englishman as steward. I don't feel you English can be trusted. Not yet, anyway."

"Thank you for being frank, my lord." Miles was starting to think he should have let Ernoul kill this fellow.

Guillame went on. "I'm telling you this now, so you can make arrangements."

"Yes, my lord."

"You have a place to go?"

"I do." If this marriage did in fact take place, Garth and his wife, Mary, would be surprised—and likely dismayed—to see Miles back in Ravenswell. Chieftain would be happy, though.

Guillame said, “There will be a substantial monetary settlement when you leave.”

“Thank you, my lord.” He wondered if that settlement would be enough for him to build a house for himself so he wouldn’t have to interfere with Garth’s and Mary’s lives any more than necessary.

Blanche rode up, still carrying the sword. There was blood on the sword’s blade. She wore the clean clothes given her yesterday by Guillame’s servants. She had discarded the despised wimple, and her dark hair flowed unbraided, her headdress having been lost in the fight. “Why are you two so serious?” she asked. “You should be happy.”

Guillame frowned. “Where did you get the sword?”

“Your hall,” she said. “I took it from the wall.”

“My God. That was my father’s sword, the one he used in the Great Battle against the English. I keep it on the wall to remind me of him.”

“Sorry,” Blanche said, “It seemed the thing to do at the time.”

Guillame relented. “I suppose it was, at that. I’m glad to see it put to good use.” He indicated the blood on the blade. “Apparently you did use it.”

“I did my bit.”

Guillame shook his head and laughed. “That must have been something to see. No wonder the beggars ran, eh?”

Miles cleared his throat, “I’ll leave you two alone, my lady, if I may. I must attend to the men.”

He started off.

Guillame said, “Oh—and Miles?”

Miles stopped. Guillame came over to him. In a voice that Blanche couldn't hear, he said, "Never, ever, touch me again."

Chapter 27

Guillame returned to Blanche. “Why are you so glum?” she asked him.

Guillame looked around ruefully. “What do I have to be cheerful about? My best horse is gone. My mill is destroyed and the miller dead. My steward, Rotrou, is dead as well; and my squire, Hugobert, is gravely injured. I don’t know how many of my villagers are hurt. Even worse, the winter wheat is almost totally destroyed. It might have been better to let the robbers take what they came for and go.”

“Nonsense,” Blanche said. “We’ve won a victory. Not a great victory, but a victory nonetheless. Yes, you lost property and people, but we killed a number of the outlaws. We’ve given Aimerie a bloody nose, and now is the time to keep him on the run.”

“Perhaps,” Guillame mused. “Tell me, how did you manage to rally so many of my villagers? I could only rouse a few.”

Blanche shrugged. "I simply told them they were needed, and to join the fight if they valued their homes and families."

" 'Told them?' You speak their language?"

"I'm learning," she said.

He spread his hands. "Whatever for?"

"We live here, Guillame. We need to—"

"I don't think that's a good idea, Blanche. We must keep a distance between ourselves and these people. You have a steward. He's impudent, true, but it's his job to talk to them, not yours. You must put yourself on a higher level, or these people will get ideas."

"What kind of ideas?" Blanche said.

"If they can talk to you, they might start to think they're your equal. On that note, I have to speak to you about something."

Blanche dismounted and held her horse's reins. Guillame said, "I'm bothered by these *capuchins* of yours."

"Why?" she said.

"The problem should be obvious. There are three classes of society—nobles, clergy, and peasants. The *capuchins* are peasants. By attacking Baron Aimerie—or his men—they challenge the nobility, and by doing that, they challenge the system, a system created by Almighty God. They challenge the natural order of things, the very fabric of society."

"That's ridiculous. They're fighting for their—"

"Hear me out. I won't pay Aimerie's tax, but I will resist him in a manner consistent with my position."

"What are you saying?"

"I'm saying that any further resistance must be led by a noble. It can't be led by you—you're a woman. So it must be led by me. And the men will no longer wear hoods."

"But the hoods keep them from being identified—"

"Hiding one's face is cowardly. The men must be under my command, not that of Miles. Otherwise, I can no longer commit to your cause."

She stared at him. "You're serious?"

"Quite serious. This skulking about in hoods is beneath my honor."

Blanche considered. "I don't know. Miles has done an excellent job so far. I think we should—"

"You must understand that I cannot put myself under the command of a peasant. Furthermore, I cannot, in good conscience, condone a peasant, especially an English one, leading an armed insurrection against a Norman noble."

"Miles's family was of the English nobility," Blanche pointed out.

"That alone proves his inferiority. Your steward has altogether too high an opinion of himself, and I have told him his services will not be required after we are married."

"What!"

Guillame said nothing.

Blanche fumed. "How dare you presume—"

"It will be my right to choose a new steward for—"

"I never said I would marry you."

"You will, my lady. You must."

"Do not presume to tell me what I must and must not do, sir. You have no authority over me, nor shall you ever."

Blanche turned and led her horse away.
Guillame watched her go and sighed.

Chapter 28

Evrard and his men headed back to Fairleigh, carrying their two dead in a cart. Evrard's wounded men were all able to walk.

Blanche cleaned the blood from Guillame's father's sword and returned it to Guillame. "We'll be going, as well."

"Wait," Guillame said.

Blanche stopped. The young lord cleared his throat. "I need to get the manor straightened out. I'm not able to speak to these people, and Rotrou is dead. Could you have Miles talk with the village leaders and find out their plans?"

Blanche looked to Miles.

Miles had no particular desire to help Guillame, but the request had been made to Blanche, and he felt sympathy for the villagers, so he nodded. He found the reeve and hayward and discussed what needed to be done.

The reeve, whose name was Burgred, said, "Reckon as how our first job should be to save what we can of the winter wheat."

"Aye," said the hayward, Edwere.

“I agree,” Miles said.

Burgred said, “Maybe we can re-plough the field where it’s most tore up, then harrow. Seed ain’t sprouted yet, might be able to re-seat some of it. Save some of it, anyways.”

“Birds are already starting to get at it,” said Edwere. “I’ll send some boys with rocks.”

“After that, you’ll probably want to start rebuilding the mill,” Miles suggested.

“Aye,” Burgred agreed. “Going to take a might o’ work, that is. Have to put that wheel back in working order, then build a new frame for it. Might have to send for the millwright in Badford.”

“Need to find a new miller, too,” Edwere said.

“Can the dead man’s son take over?” Miles asked.

“He’ll have to,” said Burgred. “He’s a good lad, should do all right.”

Miles said, “If you need help with anything, find me, or go to Evrard at Fairleigh or Hamo at Redhill.”

“What about Lord Guillame?” said Burgred. “What do we do with him?”

“Let him ride around and look important,” Miles said. “Make him think he’s being useful.”

The two men laughed.

* * *

Guillame and Blanche watched them talk. “Sounds like pigs grunting,” Guillame muttered. “I can’t for the life of me see why you want to learn that language.”

Blanche explained. “Because if you spoke English, *you* could talk to your people, instead of having Miles do it for you. For all you know, he’s telling them to kill you in your sleep.”

Guillame looked at her askance.

“Don’t worry,” Blanche said, “he’s not. It was a joke.”

“That’s not the kind of humor that goes well in an occupied land,” Guillame said.

Blanche changed the subject. “Where will you find a new steward? There’s not many Normans out here.”

Guillame sighed at the reality of what she said. “I’ll have to promote Rotrou’s son, Chretien.”

“How old is he?”

“Fifteen.”

“Young for a steward. Can he speak English?”

“Yes. He grew up playing with the village children.”

“What does he know about running an estate?”

“He can learn. If nothing else, he can relay my orders to these people.”

“You need to stop thinking of them as ‘these people,’” Blanche told him. “They’re human beings, Christians, like you and me.”

“They’re an inferior—”

“Christ save us, no, they’re not. It would be better for you to make your reeve the new steward. Rotrou’s boy could serve as a go-between until the reeve learns French.”

"I'm not employing an Englishman," Guillame said stubbornly. "This is a conquered country; they must learn their place."

"Learn their place? So, by your standards, the English can never be more than common laborers in their own land?"

"Someday, perhaps. When we've civilized them."

"King Henry married an Englishwoman," she pointed out.

"King Henry made a mistake. One that I hope does not come back to haunt us."

Blanche looked at him suggestively. "What if I were English? Would you still want to marry me?"

"But you're not English, are you? So the question is moot."

* * *

Miles finished speaking to the reeve and hayward. "Lord Guillame intends to join the fight against Baron Aimerie, and he'll need men for that. I'm not sure how he's going to communicate all that to you, so I'll have Evrard keep in contact."

"Don't worry," said the hayward, Edwere, "we'll figure somethin' out. Nothin' we'd like better'n to join your Hoods and stick it to that bastard Aimerie."

Miles relayed the plans for the manor to Guillame. Then he rejoined Blanche and Wada, and the three of them rode back to Redhill on borrowed horses. It was cloudy, the west wind damp and cold. "Rain soon," Miles said.

"I think that's what the word 'England' means in French," Blanche said, " 'Rain Soon.' "

Blanche told Miles what Guillame had said about replacing him. "I already heard," Miles said. "Our friend and ally couldn't wait to inform me that I was being removed as steward once you two got married."

"Well, we're not going to be married," Blanche said, "so your position is secure." She went on. "There's more. Guillame wants command of the Hoods. Now."

Wada swore under his breath.

"What did you tell him?" Miles asked Blanche.

"I said nothing, but how can we deny it to him? He's a noble. He won't take orders from you—he can't, by law—and we can't fight Aimerie without him."

"Do you trust his judgment?"

She shrugged. "We'll have to. The alternative is to pay Aimerie and help build his castle, and I'm not going to do that."

"And for you to marry Ernoul," Miles added with a grin.

"God, would you stop reminding me about that? Maybe seeing me in the fight today will put that desire out of Ernoul's mind."

"Knowing Ernoul, it will probably increase it," Miles said. He considered. "I guess we'll have to go along with Guillame, though I have misgivings about it."

"So do I," Blanche said, "but we have no other choice."

With that, the first drops of rain fell. The trio bent their heads and rode on.

Chapter 29

Baron Aimerie and his son Ernoul rode through the forest and into the outlaw camp. It was cold and raining.

Fromont was expecting them. As before, they met by the fire outside his hut. Hersent and the other members of the Brotherhood watched from a respectful distance. A few people went about their daily business, but not many. They knew this was an important meeting, and they suspected its outcome. Mothers struggled to keep curious children from approaching.

The three men sat on logs around the covered fire. Occasional raindrops found their way through the fire's angled roof of pine branches and hissed on the hot wood. Fromont warmed his hands. "Nasty day, my lord."

"It is that," Aimerie said. "Still, I lived in these woods through rain and snow and cold, as you well know. My family and I suffered privation here and emerged all the stronger for it."

He looked to Ernoul for validation of that statement, but Ernoul said nothing.

Aimerie addressed Fromont. "All right, let's get to it. What happened at Edsworth?"

Ernoul stared at Fromont.

Fromont didn't tell Aimerie the truth, that the raid failed because Ernoul wouldn't retreat when he was told. Fromont knew how Aimerie would react to anything bad said about his son. Ernoul's act had cost men's lives. They had been men who took their chances, men who lived outside the law—evil men, some of them—but they had been Fromont's friends and comrades, and they had died needlessly.

Fromont shrugged. "They were ready for us, and they put up a fight. We were on the verge of winning when those *capuchins* showed up again. They outnumbered us, and . . ." He spread his hands, as though the outcome had been inevitable.

Aimerie swore. "The *capuchins* knew where you'd be? Again? How is this possible? And how is it possible that the men of Edsworth knew you were coming?"

"The *capuchins* must have a good network of spies," Fromont said.

Aimerie said, "I understand Lady Blanche took part in the affair."

"Yes, she led a counterattack by the villagers against us."

"What was she doing there, I wonder?"

"Cozying up to Pretty Boy Guillame, I expect," Ernoul snarled. "Much good it'll do her."

There was silence for a moment, then Ernoul spoke, addressing his father. "Your friend Miles was there, too. I crossed swords with him myself. He and Blanche and

Guillame—the three of them are in this resistance up to their necks. And if we let them keep it up, who knows how many villeins from the other manors will put on hoods and join them?"

Aimerie stood. He paced back and forth in the rain. "I won't let three people stand in my way. I've come too far. Brightwood Castle will solidify my control over this district, and I intend to control the district tightly. It's a small step from paying taxes to swearing fealty, and that's what will come next. Soon, all the lords in this part of the shire will be my vassals. They'll furnish me with soldiers, enough for a small army." He paused and smiled. "And small armies can become big ones. This is just the start."

Fromont and Ernoul waited expectantly.

Aimerie went on. "I'm no friend of King Henry, as you well know, and there's men on both sides of the Channel who feel the same. We've kept in touch, in secret. With luck, I'll be earl of Trent soon, and more besides."

"You'd challenge Lord Galon?" Fromont asked. Fromont had experience with Earl Galon in France and knew him as a man it was unwise to cross.

Aimerie seemed unworried. "The current earl neglects his English lands. Should there be a change on the throne, and Galon loses those lands, what is he going to do about it? Mount an invasion?"

Ernoul was surprised. "A change on the throne? Are there plans to—?"

Aimerie held up a hand. "I can't speak to that, not yet. Let's just say there are plans. But that is for the future. For the present, I have sent Joubert to Redhill, Edsworth, and

Fairleigh with a last demand for those manors to pay their tallage."

"Do you expect them to reply in the affirmative?"

"No," Aimerie said. He sighed. "Fromont, old friend, I told you what would happen should there be another failure."

Fromont met his eyes. "You did, my lord."

Aimerie turned. "Ernoul, you are now chief of the Brotherhood."

Ernoul straightened haughtily. "Yes, my lord."

To Fromont, Aimerie said, "Have you any objections?"

"No, my lord. This was coming in a few weeks, anyway. Might as well do it now. Lord Ernoul has my full support."

Ernoul nodded. "Thank you, Fromont."

"You asked about my plans," Aimerie said to his son. "What are yours, now that you are in charge of the Brotherhood?"

"My plans are to teach the *capuchins* a lesson," Ernoul said. "One they'll not soon forget."

Chapter 30

The next day was dry. Hersent was in the woods, gathering firewood.

She heard a noise and turned.

It was Ernoul. His eyes probed hers. His chest rose and fell.

Hersent straightened. "I suppose I should congratulate you on becoming head of the Brotherhood."

"I've come for my reward," he breathed. "I told you I would."

He removed his cloak and lay it on the muddy ground. He advanced and motioned her toward the cloak.

She dropped the firewood. "There's no way I'll—"

He punched her in the stomach.

She doubled over, unable to breathe.

He raised her by the shoulders and punched her again.

She dropped to her knees, retching, gagging. He slapped her face once, twice, so hard it made her vision blur.

He grabbed her shoulders, picked her up, and threw her to the ground on her back.

She lay there, gasping for air, while he opened her legs and pulled up her dress. Then he had second thoughts and rolled her onto her stomach. With one hand he pressed her face into the mud and twigs and old leaves. She cried and feebly tried to fight as he raised her by the waist. He pulled down his braies and rammed himself into her. She yelped with pain and he went to work. She tried to resist, but he ground her face deeper into the mud, making her struggle for air, and he punched her in the ribs, as he pounded her and pounded her.

When he was done, he left her there, whimpering, and walked away.

* * *

Later, she returned home, hobbling and crying, her dress torn, her face covered with dirt, leaves in her blue hair. Fromont ran to meet her and carried her to his hut.

The message had been sent. Ernoul had officially taken charge of the Brotherhood.

Chapter 31

Aimerie and his wife, Oudinette, sat at the head table in the vaulted hall of Brightwood Castle, the flickering hearth to their left. Oudinette had just been served another cup of wine when Aimerie stood and took her arm. "Come on."

She looked up at him.

"Let's go on the roof and watch the Hollow's Eve fires," he said.

"I've seen them before," she told him, cradling the wine possessively.

"Not from a height like that. It should be exciting. We'll be able to look out over half the shire."

Aimerie got a horn lantern from one of the servants. He and Oudinette mounted the curving stairs to the roof, Aimerie taking the lead. A door opened onto the roof. Aimerie stepped outside onto the walkway and lent his wife a hand, using the lantern to light her way.

"Be careful. The workers have left all kinds of equipment up here. Don't trip over it."

It was breezy and cold, but the clouds were few, and Aimerie and Oudinette could see for miles, patches of light marking the villages.

"It's beautiful," Oudinette breathed.

On All Hollow's Eve, the heathen English set fires to ward off evil spirits, and to light the way for good spirits to ascend to Heaven. Children paraded through the villages with lanterns made from carved turnips.

"Look." Oudinette laughed and pointed to a string of lights that snaked along the village street below. "There go the children through Brightwood."

Oudinette had brought her cup of wine with her. She finished it and set it on the walkway by the parapet. She didn't want the cup to fall off the parapet and hit an unsuspecting passerby. "I've never been up here before, and you're right, it's a gorgeous view."

"It's full dark now," Aimerie said. "The fires should be starting any time."

As if in answer, a prick of light appeared in a distant field. It glimmered, then bloomed.

"Look!" Oudinette said. "There's one!"

"Looks like Haverham," Aimerie said.

Another fire blossomed. Another. More. All around. They lit up the night like giant glow worms.

"It's marvelous," Oudinette gushed. "Thank you, darling, I'd never have thought to come up here."

"We'll have to make it a tradition," Aimerie said, squeezing her hand.

"Yes, let's."

He leaned out from the parapet. "Look at that one. They've made it colored somehow."

She crowded beside him. "Where? I don't see it."

"To the southeast, far off, toward Badford."

"I still don't . . ."

He stepped aside for her. "Lean out. Hold on to the merlon there. That's it. Don't worry, I've got your shoulder."

She craned her head. "I still don't . . ."

"Just a bit more."

She leaned out further.

He switched his hand to the small of her back and gave her a shove.

She lost her grip on the merlon. Her arms windmilled as she fought to regain her balance.

He gave her another shove and she went over the parapet with a scream.

The scream was followed by a loud *thunk* on the ground below.

* * *

By the time Aimerie reached the ground, there was a crowd around Oudinette's body, men and women, some carrying torches or lanterns. Some of the women were crying.

Ernoul and Joubert were there. "What happened?" Ernoul demanded. His usually arrogant expression had been replaced by one of distress. Torchlight reflected moisture in his eyes.

Aimerie put his hands to his face. "She fell from the battlement. We were watching the Hollow's Eve fires, and she lost her balance." He paused, seemingly unable to control his emotion. "It's my fault, I never should have taken her up there. She'd been drinking."

Ernoul went to his knees beside the pulped body and covered it with his cloak.

"Oh, God," Aimerie repeated. "I'm so sorry."

Chapter 32

Oudinette's funeral was held on All Souls Day. The prominent nobles of the district came to pay their respects, including Lady Blanche, who had never met the dead woman.

Miles didn't want them to attend. Milli had sewn the cut above his eye; the wound was discolored and swollen. "It could be dangerous," he told Blanche.

"It's common courtesy," she said. "We'd be held remiss if we weren't there."

"Better than being held in chains," said Miles.

She waved him off.

Blanche and Miles were accompanied by Wada and Blackie, for security on the journey. Oudinette's funeral Mass was held in the castle chapel, in the bailey. It was officiated by Oudinette's confessor, Father Richard, a handsome, if weak faced, man. Blanche gathered that he had been a particular favorite of Oudinette's.

The chapel was small, and no English were allowed inside—they wouldn't have been allowed inside were the chapel five times its size—so Miles waited at the stables with Wada and Blackie. Blanche stood in the packed crowd not far from Guillame, who caught her eye and nodded. She saw Ernoul, who nodded to her, as well. His eyes were red, Blanche noted, as though he'd been crying. Baron Aimerie was stone faced.

When the Mass ended, the casket remained in the chapel. It would be buried temporarily in the chapel yard, then interred in the vault of the new stone chapel that was to be constructed next year.

Mass was followed by a meal in the keep's hall. Musicians played somberly in the gallery that ran around the second floor, and the mood in the hall matched their music. Blanche washed her hands in a basin of water by the front door, dried them on a much-used towel offered to her by a servant, then found a place at one of the long tables. Guillame took the open seat to her right. "You don't mind?" he asked.

"Of course not," she said.

"I'm sorry about the other day," Guillame said. "I didn't mean to sound so arrogant. I feel a bit of a fool. More than a bit, actually."

Blanche smiled at him. "You're forgiven."

He broke off a piece of Aimerie's best white bread and handed it to her. Sheepishly, he added, "I suppose it might not hurt me to learn a few words of English."

"It might do you a world of good," Blanche told him. "Perhaps Miles . . ."

"Not Miles. I don't think he likes me very much."

Blanche frowned.

Guillame explained. "I know this sounds silly, but I believe the fellow may be jealous of me."

"Jealous?"

"Because I spend so much time with you."

"Don't be ridiculous. He's just my steward."

"He may wish he were something more," Guillame suggested.

"Nonsense." Blanche felt herself blush, and the arrival of the food gave her an excuse to change the subject. As Guillame carved them slices of roast lamb, drizzling on the honey-wine-ginger glaze, she said, "It's a shame about Lady Oudinette. What was she like?"

"Nice enough, considering who her husband is. A devout Christian, heard Mass nearly every day. Rumor has it she'd been drinking heavily and that's why she fell."

Blanche picked some of the crisped fat from the lamb and tasted it. It was delicious—no English cooking here. She ate the rest of her slice, sucked the sticky glaze from her fingers and looked around the hall. "Where did Ernoul go?" she said.

"I don't know," Guillame replied. "I haven't seen him since the Mass."

Blanche realized that she hadn't seen any of the outlaws who'd been hanging around Brightwood Castle the last time she was here, and she thought that was odd. Or maybe not. Likely Aimerie didn't want them in sight with so many of the shire's notables about. People might recognize them and start to realize the truth about what was happening.

Up on the roof, something heavy fell, followed by laughter from the workmen there.

"Tell those men up there to be quiet!" Aimerie shouted. "We're in mourning."

His steward bowed and hurried up the stairs.

"They're working on the day of his wife's funeral?" Blanche asked Guillame.

"Yesterday was a Holy Day, so they had off. They're to halt work for the winter at the end of this week, so Aimerie must want to get as much done as possible."

Most of the guests departed early, Blanche and Guillame being no exception. "We'll be taking our leave now, Baron," Guillame told Aimerie when he and Blanche approached the head table.

Aimerie nodded, then raised a finger. "Lady Blanche—wait. Allow me to escort you."

With a questioning glance at Blanche, Guillame bowed to Aimerie and departed. Aimerie finished his wine and dabbed his lips with a greasy napkin. The chair to his left, the one that would normally have been occupied by his wife, was vacant. Aimerie rose, stepped around the high table—there was no dais—and offered Blanche his arm. She took it reluctantly, and the two of them left the hall.

"My sincere condolences on the loss of your wife," Blanche said as they started down the stairs to the entrance ramp.

"Thank you," Aimerie said. "We were together many years, and I miss her greatly."

They exited the castle and walked down the ramp, then the hill. When they reached level ground, Aimerie stopped and faced her. "Give me one good reason why I shouldn't throw you in chains right now and hang your steward, Miles."

Blanche hadn't expected this. She had no reply.

Aimerie went on. "I know that you, Miles, and Lord Guillame are behind the attacks of the *capuchins*. You and Miles were seen fighting on their side at Edsworth."

Blanche had regained her composure. "On what grounds would you arrest us?" she said airily. "Ridding the countryside of outlaws? That's not breaking the law. Nor is my refusing to pay your tallage—a tallage which you have no authority to impose."

"*I* decide the law in this district," Aimerie snapped. "It is only out of respect for my late wife that I let you and Miles leave here today."

"Why are you only saying this to me? Why not Guillame, as well?"

"Because Guillame will do what you tell him."

Again Blanche said nothing.

"I am in a position to make life very difficult for you if you don't comply with my wishes," Aimerie told her. "Remember this—a woman alone is dangerous. The Church teaches us that. A woman alone is evil, a temptress—the Church teaches us that, as well. The villeins on your estates believe what the Church teaches. They may support you now, but they can turn on you quickly, and I can help them."

"I'll keep that in mind," Blanche said.

"See that you do. My patience is near its end."

* * *

As they rode back to Redhill, Blanche told Miles what Aimerie had said.

"Nothing more than I expected," Miles replied. "He knows we're the enemy now."

"So what happens next?" Wada said.

Miles looked at Blanche. "I'm not sure, but I doubt it will be—"

Blackie pointed. "What's that?"

A large column of black smoke rose in the distance. Smaller columns rose near it.

"That looks like Fairleigh," Blackie said.

"Come on," Miles told them.

Chapter 33

The group stopped on a hill overlooking Fairleigh Manor.

Smoke rose from the burned manor house and its outbuildings. A number of the peasants' scattered houses had been burned, as well, as had the tithing barn, though the church was intact. Bodies lay in the fields and the lanes. Most of the animals were gone—stolen, no doubt. Some would be eaten by the outlaws, but most would end up as stock on Aimerie's home farm.

Blackie shook his head. "Ain't seen nothin' like this since I was a soldier in France. One of the reasons I quit that life."

They started down the hill. As they neared the manor house, the smell of charred wood mingled with the acrid smoke. There was another smell, too, a sickly smell that twisted their guts.

Burned flesh.

Miles reached over and grabbed Blanche's bridle. "Stay here. It's best you don't see."

"No," Blanche said grimly. "It's my manor. I want to see what they did. I *need* to see it."

They rode on. There was a palisade around the manor house, but no ditch. In front of the wrecked palisade gate, a pole had been set up, and something had been mounted on it.

It was Evrard's head. His eyes had been gouged out.

Wada swore. He and the grizzled steward had become good friends.

Blanche refused to take her eyes from the sight. Miles saw the rage build inside her, rage and the desire for revenge. He knew because he felt the same rage. He could tell that Wada and Blackie felt it, as well. Miles had seen this sort of thing in Wales, and he had learned to control his rage. He supposed that Blackie had, as well. Not so the other two. Neither Blanche nor Wada was hot headed, but right now their anger threatened to burst its bounds.

Part of the manor house's palisade had been burned, other parts knocked down. The animals, including the hawks, had all been stolen. More corpses lay inside the charred remains of the manor house, burned. Men and women, the manor staff—most of them in one spot, as though they had been herded together and killed. From the contorted positions of the bodies, some of them must have been burned alive.

Blanche turned away and was sick.

Miles tried to comfort her, but she shook him off. The party turned toward the peasants' dwellings. Blanche was weak from the sight of the burned bodies, and she had to dismount and walk. The others did the same. Houses that had not been put to the torch had been looted. Butchered bodies littered the lanes, mostly men, but some women and children. Survivors were beginning to emerge from the woods and fields and wherever else they had hidden. Some searched the bodies for loved ones, crying over them when they found them; others stumbled through the remains of their houses, looking for anything of value that hadn't been stolen or destroyed.

Blanche and her party went down the muddy street where the main group of houses stood, taking in the destruction. "I knew a lot of these fellows," Blackie said. "Wasn't no need for this."

"It'll take years for the manor to recover," Miles said. "That's if we can find men to work the fields."

An old woman wandered, dazed, in front of them, clutching a silver spoon which must have been the only thing she had managed to save from her property. Instinctively, Blanche hugged her. "I'm sorry," she said.

The old woman's eyes focused, and when she realized who it was, she pushed Blanche away. "Wanton. You should have paid Aimerie's tax."

"Aye!" shouted a man poking through the rubble of a nearby croft.

"Pay up!" yelled someone else. "Why should we suffer for your pride?"

Blanche stepped back, stunned by the reaction. "Believe me, no one feels worse about this than I do."

"Easy for you to say," said the old woman with the spoon. "It weren't your house what got burned. Weren't your husband they took and—oh, wait, you got no husband."

"That's enough!" Miles told her. "You've said your piece."

The parish priest, whose name was Williken, appeared. He was covered with dirt and bits of twigs and leaves, as though he'd been hiding in the woods. He held the bottom of his cowl across his face against the smell. "We're ruined, my lady," he told Blanche. "We'll not make it through the winter."

"You'll make it," Blanche told him. "I'll see that you do."

"How?" he said.

"We'll find a way."

"But—"

"Who did this?" Miles interrupted. "The outlaws?"

"Aye," Williken said. "And Baron Aimerie's boy was leading them."

Miles and Blanche were surprised. "Ernoul?" Mikes said. "Not the Viking?"

"The Viking was there, but he wasn't giving the orders. Some blue-haired girl was with him, too, and neither of 'em looked too happy about what they were doing."

A middle-aged woman wiped her eyes on a smoke-blackened apron. "They took some of the young girls. You can guess what for."

Miles and Blanche exchanged glances. "Ernoul," Miles said, and this time he made the word sound like a promise of revenge.

"I wonder why he was in charge?" Blanche said.

Hoofbeats sounded, and Guillame galloped up. "I saw the smoke," he said as he jumped from his saddle. He took in the scope of the manor's destruction and put a hand across his mouth. *"Dieu nous sauve.* This is not how the outlaws usually behave."

Blanche had recovered her bearing. "Baron Aimerie told me his patience was near its end," she said. "I guess he was right."

"This outrage cannot go unanswered," Guillame proclaimed. "It is time to go on the attack. We must end the reign of these outlaws, and of Aimerie, once and for all."

Blanche agreed. "Ready your men and join them with mine."

"I'll need to work out a plan of action," Guillame said.

The two of them sounded like they were ready to march right away. Miles brought them back to reality. "That's all well and good, but we can't do anything till we know where the outlaw camp is. In the meantime, let's get this mess cleaned up and the bodies buried."

Chapter 34

Ediva had never been this deep in the forest. It was getting late, and she'd have to turn for home soon if she didn't want to be caught out here in the dark.

Because of the danger, Father Albinus had ordered the scouts to operate in pairs now, so of course Ediva had gotten paired with stupid Hugh, the thatcher's son, who thought he was going to marry her someday. Ha. She had outrun him, though, and left him behind. She had no idea where he could be and cared less.

She made her way through the trees, not running now but taking her time, because she didn't know where she was, trying to pinpoint landmarks so she could find her way back.

She stopped and closed her eyes. Took a deep breath through her nose and let it out slowly through her mouth, becoming attuned to her surroundings, becoming one with them.

Was that a faint smell?

She closed her eyes again, took another deep breath.

Yes. It was a smell. Smoke. Smoke and what else? Cooking, maybe. And shit.

Her insides tingled. Could it be the outlaw camp? She reckoned the source of the smell was several miles distant. If she went that far, she would almost certainly be going home in the forest after dark, and that prospect terrified her.

Still . . .

Miles and Blackie and the others were desperate to find that camp. Ediva knew how popular she would be if she was the one who located it. She'd be famous in Redhill, a legend. Maybe she could even get a position up at the manor house working for Lady Blanche—as a lady's maid, maybe—instead of being married off to somebody like Hugh. Hugh would have to stop teasing her then; he'd have to stop pulling her hair and pinching her.

She moved toward the smell, picking her way, careful not to make any noise. Her parents were going to be worried when she wasn't home by dark. It was going to be cold, too. Well, she'd been cold before.

Onward she went, around hills, across a stream, the water freezing her bare feet. There was no track to follow, not even an animal track. Her feet crunched fallen leaves and she winced at the noise, but it couldn't be helped because there were so many of them.

The smell grew stronger. Ediva was sure it was the camp. It had to be. She took note of her surroundings, so she could guide Blackie and Miles and maybe even that handsome Lord Guillame back here.

She stopped, listened, heard nothing but woodland sounds. A brown leaf fluttered to the ground.

Closer she went. Bent over, senses straining. The smell was stronger now. She heard a viol playing. A drum. Raucous singing, laughter.

She went cold in the pit of her stomach. This *was* the camp. She would get close enough to actually see it, then bolt for home. She prayed to St. Edith of Wilton, her namesake.

She heard voices clearly now. Sounds of men and women walking in the forest. Animals. Metal clanging, an axe chopping wood. Camp sounds.

She crept up a low rise and lay on her stomach. Through the bare trees she saw huts and lean-tos. People milling about.

That was enough. Time to go. As she started to her feet, a strong hand grabbed the back of her hair and twisted it. Hard.

Chapter 35

Ediva was pulled to her feet and shoved toward the outlaw camp.

"Move, you little bitch," said a foul-smelling man in ragged clothes.

"No!" Ediva pulled back, tried to resist, but the man was too strong.

"Move!" He twisted her hair so tight she thought he was going to pull it out of her head.

She stumbled forward, crying, her head pulled back, doing her best to stay on her feet and keep up with the man.

A blur from the right. It hit the foul-smelling man, knocking him down and making him let go of Ediva. She fell to the ground.

The blur was Hugh. "Run!" he cried to Ediva.

Hugh wrestled with the outlaw. Ediva got to her feet, wanting to help Hugh.

"Run!" Hugh urged her.

Ediva hesitated, then turned and ran. As fast as she could.

* * *

Hugh was eleven. He stayed on the outlaw's back, pounding him with his fists, looking for a rock or something to hit the man with.

The man was bigger and stronger than Hugh. He had been taken by surprise, but he managed to throw Hugh off him and regain his feet.

Hugh knew he should run, but he had to give Ediva time to get away. He picked up a thick fallen branch and swung it at the outlaw. The man blocked it with his forearm. He yelled in pain, then fetched Hugh a blow on the ear that rendered him unconscious.

* * *

Hugh came to.

He was moving.

He had been thrown over the outlaw's shoulder like a sack of grain, his hands and feet bound, the man's strong arm holding him in place. Hugh's head still rang from the force of the man's blow. He saw the man's ragged shoes as they crunched the fallen leaves. He struggled and tried to get loose.

"Stay where you are," the man growled in heavily accented English, "or I'll smack you harder."

They were in the camp now. Hugh saw the feet and legs of men, women, children. Heard them laughing and shouting questions at the foul-smelling man. Heard squalling babes. Smelled food and the stink of latrines. Saw a puddle of piss—human or animal, he couldn't tell. He was thrown down and landed on his back, knocking the air out of him.

His eyes adjusted, and he stared up at a circle of faces. There was a bearded man with a blond topknot who must be the famous Viking, though he wasn't bare chested right now. There was a woman with braided blue hair. Others—he'd never seen any of them before.

"Found him spying on us," said Hugh's captor. "Him and some girl. Bugger damn near broke my arm."

"Where's the girl?" said a man Hugh couldn't see. "Did you kill her?"

"No," said Hugh's captor, "she got away."

"You idiot," said the voice.

Hugh's captor lifted him to a sitting position. Hugh turned his head and saw a squat, powerfully built young man dressed like a noble. The man slapped Hugh across the face so hard that Hugh thought his head was going to come off.

"What's your name?" the man demanded.

"H—Hugh."

"And the girl?"

Hugh had enough of his wits about him to know he shouldn't answer that question truthfully. "Alice."

The man slapped him again.

"Ernoul!" the blue-haired woman cried. "Stop!"

Ernoul. This must be Lord Aimerie's son.

"What's her name?" Ernoul said.

"Alice!" shouted Hugh.

"What manor are you from?" Ernoul said.

Hugh hesitated. He had to give Ediva time to get away.

Ernoul slapped him again, so hard that Hugh fell onto his side. Somebody dragged him back to a sitting position. He tasted blood in his mouth, felt it running from his nose.

"What manor?" Ernoul repeated.

"Ecc-Ecclestone." Ecclestone was in the other direction from Redhill.

Somebody said, "He ain't from Ecclestone. I spent time there, never seen him."

Ernoul slapped him again. Hugh's vision blurred. Things were spinning.

"What manor?"

Hugh said nothing. Every moment gave Ediva that much more time.

Another slap. "What manor?"

The blue-haired woman knelt beside Hugh and took his shoulders, shielding him from Ernoul. "Where do you come from, Hugh?" she said gently. "Tell us, and you won't get hurt any more."

Anything to keep from being hit again. "Red . . . Redhill."

Hugh heard murmurs from the crowd. "And what are you doing here?" the blue-haired woman said.

"Nothing," Hugh mumbled through swollen lips. "Me and—" he almost said "Ediva" "—me and Alice, we was just exploring."

"You're a long way from Redhill," Ernoul snarled.

"We was on a dare, like. See how far we could go."

Ernoul turned to the Viking. "Get your two fastest boys and send them to Redhill. Catch that girl before she gets there."

"Aye." The Viking turned away. Ernoul pushed the woman aside and pulled Hugh to his feet. "What were you really doing here?"

"Exploring, my lord," Hugh cried. "It's the truth, I swear it is."

Ernoul slapped him again.

"Please, my lord. Don't hit me any more."

"You were looking for our camp, weren't you?"

Ernoul hit him again. Hugh raised his bound hands to ward off further blows.

"Weren't you!"

Hugh started crying. "Yes."

"Who sent you? Miles?"

"Yes."

"And Blanche?"

Hugh cried harder. He had tried to be a man and resist, but he had failed. "Yes." He felt snot running from his nose and into his mouth.

Ernoul shoved him. Hugh managed to stay on his feet. Ernoul turned away, like he was done with Hugh. Then he turned back, and there was a sword in his hand.

Ernoul swung the sword. There was a moment of blinding pain, then Hugh felt nothing.

* * *

Hugh's head rolled in the mud. The body remained on its feet, spurting blood, dancing a spastic jig, then it collapsed.

The camp went quiet. Hersent closed her eyes. "You didn't have to do that, Ernoul. He was just a boy."

"Well, he's just a corpse now," Ernoul said.

"You—"

"I do what I want," Ernoul snapped. His eyes met hers. "You know that."

Ernoul went on. "If they're looking for our camp, they want to attack us here. So we'll go after them first. Fromont, gather the men. Have them armed and ready to march on Redhill in the morning. I'll go to the castle and let my father know what's happening."

Fromont inclined his head toward the dead boy. "What about him?"

"Feed him to the pigs," Ernoul said.

Chapter 36

Ediva ran for all she was worth.

Her lungs burned. Her ankles and feet hurt, and the bottoms of her feet were wet with blood. But she couldn't stop. She was being chased.

At first things had been all right, then she'd heard faint sounds behind her. Distant sounds, as of someone running. The sounds had grown gradually louder until she could make out two separate runners. That they were after her was not in doubt.

Another mile slid by. The sounds grew louder. Ediva looked back and saw two boys. They were fifteen or sixteen. They were lean and fast, had probably done some poaching and were used to the woods, and she knew she had no chance of outrunning them.

She wondered what had happened to Hugh. She hoped he was all right, hoped he had gotten away. If he was captured, she hoped he wasn't being treated badly.

Her aching feet pounded the forest floor. Up and down, around curves, through brush, over fallen trees. She splashed through a small creek that she knew the two boys behind her would be able to jump. Another step of her lead gone. Her eyes were half-blinded by sweat but she couldn't wipe it away. That would mean slowing for a step, and she didn't have a step to give. The trip to the camp had tired her, and now she had to run at full speed all the way home, and she didn't know if she would be able to make it.

The path ended at the top of a steep hill, as she knew it would. This was her best chance to lose the two boys. She launched herself down the hill recklessly, dodging trees and rock outcroppings, praying, letting her feet find their own way, not stopping to think about where to put them because as fast as she was running, that would be a disaster.

Behind her came a cry as one of her pursuers fell and bounced down the hill.

She reached the bottom of the hill and kept going. The second boy hit the bottom not long after her. He'd made it. Ediva cried in anger and frustration.

She kept running, legs wobbly, breath coming hard. She glimpsed distant fields through the bare trees—Redhill—but she didn't know if she'd get there before the boy behind her caught up.

He was getting closer, his breathing harsh but steady, his feet pounding the ground rhythmically.

The boy got closer and closer, closing rapidly. Ediva was done in. It was hard to put one foot in front of the other. She wasn't going to make it. She heard him behind her, could almost feel his hot breath on her neck. It seemed that all he had to do was reach out and—

There was a *whoosh* in the air beside her, followed by a *thunk* and a grunt of pain.

Ediva stopped and looked back. The boy was just behind her. He had stopped, as well. He had a scraggly ginger beard, and there was an arrow in his chest. He stared at the arrow stupidly, as if wondering what it was and where it had come from. Then he fell over.

Ediva rested her hands on her knees, heaving air into her lungs. She collapsed to the ground, tears in her eyes.

Footsteps. Men running. Ediva raised her head, saw a familiar mop of curly dark hair. Blackie. With him were his friends Will and Sewale.

Blackie knelt beside her. Held up her head, gave her water from a skin. "Ediva, we been looking for you. What happened?"

"I—I found the outlaw camp," Ediva said between deep breaths and gulps of water. "But I got caught. Hugh saved me. I ran."

Blackie peered in the direction from which Ediva had come. "Where's Hugh now?"

She shook her head, tears in her eyes. "I don't know." Blackie hugged her, comforting her, and she added, "There was a second one chasing me."

"Go look for Hugh," Blackie told Will and Sewale. "Keep an eye out for that second fellow that's after Ediva."

"And if we find him?" Sewale said. "The second one?"

Blackie gave Sewale a look that said they knew what to do. The two men turned and started off.

Blackie lifted Ediva and carried her back to the manor, walking with her in his arms as though she weighed nothing, murmuring, "You're all right now. You're safe."

A crowd gathered as Blackie carried her down the village street. "It's Ediva!" someone shouted.

"They found her!"

"Take her to my house," said Father Albinus, waving Blackie toward the church close. "It's warm there."

Blackie carried Ediva into Albinus's house. "That's it, that's it. Give him some room, there. Mind the fire pit."

It was dark in the house. Blackie laid Ediva on a spare bed. Those of the villagers who could, crowded in behind, with Ediva's mother, Ailova, in their lead. Ailova was tall and had probably been quite attractive—maybe even beautiful—at one time. The passing years and hard work had ground her down, though, wiping out any youthful dreams or ideals she might once have possessed. A once fetching figure was now lumpy; her blonde hair was going grey.

Hugh's father, Matthew the thatcher, pushed into the house. "Where's Hugh?" he demanded.

"Now, now, we'll get all that straightened out," Albinus told him. "Move back, give the girl room to breathe. Ailwyn, fetch your daughter some of that ale and a bit to eat. Not too much, mind, she's weak." He examined her swollen and bleeding feet. "I'll tend her feet."

"No," said a voice, "I'll do it."

It was Blanche's maid, Millicent, making her way through the crowd.

Albinus said, "Now, sister, I'm trained in—"

"I'll *do* it," Milli said. "I've tended more wounds than you ever dreamed of. Open those shutters so I can see. Somebody find a candle."

Millicent was followed into the crowded house by Lady Blanche and Miles, with Wada waiting by the door outside.

While Millicent cleaned Ediva's battered feet and put salve on them, Miles knelt beside the bed. Miles would make it right, Ediva thought. He was the kind of man you naturally thought would make things right. "Tell us again what happened," he said to her.

"I found their camp," Ediva said, still short of breath. "The outlaws."

"You and Hugh," Matthew corrected. Matthew had a bulbous nose, veined in red.

"No, just me. Hugh and I got separated." She broke down and started crying. "That's not true. We didn't get separated, I ran away from him."

"What!" said Matthew.

"Why?" said Blanche.

"I don't know!" Ediva cried some more.

"Hold still!" Millicent said, bandaging her feet.

Still crying, Ediva said, "I thought I was better than him. I wanted to find the camp on my own, without him. I wanted all the glory for myself. Hugh must have tracked me, though, because he saved me from the man who caught me. Oh, I'm so sorry. If we had just stayed together . . ."

"Too late to worry about that now," Miles told her, putting an arm around her shoulder. He turned. "Any sign of Hugh?" he cried toward the door.

"Not yet," said Wada from outside.

Blackie said, "I've got Will and Sewale looking for him."

"The outlaws must have caught him," Ediva sniffed. "What do you think they'll do to him?"

Miles shared a glance with Blanche, who looked worried.

To Ediva, Miles said, "It's hard to say. With luck, he got away. Took a different route back here."

"If not?" Ediva said in a weak voice.

"If not, they have him prisoner. He's young, so likely they won't treat him too bad. We'll get him back, don't worry."

Hugh's father, Matthew, said, "I was against the idea of using children as scouts from the beginning, Miles. No good could come of it, I said. In fact, I told you that—"

"In fact, you told us how proud you were that Hugh had been chosen," Father Albinus said. "Matthew, what's done is done, and it's the Lord's will that it's done that way. We're praying for your boy, and at this point, that's all we can do. The Lord will watch over him."

Matthew stepped back, chastened. Miles turned to Ediva. "Could you find that camp again?"

Ediva nodded. "Yes."

Ediva's mother, Ailova, stepped forward. "Oh, no. She's not going with you. I lost three children to disease and one to injury. I'm not losing another for your fool ideas about freedom and glory."

"We'll make sure she's safe," Blanche reassured the woman. "I'll personally see to her."

"So will I," Blackie added.

Ailova still didn't want her daughter to go, and while Blanche and Father Albinus tried to persuade her, Miles stood. "Wada, ride to Edsworth. Tell Lord Guillame to gather his men and meet us at the crossroads first thing tomorrow. Blackie, get our men together. We leave before dawn."

Chapter 37

The men waited at the crossroads where the road to Badford Town met the path to Redhill. There was an ancient shrine there, its carved wood worn smooth, dedicated to some English saint that Miles had never heard of.

It was not long after dawn, windy and cold, the sun peeking in and out of fast-moving clouds. Father Albinus stamped his feet. "Where are they?"

"No doubt Lord Guillame wants to make a grand entrance," Blackie said.

"Guillame and his men have farther to come," Miles reminded them, trying to be diplomatic. "Still, it wouldn't have hurt them to leave early. We've got a long march ahead of us."

Next to Miles, Blanche sat her white horse, Ediva on the saddle before her. Blanche wrapped her cloak around the girl. "Are you all right?"

Ediva nodded. "Yes, my lady."

"You're sure you want to do this?"

"I'm sure, my lady."

Wooly-haired Father Albinus patted Ediva's knee. "Don't you worry, child. Lady Blanche will start you back to safety as soon as we're close enough to that camp to find our own way."

"I'm not worried," Ediva said, though Blanche could tell that she was. Hardly surprising, after what she'd been through yesterday.

"D'ye think we'll find Hugh?" It was Matthew the thatcher, Hugh's father, his red-veined face lined with worry.

"Your boy could still be hiding, Matthew," Father Albinus said. "Or lost, maybe. We'll get him back, never you fear."

"If he's been captured, we'll ransom him," Blanche added.

Will and Sewale had found no trace of Hugh yesterday. But they had found the second boy who'd been chasing Ediva. "He was dead, my lady," Sewale reported to Lady Blanche. "Broken leg."

Blanche arched a brow. "He died from a broken leg?"

"Well, his throat was slit, too," Will added with a straight face. "Must of done it while he was fallin' down that hill."

Blanche tisked. " 'Running with knives.' I learned not to do that when I was first able to walk. You think he'd have been more careful."

"Indeed, my lady," Will said.

Miles had an axe and short sword in his belt. He'd found some shields in the main hall. He had one; Wada had another, to go with his iron bar; and Albinus had the third.

Blackie and his men carried bows. Ivor the smith was there with his hammer. Ailwyn, Ediva's father, was there, as well. Hamo wasn't there; he still disapproved of what they were doing. So did Simon, the new reeve. Albinus had left his gangly deacon, Tostig, to watch the church. Men were armed with bills and pitchforks, a few spears, short swords pulled from the rafters of their houses. The slingers, who were mainly younger teenagers, stood off by themselves, making jokes and talking about girls.

Giles the potter and a few of the other men had pulled their grain-sack hoods over their heads, as much for warmth as for anything else. Most of the others had the hoods tucked into their belts.

"Come on, come on," Blackie muttered impatiently.

As if in reply, from down the road came the sound of a drum.

A man appeared, carrying a square blue banner with two white chevrons on a blue field. He was followed by the drummer, pounding his drum solemnly, one beat to each second fall of his right foot. After him came Guillame, on horseback. Then Guillame's men. Fairleigh had sent a small contingent, as well, despite the losses they had suffered, and they brought up the rear.

Guillame wore a knee-length mail shirt and a steel cap. Around his neck was a shield painted blue with the two white chevrons, and his horse pranced in the road.

"Frenchy fancies himself, don't he?" Will said, leaning on his bow.

"Aye," said Sewale, "he does that." Sewale was married with a large family, and because of that he took his work in the fields seriously. He was a poacher, but he poached to put food on the table. Will was unmarried and worked in the fields only when he was forced to. Poaching provided him money for the ale house.

Guillame drew even with Blanche and bowed deeply from the saddle. "Good morrow, my lady. You look radiant, as always."

"Lord Guillame," Blanche said.

"Let's hope for happy hunting today." He indicated Ediva, huddled in Blanche's cloak. "Is this the brave child I've heard so much about?"

"It is. Ediva. She was the one who found the outlaw camp."

"Her and Hugh!" Matthew cried, wanting his son to get credit.

Guillame threw Matthew a warning glance for speaking without being asked, and Blanche corrected, "Ediva and a boy named Hugh located the camp. Hugh hasn't returned home yet."

Guillame didn't seem overly concerned about Hugh. He put his hand over his heart, flashed his broad smile, and bowed to the girl. "Lady Ediva, it is a great pleasure."

Flattered by such attention from the handsome young lord, Ediva didn't know how to reply. Meekly, she said, "Thank you, my lord."

" 'Ediva,' " Guillame repeated the name. He looked to Blanche. "Almost sounds French, doesn't it?" He reached into his purse and handed the girl a silver coin. "Take this as an expression of our thanks."

"Thank you, my lord," Ediva said.

There were tears on Ediva's cheeks as she turned and handed the coin to Matthew. "This should go to Master Matthew, my lord, Hugh's father. Hugh saved me. Wasn't for him, I'd never have gotten back." Matthew was crying, as well.

Nearby, Ailwyn's shoulders slumped. He understood his daughter's motive, but that silver coin would have gone a long way for his family.

Guillame was taken aback, but he recovered. "As you wish. A noble gesture. And the girl is to guide us?" he asked Blanche.

"She is."

"Excellent, excellent." Guillame rubbed his gloved hands together and sat straight in the saddle. "All right, let's get these fellows organized. Look like soldiers, not some peasant rabble."

"We *are* a peasant rabble," Will joked, but Guillame chose not to hear him.

Guillame said, "You men with the hoods, take them off." His new steward—Rotrou's boy, Chretien—repeated the order in English.

The men wearing the hoods hesitated. They looked to Miles for instruction, and Blanche could tell that Guillame didn't like that. Miles nodded to the men to obey.

"I told you there were to be no hoods," Guillame reminded Miles.

Miles said nothing.

Grudgingly, the men removed their hoods and put them in their belts.

"Now," said Guillame. "Men with bows, over there." He motioned with a hand. Chretien, the steward, repeated the order in his breaking voice.

Blackie, Sewales and the others shuffled over.

Miles said, "My lord, we need to make haste if we are to—"

Guillame held up a hand, stopping him. Blanche gave Miles a look. She knew they were wasting valuable time, but she would be undermining Guillame's command if she said something, and lack of a defined leader could prove disastrous in a fight. Guillame had told her he was 27, and she hoped he was up to the task ahead. Well, Alexander the Great had conquered the world by the time he was 33, or so she'd heard. Defeating a bunch of outlaws shouldn't be that difficult.

Guillame next separated the men with longer weapons—bills, scythes, spears; then the men with shorter weapons—axes, short swords, knives, Ivor and his hammer. Lastly, the slingers. He formed them up with his own men, who had been separated the same way, taking his time.

"Time we get started, it'll be time to turn back," Will said.

A few of the men who'd heard the remark stifled a laugh.

Guillame's chaplain, Jean, had not come; he was too busy—"Too scared, belike," Sewale said—so Guillame had Father Albinus lead the company in prayer.

The men knelt, and Albinus intoned, "Heavenly Father, bless us today, and give us the strength to overcome the forces of Satan. We humbly put our trust in You." He made the sign of the Cross. "In the name of the Father, and of the Son, and of the Holy Spirit. Amen."

The men rose. Blanche dismounted and Miles handed Ediva down. "What are you doing?" Guillame asked her.

"Walking," she said. "Horses will hold us back in the forest."

"No, no, no, I won't hear of it. You're a great landowner, Blanche, it's not for you to walk. You must set an example to these men. They can't see you on foot, like a villein. Besides, young Ediva, here, deserves to ride after what she's been through."

Reluctantly, Blanche remounted, and Miles lifted Ediva back up to her.

Guillame motioned to the drummer, who began his steady beat. With Guillame and Blanche in the lead, the company started forward.

* * *

The line of men shuffled through the woods. The drum had long since stopped; the man with the flag had wrapped it around its staff. The men were in good spirits. They were going to rid the district of the outlaws who had plagued the roads for years. They were going to eliminate the constant demand upon them for taxes and forced labor.

"Baron Aimerie can take his fancy new castle and stuff it," Will said. "Who's he think he is?"

"Aye," Sewale said. "We're free Englishmen. We don't pay taxes to no one who's not our lord."

Will lowered his voice. "And not even to him—or to her—if we can get away with it."

"I heard that, Will," Blanche called from up ahead.

Will cleared his throat. "Sorry, my lady. I was speaking in what you might call kind of a fanciful way."

"That's what I thought," Blanche said. "Carry on."

They marched on, Guillame and Blanche in the lead, Ediva pointing the way. At the more difficult spots, the horses had to go around, taking up yet more time. Blanche dropped her horse back to where Miles walked. "I came here looking for peace and quiet, and I find myself in a war."

"Sorry," Miles said. "I feel responsible somehow."

"Why?" she said.

"I don't know."

"You blame yourself too much. None of this is your fault. Anyway, it's almost over now."

"Aye," said Miles, "but in whose favor?"

Guillame heard that and dropped back as well. "Come now, Miles, you must have faith. Our cause is just, is it not?"

"Our cause was just at Sand Lake," Miles said, "but that didn't stop your lot from stealing the country from us."

Guillame bristled, but before he could say anything, there was noise ahead of them. Two scouts who had been sent ahead came running back.

"The outlaws, my lord," the first one told Guillame. "They're coming!"

Chapter 38

If Guillame was surprised by this news, he didn't let on. "Excellent," he said. "Saves us the trouble of tracking them to their lair. How far ahead of us are they?"

Guillame's new steward, the gangly youth Chretien, repeated the question to the scouts.

"Two miles, maybe," said the first scout, a steady fellow who was one of Guillame's men from Edsworth. "There's a lot of them, and they'll be here quick."

Guillame said, "We must find a place to fight. Not here amongst the trees."

Miles would have preferred to fight amongst the trees, but, as Blanche kept reminding him, Guillame was in charge. Chretien questioned the scouts, and the second one replied, "There's a brook up ahead. And a clearing."

Chrettien relayed this information to Guillame, who said, "Perfect! We shall fight there." He turned to Blanche. "Alas, my lady, it is time for you and young Ediva to leave us."

Blanche looked at Miles before answering. "I've changed my mind. Someone else take Ediva back to Redhill. I'm going to stay here and fight."

"That is not possible," said Guillame. "I cannot permit you to put yourself in a place of danger."

"I don't care what you permit. I'm not going to run—"

"Blan—my lady," Miles cut in. "Lord Guillame is right. You'll be little help to us in a fight. Even worse, the outlaws will make it their goal to capture you, and we'll be too busy worrying about your safety to concentrate on what we're doing. It's best that you leave."

Blanche's jaw set in that way she had. "I'm not—"

"Please?" Miles said.

She paused, then let out her breath. "Very well. Come, Ediva, we shall return to Redhill." With a furious glance at Miles, she turned her white horse. As she rode down the line, she held out her hand. "Good luck, men."

The men from Redhill and Fairleigh—and some from Edsworth—touched her outstretched hand as she passed. "Thank you, my lady." "Bless you, my lady."

Guillame looked on with disapproval. "Shaking hands with villeins—what is she thinking?" He turned to Miles. "You are far too familiar with Lady Blanche, Miles. She's a noble, and you need to learn—"

"You've told me that before, my lord. More than once. Let's get these men forward, if you want to reach that brook before the outlaws do."

Miles and Guillame's steward, Chretien, barked orders, and the column hustled forward, Miles and the two scouts in the lead. Guillame held his horse aside for them to pass, because if he went first, the big horse might hold them up on the rough ground. "No unnecessary noise," Guillame said through his steward as the men filed by. "We want our presence to be a surprise to these fellows."

They came to the brook. The clearing, a large one, was on this side of the brook, totally open save for a large oak tree. On the other side, the woods ran right to the water. There was a three-foot bank on this side, as well. Not a huge obstacle for the outlaws to surmount, but better than none.

The men debouched into the clearing, and as they did, Miles waved them into line. Those with shorter-bladed weapons were in front, at the lip of the stream bank. The men with longer weapons were behind them. The archers and slingers held the flanks.

Guillame came up, and Miles said, "With your permission, my lord, I'd like to try a trick the Welsh used on us to great effect. We'll form the main body here, as if to fight, then I'll take the archers and slingers, cross downstream, and wait in the woods. When the outlaws advance on you, we'll hit them from the side and the back."

"The Welsh?" Guillame said. "We can learn nothing from them, sir. They're barbarians, savages. Why would I use a tactic of theirs? No, we'll have a straight-up fight, like men. Good versus evil. We're in the right, God will provide."

"But—"

"I'm getting tired of my orders being questioned by a peasant," Guillame snapped. "You have a habit of forgetting your place. Now get these men ready to fight. And if you have any more brilliant ideas, I'd be obliged if you'd keep them to yourself."

"Aye, my lord."

From the right flank, Blackie approached Miles. "Why don't we take some of the men and cross—?"

"I already suggested it," Miles said. "Guillame didn't like the idea. Offends his noble sensibilities."

Blackie shook his head. "French fool. We could ambush them and—"

"I know, I know," Miles said helplessly.

Guillame planted his blue-and-white banner near the oak tree, and left his young steward, Chretien, to guard it. He rode behind the line of men, sword drawn, waiting.

"Look," Wada said, pointing.

Figures had appeared in the trees across the brook. Three men.

"Scouts," said Blackie.

The scouts stared at Guillame and his men, then vanished back into the trees.

Miles walked down the ragged line of men, shield on his arm, axe in hand. These men were peasants, some of them eager for a fight, others less so. This wouldn't be a battle, it would be a giant tavern brawl. Miles's men were tough and strong, but a lot of the outlaws probably had experience as soldiers, and that would give them an advantage not only in using weapons, but in maintaining cohesion and working together.

"Be ready," Miles said. "Shouldn't be long now."

Soon after, the outlaws' main force began spreading through the trees along the opposite bank of the brook. Ernoul appeared, on horseback. Ernoul was dressed much the same as Guillame, with a mail shirt, helm, and shield.

The Viking, bare-chested as always, was behind him. The blue-haired girl was there, as well, with a bow.

Ernoul walked his horse into the shallow water. "Baron Guillame!" he cried jovially. "What a coincidence. We were on our way to visit you."

"And we were coming to visit you," Guillame said.

"I know," said Ernoul. "That boy, Hugh, told us everything."

"Where is Hugh?" Miles shouted.

Guillame cast Miles an angry look for interrupting him, but Ernoul was happy to answer. "He's where you'll be if your mistress doesn't swear fealty to my father and pay her taxes."

Miles felt a chill run through him. Hugh's father, Matthew, ran forward, crying with rage, but Miles grabbed his arm and held him back. "No," Miles said.

Guillame spoke. "Neither I nor Lady Blanche will swear fealty to your father, nor will we pay his taxes."

"Then I find you to be in a state of rebellion," Ernoul proclaimed.

"You can't rebel against something that is illegal," Guillame told him. "All you can do is resist."

"Noble sentiments," Ernoul said. "Resist, then, by all means."

"Why all the yapping?" Father Albinus muttered. "They're wasting time. Why don't they just get on with it?"

Ernoul went on. "I have one request to make."

"Yes?" said Guillame.

"Let us cross the stream unimpeded and mount the bank. That will make it a fair fight. This way, we are at a disadvantage, which you'll agree is unchivalrous."

Miles was afraid Guillame might agree to Ernoul's request, but Guillame surprised him. "Chivalry does not apply to outlaws, *seigneur*," he said.

"As you wish," Ernoul told him.

As he spoke, the blue-haired woman stepped forward and shot an arrow. The arrow struck Guillame's gangly young steward, Chretien, who clutched his chest and fell to the ground near Guillame's banner.

Without being ordered, Blackie, Will, and Sewale nocked and shot arrows at the blue-haired woman, but she had already retreated to the safety of the trees.

Blackie and the others switched their target to Ernoul, but he blocked their arrows with his long shield and backed his horse into the trees, as well.

"Get ready!" Miles shouted.

"*Attendez!*" Guillame cried.

Miles expected the outlaws to burst from the trees and cross the brook, but nothing happened.

Time passed.

The only sound was the wounded steward's crying.

The short November afternoon drifted by. The men grew edgy.

"What are they waiting for?" Wada said.

"No idea," said Miles.

"Maybe they ran away," Will suggested.

"They didn't run away," said Blackie. "That Ernoul fellow seems like a hot head, and if he ain't, the Viking sure as hell is."

"They got something in mind, then," Sewale said.

Father Albinus said, "Wish I knew what it was."

Blackie said, "What I wish is that we'd crossed the stream and attacked them from behind."

"Too late for that now," Miles told him.

The blue-haired woman stepped from behind cover and let another arrow fly. A man in the front rank cried out and toppled off the bank into the brook.

Blackie and his men fired arrows in retaliation, but the outlaws were too well covered by the trees. "Hold off," Miles told them. "You're wasting arrows."

"Watch that spot where she was," Blackie told his men. "When she shows up again, be ready."

A few minutes later, the blue-haired woman popped up again, but in a different spot. She shot an arrow. Another man went down. She was back in the trees before Blackie and his men could adjust their aim and get arrows off.

Blackie said, "We can't stand here and let that girl shoot us to pieces."

Miles hated to give up this position. The three-foot bank was as close as they were going to get to a fortification. But Blackie was right. Plus, the day was dragging on.

Miles approached Lord Guillame. "Should we attack, my lord?"

"Why are they waiting?" Guillame asked Miles.

"No idea, my lord."

"I think they *want* us to attack," Guillame said. "I think it's a trap."

The blue-haired woman fired another arrow. Another man went down with the shaft in his leg.

"Maybe," Miles said, "but we won't be able to get this many men together again. They have too much work to do at home. The day's wearing on, and we don't want to fight in the dark."

"I know that!" Guillame said. "Now will you please stop bothering me?"

There was a noise in the trees behind them. Miles looked over his shoulder, and then he knew why Ernoul had declined to fight until now.

Emerging from the trees into the clearing were Baron Aimerie and five armored knights, spears in hand.

Chapter 39

Aimerie and his knights broke into a lumbering charge. At the same moment, Ernoul and the outlaws attacked from across the stream, cheering. Both the knights and the outlaws aimed for the center of Guillame's line, Ernoul going for Guillame himself.

Miles doubted that even the men he'd had in Wales could have maintained their discipline under such circumstances. Guillame's men were not trained soldiers. They dissolved into a mob, running for safety, throwing down weapons.

The knights slammed into them, bowling men over, transfixing them with spears, then dropping the spears and hacking at them with swords, the big horses and armored men invulnerable. The outlaws caught what was left of Guillame's men from behind.

The men from Redhill ran like the rest. After the initial attack destroyed Guillame's center, knights and outlaws turned left and right. Men were running, colliding with one another, falling, screaming in terror and screaming for mercy. Splashing across the brook in their desperation.

"Come on!" Miles cried. He grabbed Wada, along with Blackie, Sewale, and Will, who still plied their bows. "There's nothing we can do. Let's go."

Father Albinus joined them, along with a few others. They ran along the bank of the brook, then turned into the trees. They were at the far end of the line, so were given a bit of breathing room. Behind them were screams and cries. Will tripped, and as he rose, a knight galloped up, his shield painted red. The knight leaned in his saddle and swung his sword. Will's head went flying. The rest of Miles's men made it into the trees, and the knight with the red shield turned away, looking for easier pickings.

The little party ran through the woods, the sound of battle growing more distant behind them. Heaving for breath, they slowed to a walk.

"Get rid o' these shields?" Wada asked.

Miles considered; the shields were heavy. "No, they may come in handy. Sling 'em across your back."

Wada took off his thick cloak and stuffed it behind the shield on his back. They heard noises to their right, turned, ready to fight. But it was Ivor the smith, carrying his hammer, along with two men from one of the other manors.

Miles waved them toward his own group. "Come on."

There were other, distant, noises in the forest, occasional cries and screams, but Miles and his group ignored them and pressed on.

"We were well and truly tricked," Father Albinus said.

"That we were," Miles agreed. "I'll give Aimerie credit."

"What now?" said Wada.

"Let's see if we can get home safely before we worry about that," Miles said.

They stopped to drink from a muddy rivulet, so thirsty they didn't care, the water full of dirt and God knew what else.

"S-h-h-h!" said Blackie.

The group came alert.

Blackie cupped a hand to his ear in warning.

They listened.

There was a noise behind them. A clopping of hoofs. Big hoofs.

Miles motioned the men off the path, into the trees and brush.

The sound of hoofs grew louder.

A knight rode into view, mounted on a charger. Helmet, hauberk, his long shield painted red, the lower part of his face covered by an aventail. Sword in hand. Looking for survivors of Guillame's force.

"Let's get one of the bastards, anyway," Miles whispered. He told the others what he wanted them to do.

Quietly, the men spread out, keeping under cover.

The knight rode by, eyes searching the trees, sword ready.

When he was past, Blackie jumped up, ran down the hill, and with his dagger, hamstrung the knight's horse.

The animal screamed piteously, pawing the ground with its forelegs. The knight jumped from the saddle and chased Blackie but couldn't catch him due to the weight of his armor.

The knight stood in the path, turning slowly, sword in hand, ready to fight.

Miles and Father Albinus rose and started forward. They spread out, shields up. The knight prepared to face them.

Just then, Ivor ran at the knight from behind. He raised his hammer and brought it down. The knight heard him and turned, so the hammer blow, which was supposed to hit the knight in the head, fell on his shoulder instead, shattering bone beneath the mail hauberk.

The knight screamed and dropped his sword. He faced his attackers, red shield up, his now useless right arm dangling at his side.

Miles and Albinus circled him. Sewale drew his bow and put an arrow in the knight's back. The knight grunted. He moved more slowly, the back of his hauberk wet with blood.

Miles ran forward. He bashed his shield into the knight's shield, stepped to his left and stabbed his short sword into the knight's right side. The knight grunted again. His steps faltered.

One of the new men took his axe to the rear of the knight's left leg. The knight fell to a sitting position. There was blood all over the ground and the fallen leaves. The red shield still protected the knight's face. Ivor hit him with the hammer again, and this time the blow struck his helmet.

The knight fell on his back. Wada grabbed the knight's shield and pulled it away, and Miles plunged his sword into the knight's chest, feeling the point go through mail and leather, through bone and flesh.

Blood bubbled over the knight's aventail. He kicked weakly, then fell still.

Miles was breathing heavily. They all were.

It started to rain.

"Finish off that horse," Miles told Wada. "Then let's get out of here before more of these bastards show up."

Chapter 40

The fight was over.

It was raining, cold and steady. Bodies littered the clearing, most of them belonging to Guillame's men. The outlaws went about dispatching the seriously wounded. The lightly wounded and prisoners were herded together.

Ernoul rode up to join Baron Aimerie. "Why are you sitting your horse like that, Father?" he said, waving a hand. "There's work to be done. What's left of the *capuchins* are getting away. Let's finish them off."

Aimerie changed the subject. "Where is Guillame?"

Ernoul gave a satisfied smile. "Lord Pretty Boy isn't so pretty anymore. I opened a wound in his side that should send him to the worms. I wanted to carve his face, but this will have to do."

"You believe he'll die, then?" Aimerie said.

"I do."

"So much the better for us. As he has no heir, I'll give his manor to you."

"That's for the future," Ernoul said, "what about now? We have the *capuchins* on the run, we can—"

"No," Aimerie said.

"Why?" said Ernoul.

"Think, son. If we kill these people, who will work the fields? Who will pay us taxes? Thanks to your ham-handedness, we already have one manor that needs to be repopulated. Where are we going to find the men—and women—for that?"

"You told me to teach them a lesson," Ernoul reminded him.

"I didn't tell you to turn the place into a desert," Aimerie said.

"We could use Fromont's men to work the fields," Ernoul suggested.

Aimerie didn't think much of that idea. "If Fromont's men wanted to be farmers, they wouldn't be living in the woods, robbing travelers."

Four of the knights had rejoined Aimerie, their lower legs and the lower bodies of their horses splashed with blood. Aimerie looked around for the fifth. "Where is Francois?"

"Haven't seen him, my lord," said a blond knight named Blaise.

"He'll turn up," said another. "Maybe he found some wine."

"Maybe he found a woman," said a third knight, and they all laughed.

Ernoul didn't care about Francois. He was irritated. "What about these prisoners? I suppose we're not going to kill them, either?"

"That's right," Aimerie said. "We'll question them, then hold them until peace is made."

"That could be a long time."

"I don't think so, Aimerie said. "Blanche will give in quickly now." He turned to the former steward, Joubert, who had accompanied the outlaws. "See if Miles is among the dead."

"Aye, my lord." Joubert moved off.

"And if he's not?" Ernoul said.

"If he's not, I want him taken and hung as a rebel. I'll take particular enjoyment in watching that."

"What about Blanche?"

"What about her?" Aimerie said.

"You're not going to hang her, too, are you?"

"Of course not, she's a noble."

Ernoul looked relieved.

Aimerie said, "Now, this weather is atrocious. I'm going back to the castle and warm my bones."

Ernoul grinned. "Good idea."

He turned in the saddle and beckoned to Hersent, who stood nearby. He extended his arm and removed his foot from the left stirrup so that she could mount behind him.

Hersent hesitated, but she saw the look on Ernoul's face and decided it was wiser not to say no. She mounted behind Ernoul, put her arms around his waist.

Ernoul glared at bare-chested Fromont. "Any objections?"

Fromont growled, "No objections, my lord."

Ernoul turned his horse and rode away.

Chapter 41

Blanche waited at the end of the village street, in the rain, the hood of her white cloak drawn over her head. Millicent stood beside her. The village women—wives and daughters—were there, as well. Around them, the grey dusk deepened.

The first survivors of the battle returned, singly and in small groups. Tired, heads down. Limping, some of them; others, wounded.

Blanche put a hand to her mouth at the sight. "What happened?" she asked as the first men came up.

"It was a trap, my lady," said a man with a bloodied rag around his head.

"We never had a chance," added another. It was Giles, the potter.

"Where is Miles?" she asked.

They shook their heads. No one knew. "Ain't seen 'im since the start of the battle."

"Battle?" said Giles. "Massacre's more like it."

More men trickled in, nodding to Blanche as they went by. “My lady.” Their women went off with them—or helped them, if they were wounded—until Blanche was left alone, staring up the path that led to the forest.

It grew dark. No more men came. The only sound was the rain.

Millicent approached. “My lady, perhaps we should . . .”

“No!” Blanche said, and she stood there, alone, her back straight so that it wouldn’t be obvious that she was crying.

She stood in the darkness, in the rain, refusing to give up.

She didn’t know how long she’d been there when she heard sounds. Weary feet trudging the muddy path.

There was movement before her, and from out of the darkness came Miles, followed by Blackie and Sewale and Father Albinus, Ivor the smith, and some men she didn’t know.

Miles saw Blanche and stopped. His clothes were splashed with rain-washed blood.

Blanche’s hood came off as she ran to him. She threw her arms around him and buried her tear-stained face in his chest. He wrapped his strong arms around her and laid his cheek against her wet hair. They stood there, saying nothing, holding one another.

The other men looked at them as they passed. Some of them might have suspected the relationship before, but here it was in the open. By tomorrow, the whole manor would know. By the next day, the other manors would know, as well. Within a week, the shire would know, but Blanche didn’t care.

Father Albinus wordlessly nudged the men on up the street. Millicent took charge of the men from the other manors, leading them to shelter for the night.

Miles and Blanche remained there for what seemed like a long time. Then they broke apart and walked, hand in hand, to the manor house.

Chapter 42

Servants were building up the fire in the hall when Miles and Blanche got there. The hall was packed and noisy. It smelled of wet men and mud and untended wounds. It was busy, as well, and Miles and Blanche didn't have any more time to themselves. The men from the other manors had to be fed and given blankets and places to sleep beside the fire. Miles and Wada oversaw that, while Blanche and Millicent tended the wounded as best they could.

After a long time, they were done, at least for the night. Blanche was thoroughly chilled from standing in the cold rain, but she was too tired to put on dry clothes, so she threw off her wet cloak, wrapped herself in a blanket, and lay as close as she could to the fire, with wounded men and servants jumbled around her. Miles lay beside her and put his arms around her for warmth, not caring who saw or who disapproved.

"It was better when we did this in the summer," Blanche murmured, placing her hand over his. Before they had become lovers, or even friends, the two of them had been forced to spend a night in the forest, in the rain. Blanche had fallen asleep on Miles's shoulder, and he had held her all night, shifting her to make her more comfortable.

Miles was surprised. "I didn't know you were awake when that happened. I thought you slept through it."

"Let's say I knew it was happening," she told him. She smiled. "And I liked it."

He kissed her damp hair, and they slept.

* * *

The servants and cooks awakened before first light, rebuilding the fire and putting away their bedding. They were followed by the rest of the manor staff, who slept in the hall. Only Millicent had gone to the solar. Sleeping in the hall was beneath her, even though her mistress was there. Dogs wandered through the hall, sniffing the unfamiliar bodies, digging in the rushes, peeing.

Miles and Blanche rose. Milli came down from the solar, resignation mixed with the disappointment on her face when she saw Blanche and Miles together. One of the wounded men had died during the night, and his body was taken away to be buried. With the aid of Millicent and Wada, the men from the other manors were fed and seen off to their homes, some, no doubt, to die from their wounds. The hall rushes were stained with blood and vomit, with bits of bandages in them.

Blanche said, "Milli, find me fresh clothes—these are still damp. Then have the hall swept out and the rushes changed."

"Yes, my lady," said Milli.

Miles went to his quarters and changed clothes, as well. He came back to the hall, where he had a thick slice of barley bread, spread with butter from the spring house, and a small pot of ale.

When he was done, he and Blanche went to the village. "At least it's stopped raining," Miles said.

"What happens now?" said Blanche. "Will Aimerie and his men attack us?"

"I don't think so," Miles said. "They hurt us enough. Now they'll wait for us to give up."

Blanche was grim faced. "They'll have a long wait then."

It had just grown light, but the villagers were already up—getting water, some of them breaking the thin film of ice that had formed on their cisterns, turning out the sheep and pigs and cattle, hauling carts to fetch firewood. Led by Simon the hayward and Ralf the carpenter, a group of men gathered to put up a new house for Giles the potter, to replace the old house that was being propped up by a log. A few of these workers blew on their hands to warm them, while others sorted out the different-length poles that would be used for framing the house, and Simon and Ralf marked where the post holes would be. Yesterday, some of these men had been fighting for their lives; today it was back to village work. Somewhere, someone was hammering.

Blanche and Miles received sullen, resentful looks as they walked down the street. A crone spit in their direction.

"Got my husband killed," muttered a woman of about Blanche's age. "Now I guess you'll be taking heriot. That's what you come here for, ain't it?" When the head of a household died, his—or her—best animal was taken by the manor's lord as heriot.

There was angry shouting. "Our men die, and you get rich."

"That's the way it always is."

"You watch," cried the woman, "her and Aimerie will make up now, and the only ones who'll be the worse for it are us."

"Maybe she planned it that way."

More angry shouting.

"I'll take no heriot," Blanche told them. "I'll not profit from your loss."

Her words were received with jeers.

A woman carrying water confronted Blanche. "My Jorvik, 'e had 'is arm crushed 'cause of you. 'E may never be able to work again, and where will we be then?"

Ediva stood outside her house. She waved at Blanche and Miles timidly.

Blanche entered the yard. She knelt and took the girl's shoulders. "How are you, Ediva?"

"Good, my lady," Ediva said. "Except . . ."

"Except what?"

"My dad, he's not come home."

Blanche tried to remember the father's name. "Ailwyn?"

"That's right," snapped Ediva's mother, Ailova. She took the girl from Blanche's grasp and turned her away. "You got him killed, you and your Godless French ways. And I'll thank you to leave my yard."

As Miles and Blance went back into the street, a man shouted, "Pledge yourself to Aimerie and pay his tax."

"Aye," said one of the men who'd been in the fight. "We've had enough."

"God help us, but I'd rather they bring back Joubert." That hurt Blanche the most, because it came from Winchelsey, the old woman they'd saved from Joubert on their first day here.

There were angry mutters of agreement. "We shouldn't have a woman for a lord," Ailova said from over her gate. "T'ain't right."

"Specially one what's livin' in sin," said the woman carrying water.

Shouts of agreement.

Blanche held her head high, fighting back tears.

Others weren't ready to give in. "We can still fight," Blackie told the villagers.

"Aye," said Sewale. "We ain't beat yet."

Father Albinus heard the commotion and left the church, where he and Tostig had been treating more of the wounded. "All right, all right," he told the crowd, motioning with his palms out. "Calm down."

"How can we be calm?" said Hamo, the grizzled steward. "We lost half our young men, and half the rest is unfit to work. I told you how this would end up, but you wouldn't listen. You can't challenge the lords. They always win."

"*I* am a lord," Blanche reminded him.

"Beggin' your pardon, my lady, but you're not. Not really. You're a woman. I'm grateful that you and Miles made me steward, but it's my job to tell you how things are."

Albinus turned to Miles. "Any word from Lord Guillame?"

Miles shook his head. "We don't even know if he's still alive."

Hamo pointedly ignored Miles and Blanche spoke to the priest. "What do you think we should do, Father?"

Albinus wiped a hand across his rugged face. His arms and clothes were covered with blood. There was blood in his beard, and judging by the dark circles under his eyes, he'd gotten no sleep. "I don't like giving in. By all that's Holy, I don't. Not to the likes of Aimerie and his son. Not to those outlaws. But . . ."

Blanche finished for him. "But you don't see how we can go on?"

"No, my lady, I don't."

Blanche nodded. "I appreciate your honesty, Father. I'll send Milli to help with the wounded. Wada and the manor staff will bring food and drink."

"Thank you, my lady," said Father Albinus.

Blackie said, "Me and Sewale, we'll scout around. See if Aimerie's men are coming."

"Good," Miles said.

Hamo blocked Blackie's path. "No, you don't. You two got work to do. You're done playin'—"

"Let them go," Miles told him, and there was something in Miles's voice that warned Hamo not to cross him.

Hamo hesitated, then nodded reluctantly to Blackie and Sewale, who went to get their bows.

Miles and Blanche started back to the manor house. The sun had come out, but it provided little warmth.

"That went well," Miles said.

"Aimerie said they'd turn on me," Blanche said. "He didn't say it would be this quickly."

"It's my fault," said Miles. "I failed you. I started a fight we had no chance of winning."

"I'm as much to blame as you are," she said.

"Yes, but I'm the soldier, I should have known better. I let pride get in the way of my common sense. Now I've wrecked two manors—three, if you count Guillame's."

Blanche took his hand; she didn't care if the villagers and servants saw. "You could say the same about me."

Miles went on. "I'm ashamed to show my face around these people. God knows, they'd be happy enough not to see it."

"Stop feeling sorry for yourself," Blanche admonished. "Like Sewale said, we're not beaten yet."

"It certainly feels like it."

"We can—"

"I don't want to fight to the last villager, Blanche, not when there's no chance of winning."

"So shall we do?" she said. "Surrender?"

Miles sighed. Like Father Albinus, he hated to give in. "Before we make a decision, let's see how Guillame is."

Chapter 43

Miles and Blanche set off for Edsworth, attended by Millicent. Miles left Wada behind, to help Blackie should Aimerie and his men—useless to think of the outlaws as anything but "Aimerie's men" now—attack. The day was dry and cold, with drifting clouds.

Miles watched a high-flying hawk and breathed deep. " 'Blood Month,' we call November."

Blanche seemed to have gotten over her confrontation with the villagers. "Because that's when the animals are slaughtered?" she said. In November, animals that could not be kept over the winter for lack of feed—pigs, goats, cows, geese—were killed.

"Aye," said Miles, "best time of year. Soon the rafters will be groaning with hams and slabs of bacon. There'll be sausages and blood pudding, mutton and roast goose. Today's the Seventh of the month, first day of winter here in Trentshire, though I've heard that in some places winter starts on November First."

"Where I grew up, it starts on Martinmas," Blanche said, "but it depends on the parish. In a parish near ours, winter didn't start until the First of December."

"Huh," said Miles noncommittally. The French were strange.

The ruins of Fairleigh were on their way. They stopped there long enough for Miles to appoint a new steward, Toli. Toli was the man with the face wrinkled by burn scars. He had led the small Fairleigh contingent in yesterday's fight and been lucky to get out alive.

"You have a big task," Miles told him, "getting this manor reorganized. Especially with winter here."

"We'll get it done, don't fear," Toli said.

"Good luck," Blanche told him.

"Thank you, my lady," he said. "What's to happen now? With the Hoods, and all?"

"I'm not certain," Blanche said. "We'll keep you informed, though, don't worry."

They rode on to Edsworth. Upon arriving, they learned that Guillame was alive, but that he had been badly wounded in yesterday's fight. He was in the manor hall. It was an older hall, dimly lit by a few candles and the fire. A bed had been made for Guillame near the fire pit, where he was tended by his chaplain, Jean, the same chaplain who had been "too busy" to join Guillame's force in the battle.

Jean sat in a chair beside the bed, head down and hands clasped together, his eyes closed, lips moving silently. Guillame's side had been gashed open. Grimy, blood-soaked bandages swathed his lower torso. His head was propped up, and he smelled of blood and dirt and feces.

"How is he?" Blanche asked the priest.

Jean looked up. He had a pale, humorless face. "Not good, my lady. Our only hope is to trust in the Lord and—"

"What have you been doing for him?"

"Why, praying, my lady. Praying. There's naught else we can do—"

"What a mess!" Milli exclaimed, pushing forward. She shooed Jean from his chair, then moved the heavy chair out of her way.

Jean took offence. "What—?"

Milli examined the bandages and sniffed them.

"You're supposed to smell his *urine*," Jean told her, "not the bandages."

"You smell it if you want. Get me water and soap. And wine, the strongest wine you have."

"Soap?" said Jean.

"Yes. You've heard of it, haven't you?" Milli said.

"Of course," said Jean. "But what good will soap—?"

"Just get some!"

Jean drew himself up. "See here, I don't know who you think you—"

"Do as she says," Blanche told him.

Jean moved off in a huff.

"You're lucky he hasn't killed you," Milli told Guillame. She turned to a serving girl. "Clean bandages—hurry! And a needle and thread."

"Thank you," Guillame murmured to Milli. He turned to Blanche. "Thank you, as well, my lady."

"We came to see how you are," Blanche told Guillame.

"I've been better," Guillame joked weakly.

"We also . . . well, we also came to learn your plans for the future."

Guillame's handsome face was pale and drawn. His hair was matted with sweat. Milli held a cup of water to his lips and let him sip. "Don't tax him, my lady. He's sore hurt."

Guillame's voice was as drawn as his face. "Sorry . . . but I'm beaten. I sent messenger to Aimerie . . . told him that when I'm well . . . if I live . . . I'll go to him . . . pledge fealty. Pay taxes. You should . . . you should do the same, Blanche. It's over."

Blanche wanted to argue with him, but she knew it was useless. There was no fight left in him. She felt sorry for him. He had been so bold and brash and proud. And now . . .

"Will you?" Guillame asked her weakly. "Give in?"

Blanche looked to Miles. "I must think on it."

The serving girl arrived with an armload of clean cloth to be cut up for bandages. Jean sent another servant with soap and water and wine. Milli cleaned Guillame's wound first with wine, the alcohol in the wine making Guillame hiss and take in his breath, then with soap and water,

"Why the wine?" Miles asked Blanche.

Blanche shrugged. "Don't know, really. We found that it works. No idea why."

Milli looked up from what she was doing. "Beg pardon, my lady, but can I stay here and see to him? That priest will kill him."

"Of course," Blanche said.

"That English girl, Estrild, can handle my duties until I get back."

"Very well," Blanche said. "Stay as long as you deem necessary." Blanche bent and kissed Guillame's damp forehead. "Get well, my friend, by God's grace."

"Thank you," he said.

"Good luck, my lord," Miles added.

Guillame nodded to him.

"Now let me finish with this wound and sew you up," Milli told Guillame. She had completely forgotten about her mistress and Miles, who turned away and took their leave.

"Guillame is done," Blanche told Miles as they left the hall.

"Aye," said Miles. "We're on our own, now."

Chapter 44

Blanche and Miles made their way back to Redhill, their horses plodding along the path between the empty fields. “Do you think Guillame will live?” Blanche said.

Miles shook his head. “It doesn’t look good for him.”

“I was hoping he would keep up the fight, but now . . .”

“Now he’ll be lucky to last the week. There’s little else he can do but surrender. If he doesn’t swear fealty to Aimerie, Aimerie will simply take Edsworth away from him.”

“And what about us? Will Aimerie take Redhill and Fairleigh from us? Will he give me to Ernoul?”

“He may well try,” Miles said.

“So what are our options?” said Blanche. “We can leave, but I don’t know where we’d go. I have no land in Normandy, no family there, save for my ex-husband’s relatives, and they won’t welcome me. The only other option is to stay and fight.”

“We’ll lose if we do that,” Miles told her. “We can’t beat Aimerie’s knights. Anyway, the people no longer support us. You heard them back at the manor.”

"Then I should surrender? Pledge fealty to Aimerie and marry Ernoul? Believe me, I'll kill myself before I let him—"

"There is another option," Miles said.

Blanche waited.

"I still have land in Ravenswell. You could come back there with me."

She frowned. "As what? Your guest? Your . . .?"

"As my wife."

She arched an exotic brow. "Well. You certainly have a romantic way of proposing marriage."

"I'm serious," he said. "We'd be safe there. Aimerie's writ doesn't extend that far. Not yet, anyway, though God knows what he's got planned for the future."

"So I'd be a peasant again," Blanche said.

"You'd be my wife. And, as you know, I am a free man."

"What about your son and his family?"

"The land is still mine. We would build our own house. Anyway, they know you and like you."

Blanche sighed. "I was a peasant once, I can be a peasant again." She looked at her lacquered nails, imagining what they would become like with farm labor. "Pity about the nails, though. Oh, well."

Miles arched his own brow. "You certainly have a romantic way of accepting a marriage proposal."

"Actually, I have a much better way of accepting," she told him with a sly look. "Let's go into that patch of woods over there and I'll show you."

Miles grinned. He was about to pull off the path when he noticed something.

A rider was approaching. At a canter.

"Of all the luck," Miles moaned.

"It's all right," Blanche said. "We'll wait till he's gone past."

Miles squinted. "That looks like Wada. He must be looking for us."

Indeed it was Wada. He grew closer, then reined in before them. "My lady," he said, bowing his head to Blanche. "Thank God I found you. Ernoul and his father's bailiffs have been to Redhill. Baron Aimerie has declared Miles outside the law. There's a bounty on his head, and Aimerie's men have been instructed to hang him on sight."

Chapter 45

"Hang you on sight?" Blanche said to Miles. "Aimerie doesn't have the authority to do that."

"He doesn't have the authority to make me an outlaw, either," Miles said. "Think about it, though. If he hangs me, there's no trial. My side of the story never makes it onto the court rolls. For all intents and purposes, I vanish. So does what Aimerie has done in this part of the shire."

"He says that anyone that aids you is subject to punishment, too," Wada added.

The three of them dismounted, to rest their horses. The sun still played hide-and-seek with the clouds. The land was brown, dead, awaiting spring's rebirth.

"You can't go back to Redhill," Blanche told Miles. "They'll be looking for you there. The same with Fairleigh and Edsworth."

"We'll go to Ravenswell," Miles said, "like we talked about."

"Won't Aimerie expect you to do that?"

"I told you, it's beyond his writ. He used to be lord there, but the new lord, Stigand, is the earl of Trent's steward, as you know. Stigand doesn't particularly like me, but he's prickly about anyone infringing on his new-found authority. As for your former stepson, Earl Galon, he'd like nothing better than to see me hang, but he wants to do it himself. He'd take a dim view of somebody else doing the job. Aimerie's bound to know that, so he'll stay away. He doesn't want to make an enemy of Galon. Not yet, anyway."

Wada kept looking over his shoulder, as if expecting to see riders. "You'll have to take back roads, my lady, or maybe go where there's no roads at all. Aimerie's got patrols out."

"I'm not going," Blanche said.

"What!" said Miles. "We just talked about this."

"You go," she told him. "I'll stall them. Negotiate with Aimerie about marrying Ernoul. In the meantime, you get a message to Lord Tutbury." Tutbury was sheriff of Trentshire. "Tell him what's going on here."

"I don't know where Tutbury is," Miles said. "He may still be in France."

"Then you'll have to go to France and find him."

"That could take months. Can you hold off Aimerie and Ernoul for that long? Ernoul's to be knighted in two days, and he'll want to marry you right away."

"I have my ways," she said.

Miles kicked at the ground. "I don't like this, Blanche. Come with me. It's too risky for you to stay here."

"Nonsense," she said. "What can they do to me? I'm an earl's widow, under the king's protection. They wouldn't dare hurt me." She drew herself up. "Besides, I'm lord of Redhill and Fairleigh. I can't abandon my lands. I can't abandon my people, even if they've turned on me. I have a responsibility toward them, a duty. You would feel the same were you their lord."

Miles made no answer, because what she said was true.

She removed the purse from her belt and handed it to him. "For food. And lodging, should you need it."

Wada kept looking back the way he'd come. "You'd better get going," he told Miles.

Miles took Blanche in his arms and kissed her, molding her lithe body to his. Pressing her mouth to his, feeling the warm softness of her lips. Absorbing it.

"Good luck," she breathed.

"And to you," he said. "I love you."

"I love you, too."

She kissed him again, and her cheeks were wet.

He mounted and rode off.

Chapter 46

Miles headed southeast, towards Ravenswell. After that, he would go to Badford Town or France, wherever Lord Tutbury might be.

Or maybe he would send Tutbury a message.

Father John, Ravenswell's pastor, could write the message; Ravenswell's steward, Pierre, would know how to get it delivered. That would be the soundest plan. Then Miles could go back to Redhill. He didn't like leaving Blanche. He felt guilty, like he was abandoning her. He didn't know what Aimerie would get up to in his absence, but he was sure it wouldn't be good.

He had to swing wide of the Badford Road. That was the first place Aimerie's men would look for him. The river road to the north would be the next fastest route, but he couldn't use that because it would bring him too close to Brightwood and the castle. So he took a long detour south, down seldom-used paths and narrow lanes, through country he didn't know. He had no idea how long it would take. He kept to the woods as much as possible, avoided travelers and passed through no villages. He dared not trust anyone he encountered out here. Once, he saw riders in the distance, and he moved deeper into the forest until they were past.

The short November day was already waning. The northwest wind was freshening, with the smell of rain. The air was heavy. A storm was coming. A big one. He could feel it. Not tomorrow, but soon. The steward in him thought of houses blown down, rivers flooded, people and animals drowned. That would be someone else's responsibility now. He hoped Hamo and Toli were up to it.

He slept in the woods that night, in a hollow, building a small fire that couldn't be seen for any distance. Despite the fire, he was freezing. This would be the Devil of a way for things to end—with him freezing to death. Tomorrow he would use Blanche's money to seek lodging at a manor, or at least to buy food for himself and grain for his horse. With luck, he would reach Ravenswell the next day.

He was back in the saddle at dawn, his back and limbs stiff with cold. When he thought he'd gone far enough to be out of reach of Aimerie's patrols, he angled north again, and eventually came to the Badford Road. He should be all right from here. He kicked the horse into an easy canter.

He heard a noise behind him and stopped.

Bare feet slapping the mud.

Someone running.

There was a curve in the path, so he couldn't see whoever it was. The steps were light, maybe belonging to a woman or a boy.

He thought about getting off the road, but the runner was too close, and, anyway, he didn't see a good place to hide. He wheeled the reluctant horse, at the same time drawing his short sword.

Around the curve came a girl, running.

Ediva.

He rode up to her. She stopped, hands on her knees, out of breath. He threw himself from the saddle and took her heaving shoulders.

"Baron Aimerie has kidnapped Lady Blanche," she blurted. "He means to marry her."

Chapter 47

Miles couldn't get his head around what Ediva was saying. "Wait. What? *Aimerie's* going to marry Blanche? I thought he wanted her to marry Ernoul."

Ediva's breathing slowed, and she shrugged. "That's what he said."

Miles gave Ediva water from a skin. He changed the subject. "You shouldn't be out here by yourself, young lady. How did you find me?"

"They sent a bunch of us after you. Just happened to be me what found you. Figured you'd go off the road, then double back onto it after a bit."

"Still, I have a horse. How did you . . .?"

"I stayed on the road. Aimerie's patrols paid no attention to me. I'm just a little girl."

Ediva lowered her eyes. "Actually, I wasn't supposed to be one of the ones that went after you. I kind of done it on me own. Sneaked out of the house. Mum'll kill me, but I don't mind. Lady Blanche, she was nice to me, and . . . and I thought you should know what happened to her."

"You're a brave girl. Where did you sleep last night?"

"Under a pile of leaves," she said.

"Alone? Weren't you scared?"

"Real scared." She shivered as her body cooled down after the running. "Real cold, too."

Miles led her to a fallen tree branch and let her sit. He wrapped his cloak around her and gave her more water. He took a chunk of bread from his scrip—all the food he had—and handed it to her. "Now breathe deep, and tell me everything that happened."

Ediva drank more water, munched the bread. "Well, Aimerie, him and his knights showed up at the manor house. All in armor they was, and they had some other men with 'em. Soldiers. Lady Blanche bolted the door, but they knocked it down, threatened to burn the place if she didn't come out."

"Did anybody resist?"

"Your beadle, Wada. It happened so fast, Blackie and the others didn't have time to get their weapons and try to stop them."

Miles drew in his breath. "Is Wada all right?"

"Bit of a headache, I reckon, but he'll live. Anyways, Lady Blanche wouldn't go with them, so they dragged her. Aimerie slapped her. Knocked her silly. That's when he told her she was going to marry him."

Miles pressed. "You heard him say that?"

"Aye. Shouldn't have got that close, I guess, but I did." She shrugged again. "Curious."

Miles rubbed a hand across his bearded jaw. He'd never actually heard Aimerie say that he wanted Ernoul to marry Blanche. It had been Ernoul who kept saying that.

Then there was the convenient death of Aimerie's wife. Did she fall? Or was she pushed?

It started to make sense. Still . . . how would Aimerie manage it? Blanche would never agree to marry him.

He remembered that a priest *could* conduct a marriage if the prospective bride was absent or refused to participate. Maybe Aimerie had a priest who would perform such a ceremony. If so, it would be legal, and when it was over, Aimerie would own Blanche's lands as well as Brightwood and the castle, giving him a strong base in Trentshire, especially with Guillame and the local lords pledging fealty to him.

He would also own Blanche.

Ernoul's knighting ceremony was tomorrow. Aimerie would want to have his marriage then, as well, since the guests had already been invited for the first event. Some of them would be coming from a distance and would stay overnight. No sense having them do it twice.

"Let's get you home," Miles told Ediva.

He put her on his horse and mounted behind her, settling his cloak around her. Ediva said, "I wish . . ."

"You wish what?" Miles said.

She looked up at him, blonde hair matted and stuck with bits of leaf. "I wish Hugh was here. Funny, I hated him when he was alive, but now he's gone, I wish he was back."

"I do, too," Miles said. "Hugh was a hero. We'll never forget him. I'm certain he'd have grown up to be a fine man."

They started off. Miles didn't take as wide a circle as he had before. He would have to risk meeting Aimerie's patrols. With any luck, the cold and damp would keep Aimerie's men close to a fire. Plus, there was a storm coming . . .

Chapter 48

Aimerie and Ernoul sparred on foot, on the open ground east of the castle. They wore full armor, with the only difference between this and an actual trial by combat being that they carried blunted wooden swords.

Ernoul, though technically still a squire, was strong and vicious. He had injured some of his father's knights in these sparring sessions, and Aimerie had to constantly remind him to take it easy on them. He was paying those men a lot of money, and he couldn't afford to have them incapacitated. They were no good to him that way.

The two combatants were surrounded by curious onlookers, who were kept at a respectful distance by guards. The castle battlements were full, as well, as were the walkways along the bailey wall. The wind had picked up; the skies were darkening.

"Look at all those people," Aimerie said as he loosened up.

"Don't they have work they should be doing?" Ernoul growled.

"They're here to see if you'll finally beat me."

Ernoul stretched the kinks out of his neck. "I will."

"Don't be overconfident," Aimerie told him. "I've warned you about that."

"We didn't come here to chat. This storm promises to be a big one. Let's get to it before it hits."

The two men touched their wooden swords in salute and circled.

"Why did you want to do this today?" Aimerie asked. "Just before your knighting ceremony."

"Because I want to know why you killed my mother."

Aimerie's jaw fell; his eyes widened. "I didn't kill her."

"You swear it?"

"Of course I swear it. What do you take me for? She was drunk, she fell. It was a tragedy, but life goes on. I loved Oudinette."

"And if I don't believe you?"

"You have to—"

Ernoul attacked without warning, all brute strength, slashing furiously, trying to beat Aimerie down. Aimerie blocked the blows with his long shield, but he felt each one of them, pounding into his forearm and up his shoulder. It wasn't the overhand blows Aimerie worried about so much as it was Ernoul's wild backhand slashes. If one of them got over the top of his shield, Aimerie could have his face caved in. He wouldn't be the first man to die in a practice fight.

Ernoul backed away, scarely breathing hard. Twirling the sword in his hand.

Aimerie's shoulder hurt; his forearm was already going numb. Ernoul's goal was to wear him down. Eventually

Aimerie would no longer be able to raise his shield, and then he would be easy prey. He was getting too old for this.

"And now you plan to marry my woman," Ernoul said as they circled each other once more.

"You have no call on Blanche," Aimerie replied.

"The Devil I don't," Ernoul said. "I claimed her first."

"And I am lord here. I say who marries Blanche, and I say it's me."

"Why?"

"Two reasons. One—" Aimerie swung his sword, trying to catch his son off guard. Ernoul blocked the blow, blocked the quick follow-up backhand as well. "I love her. Two—" Aimerie swung again; the sword hit Ernoul's curved shield and slid down it. "I need her."

"Need her for what?"

Before Aimerie could answer, Ernoul charged, battering his father's shield again. Aimerie countered with a thrust, hoping to catch his son off guard while he was stepping back, but the blow bounced weakly off Ernoul's hauberk.

Aimerie said, "Besides, I know what you do to Hersent. Oh, you take care only to hit her in places that don't show, but I've seen the bruises on her arms. I don't want that to happen to Blanche. She doesn't deserve that. She doesn't deserve you."

With a yell, Ernoul feinted an overhand blow, went low at the last moment. Aimerie saw it and tried to get out of the way, but the blow caught him on the ankle, and Aimerie howled with pain.

"Ha!" Ernoul cried, raising his arms in triumph. "Were we fighting with real swords, that blow would have taken off your foot. I win."

"These aren't real swords," Aimerie gasped, hobbling, his ankle bone throbbing with pain. "I'm still in the fight."

Ernoul attacked again, driving Aimerie back, cracking his shield down the center. "You planned this all along, didn't you? Marrying Blanche."

"After Oudinette died, yes."

"You said that you loved Mother. But now you love Blanche."

"I also said life goes on. Oudinette is dead."

Ernoul rushed his father. Banged his shield against Aimerie's, the broken half of Aimerie's shield falling away, the force of the attack driving Aimerie back, stumbling. Ernoul swung an overhand blow with the sword. Because of his tired arm, Aimerie couldn't raise his shield high enough or fast enough, and the blow caught him on the helm.

Aimerie was wobbly. Ernoul crowed, "I just sliced your head in half, Father. Your brains are spilling over your chest.

"Wooden sword," Aimerie mumbled. His helmet was knocked askew; his shield was broken. His eyes swam.

Ernoul rushed Aimerie again. Banged what was left of Aimerie's shield, then stuck his foot in and tripped him. Aimerie landed on his rear. Ernoul moved in, raised his sword for the decisive blow, exposing his chest as he did, but before he could bring his weapon down, Aimerie got to one knee, and Ernoul found the point of Aimerie's sword at his breastbone.

Ernoul stared in disbelief.

"I told you not to get overconfident," Aimerie said.

There was a buzz of noise from the crowd. A scattering of applause, but not much. Most of these people disliked Aimerie and Ernoul in equal measure.

Ernoul swore foully. He switched his sword to his shield hand, reached out, and helped his father up.

Aimerie slapped Ernoul's shoulder. His head was spinning; he hoped his ankle wasn't cracked.

"You never told me what you need Blanche for," Ernoul said.

"For my plan," Aimerie said.

"Does that plan have something to do with all those new soldiers at the castle?"

"It does."

"And?"

"I need Blanche because marriage to Blanche gives me a solid base here in Trentshire. And with that base, I can become earl."

"That's it?"

Aimerie hesitated. "I've been in touch with other nobles who are unhappy with King Henry, men like the earl of Shrewsbury. Henry tries to rein them in, to take away their powers. Members of the Church aren't happy with him for the same reason. Even the archbishop, Anselm. As you know, old King William's eldest son, Duke Robert of Normandy, is being held prisoner in Devizes Castle. Once I have attained the earldom of Trent, a group of us intend to rescue Duke Robert. From Devizes, we will go to Winchester, which is but a short distance away. We will seize the royal treasury and proclaim Robert the rightful king of England."

Ernoul took that in. "Henry will fight," he warned his father.

"And he'll lose," Aimerie assured him. "After that, I will become one of King Robert's chief advisors. Robert is weak; he's not a leader. He won't be an effective king. It's possible he could meet with an 'accident,' leaving his son, William Clito, as king. William is scarcely more than an infant, so he will need a strong regent until he is of age."

"And that regent will be you?"

"Yes, though I prefer the title of 'lord protector.' Has more of a ring to it, don't you agree?"

"So you want to be the power behind the throne? Not the king?"

Aimerie smiled. "Being king is too dangerous. Kings' advisors can always change sides if things go bad."

Ernoul said, "I assume I have a part in this?"

"Indeed you do. I'll need someone I can trust beside me."

"So I won't be going to Normandy for the tournament circuit, after all?"

"Not this year. Perhaps not for the next few years, while we consolidate our position here." Aimerie's smile widened. "Naturally, once I'm in a position of power, I'll need to add to the family's power base."

Ernoul understood. "Ah, and that's why you didn't want me to marry Blanche?"

"Exactly. Once I'm lord protector, I'm thinking we could negotiate you a bride from the French royal family, or maybe from the ruling houses of Flanders, or Burgundy, or Acquitaine. Maybe even a German princess from the Empire. We'll see if e can get you a title with the marriage. Count, perhaps, or marquis—no idea what kinds of titles the Germans use. With a title, your prospects—and the family's—are boundless."

"And if I can't get a title through marriage?"

Aimerie shrugged. "We'll kill someone and take his."

Ernoul contemplated this lofty change in station. "How long have you been planning this?"

Aimerie's voice grew steely. "Since the day I returned to England."

Ernoul raised his brows in surprise. "Yet you never thought to tell me?"

"You were too young, too liable to talk. I was going to tell you on the day you were knighted, but as that is tomorrow, I'm telling you now."

"The soldiers are here. You'll need to use them soon.

"I intend to. And I can't do any of this without Blanche. Without her estates, I can't become earl. And if I'm not earl, the rest of the plan won't work. Also, her position as widow of the former earl provides me the appropriate social standing."

Ernoul had to smile. "You're a devious bastard, Father. I commend you."

"Thank you, son. Now let's get some wine. My head hurts like the very Devil, and my throat is dry from all this talking."

Ernoul said, "I still won the fight, though."

“Wooden swords,” Aimerie countered.

They headed back to the castle.

Chapter 49

It was dusk when Miles and Ediva reached Redhill. The wind had picked up ahead of the approaching storm.

Ediva had fallen asleep in Miles's arms. She woke as they entered the village, shaking her head and blinking her eyes rapidly. The first people who saw them spread the word, and soon the entire village was in the street, along with the manor staff. Miles saw Wada hurrying from the manor house, with his head bandaged.

Ediva's mother, Ailova, ran up, crying. Miles handed the girl down to her. Ailova hugged Ediva to her breast and dragged her back to the house without a word to Miles. Ediva cast a last look over her shoulder at Miles, who smiled at her and touched a finger to his forehead in salute.

Men and women gathered around Miles as he climbed from his horse. Father Albinus was there, with his lanky deacon, Tostig. So were Hamo and Simon, as well as Ivor and Blackie and Sewale. "You heard what happened?" Albinus asked Miles.

"I did," Miles replied.

"We sent runners after you. Didn't think Ediva'd be the one to find you, though. She wasn't even supposed to go. Anyway, we know how close you and Lady Blanche . . ." His voice tailed off. Akwardly, he added, "We thought you should know."

Hamo stepped up. The grizzled steward looked embarrassed as he cleared his throat. "Miles, I've said what I said about having a woman for a lord. I still don't hold with it, but I hold with what Aimerie done to Lady Blanche a lot less."

"We don't want Aimerie as our lord," Simon added.

"Aye," growled a bunch of the other men.

"French bastards," snarled a woman. "Think they can do whatever they want."

Sewale said, "They can't get away with this, can they? There must be a way to stop them."

Father Albinus agreed. "Lady Blanche has never been anything less than good to us. We owe it to her to do something."

"Aye," said Blackie. "The bit with the Hoods went bad, but that was more Lord Guillame's fault than hers."

Wada pushed his way to the front, confronting Miles. In addition to the bandaged head, he had a black eye. "So what are we going to do?" he demanded in a tone of voice he had never used with Miles before.

Miles drew himself up and looked them over. Men and women, they were all watching him, waiting for him. Expecting him to lead them. Expecting him to win. He had to show a confidence, a resolution, he did not feel. "What we're going to do, my friends, is capture a castle."

"Thought you said that couldn't be done," Wada reminded him.

"I changed my mind," Miles said.

On their stunned reactions, he added, "Now, if you don't mind, I could use a cup of ale, and could someone find me a bowl of real English pottage? I'm tired of that French swill they serve at the manor house."

Chapter 50

Even in the forest depths, the wind howled. Trees bent. Branches snapped off and were whirled away. Rain lashed down almost horizontally. Snow and sleet mixed with the rain, stinging the cheeks of the men and women advancing toward Brightwood Castle.

"Do you think this plan of yours will work?" Father Albinus shouted at Miles above the noise of storm.

Miles forced a grin. "Except for the part about us burning the palisade."

Blackie laughed at that and added, "Maybe the thing'll just float away."

"More likely we'll float away," Sewale said. "That's if we don't freeze to death first."

Some of the men carried hastily constructed scaling ladders; all carried weapons. Most of the surviving men who'd been with the Hoods were there. Hamo and Simon and some of the villagers who hadn't been with the Hoods had come, as well. Will's place with the archers had been taken by his older brother Edwine, who had brought his bow. Because of family responsibilities, Edwine didn't poach much anymore, but he'd been a terror in his day, and he had taught Will to shoot.

Five women had joined the group. They would hold the scaling ladders against the palisade. They wanted to do something, anything, to help. One of them was Ediva, who had sneaked away from her house yet again. She had been sent ahead, scouting.

The men hadn't needed much urging to come. "That beating we got by the stream kind of sticks in my throat," Blackie had said when they met in the church after Miles returned.

"Aye," said Sewale. " 'Specially since we could've taken the buggers. Wasn't for Lord Guillame and his fancy ideas about—"

"Let's hear nothing bad about Lord Guillame," Miles told them. "He's a brave man. He did his best."

Ivor the smith flexed his huge hands. "He did, but now I reckon it's time to get some of our own back."

Wada wore his old cloak. The bandage around his head was soaked and useless, and he ripped it off. "We ain't lettin' Aimerie have Lady Blanche," he said, "not without a fight."

A squat woman named Bertha said, "And I want Ernoul to pay for what he done to my girl Agnes last year."

The party had left Redhill before dawn. Miles had sent word to the other manors about what they were doing, and they had not been marching long when they were joined by a contingent of ten men from Fairleigh—all the able-bodied men that were left—led by the scarred steward, Toli. "You don't get to do this by yourself," Toli told Miles. "If we're going to die, we'll die as men, not slaves."

Not long after, a similar-sized group from Edsworth caught up to them, a rough-looking ploughman named Brand at their head. "How is Lord Guillame?" Miles asked him.

"Still alive," Brand said. "That maid of Lady B's, she might be stuck up, but she stays with him day and night. He'd have died by now, wasn't for her."

The force moved on, heads lowered against the storm, like oxen. There was little talking. They needed to reach Brightwood before Aimerie's priest pronounced the marriage complete. Once he spoke those words, there would be no breaking the marriage, save by death or annulment. And death was the easier method because, unless you were a king, annulments were difficult to get and could be tied up for years in Church court. If the marriage was joined, Redhill and Fairleigh would belong to Aimerie; and this rescue mission would become an act of rebellion, punishable by torture and death. Miles pictured Blanche with Aimerie, pictured her in his bed, and that thought drove him to fury. Fury at what Aimerie was doing to Blanche, fury at what he'd done to Fairleigh, at what he'd done to the Hoods, to every manor in the district.

They found Ediva waiting for them at the bank of a creek. "This is as far as I could go," she said, and it was obvious why.

Two days ago, this creek had been a trickle. Now it was a rampaging river, its swift-flowing water carrying dirt and brush and tree branches, even a dead deer.

"Shit," Blackie said. He turned to Ediva, "Sorry, miss."

"You must watch your language, Blackie," Ediva admonished.

Blackie grinned. "Yes, miss."

Toli was dispirited. "What do we do now?"

"Turn around?" suggested Hugh's father, Matthew. "Look for another place to cross?"

"There's no time," Miles said.

Miles spied a young tree, an oak, that had once bordered the creek. Now its trunk was in the stream. Almost directly across the stream from the young oak was a clump of what looked to be sturdy brush.

"We'll link arms," Miles said, "the strongest of us. The others can cross using us as a kind of . . ." He tired brain labored to think of the term.

"As a human chain," Father Albinus finished for him.

"Right. I'll go first, then you, Albinus. Then you two—" he pointed at a pair of burly fellows from Edsworth, who looked like brothers. He put his two biggest men in the center, where the current would be strongest. "Wada, you're next. Then Ivor. Then you—" he indicated a man from Fairleigh "—then Brand. Simon, you go last. Hook onto that brush on the far side."

Some of the men—and women—looked doubtful about the plan, but Miles gave them no time to argue. The longer they thought about it, the more chance they'd decide it was too risky. Before anyone could raise an objection, Miles half-scrambled, half-slid down the slippery creek bank, grabbing roots to keep from falling. He reached the bottom and made his way through the swift-flowing water to the oak, about fifteen yards away. The rushing water rose mid-way up his legs, stunning him with its cold. Fighting to stay upright in the current, he hooked his right arm around the young oak's trunk. He tested the trunk. It would hold. He hoped.

He beckoned Albinus, who worked his way down the bank, crossed to Miles's left and linked arms with him. The two brothers from Edsworth came next, then Wada. Miles braced himself against the rushing water, digging his feet into the rocky creek bottom, wedging one under some kind of root for extra support. The raging stream beat against his waist now, and he leaned back into it, almost as if he were relaxing against it. After Wada came Ivor, then the man from Fairleigh, then Brand and Simon the reeve, who hooked his free arm into the clump of brush on the opposite bank.

The others came down the bank and began to cross, bracing themselves against the current, holding the waists and shoulders of the human chain for support, inching their way over, weapons stuck in belts or held awkwardly over their heads with their packs. It seemed to take forever. Miles was numbed through by the wet and cold and the energy needed to fight the force of the rushing stream. His arms were getting tired, but he tried to ignore them.

Sewale lifted Blackie's bow above his head, along with his own bow, as he crossed, while Blackie carried Ediva down the bank and hoisted her onto his shoulders. "Hold on tight, Princess," he told her. "You'll be all right. Close your eyes if you're scared."

"I'm not scared," she said. Then her usually bold voice trembled. "What if I fall off?"

"You won't. I promise."

After Blackie and Ediva, the other women crossed, fearful but resolute. Miles felt enormous strain on his arm holding the oak. The strain on the arm linked with Albinus was almost as bad. He grit his teeth. Something crashed into the small of his back—a tree branch, maybe, he didn't know—and it almost knocked him over. He nearly lost his grip on Albinus's arm. Whatever hit him went swirling downstream.

The scaling ladders were tricky to get across. Two men carried each one, holding ladder rungs in one hand, grasping members of the human chain in the other. One of the men from Fairleigh stumbled in the current and lost his grip on a rung. The ladder was caught by the wind, wrenched from the man's hand, and somehow got hooked onto his forearm.

"Get rid of the ladder!" Ivor yelled at him.

"Shake it off of you!" shouted Hamo.

The man ignored their advice. Using his other hand, he tried to get the ladder back, slipped on an unseen rock as he did, and went into the water. His partner let go of the ladder lest he be taken, as well. The first man came up for a second, then he and the ladder were swept away, the man's screams soundless in the noise of the storm. He bounced off something and disappeared. Shaken, his partner continued to the other side.

Miles's arm felt like it was coming out of his shoulder. His bicep was on fire. He was losing his grip on the oak as the last man crossed, and he thanked God because he couldn't hold on much longer.

When the last man was across, it was time to bring in the human chain. Miles's legs were so numbed by the icy water, he didn't know if they would move. He let go of the oak's trunk. He stumbled at the sudden release of tension and the force of the water on his wobbly legs. He overcompensated and threw his free hand onto Albinus's shoulder for balance, almost bringing the priest down. Then he recovered. He worked his way down the line of linked men, banging his feet on submerged rocks and roots, strong arms hauling him in when he reached the other side.

"Careful there!"

"Don't let him go!"

Miles was followed by Albinus, then the brothers from Edsworth, then the others. One at a time, making their way across the rushing stream until Simon was the only one left, and he was pulled from the clump of brush to safety.

Miles was so tired that he had to be dragged to the top of the bank. He and the rest of the party lay on their backs in the storm, breathing heavily. Miles had never been so cold, so wet, so tired, not even in Wales. He just wanted to sleep. But he knew they had to keep going, and they weren't going to do it unless he led them, so he forced himself to stand, willing his body into motion.

A few of the others rose with him. Ediva had been sent ahead again, with Blackie behind her. Simon stared at the raging stream, with the storm still howling and the rain and snow beating down. "How will we ever get back?" he said.

Sewale laughed uproariously at that. "There'll be no need to get back. We're all going to die at the castle."

"Come on," Miles told them. "We have a wedding to attend."

The rest of the group climbed to their feet. Miles helped some of them. They started off, exhausted by the stream crossing. They were going to miss that ladder that had been lost, but there was no use worrying about it. Miles's right arm blazed with pain. He shook it as he walked down the line of men and women. "Keep going. Not far now."

The frozen, sodden column trudged on. Miles's shoes were ruined; everyone's were. His feet squished in his wet hose. It was like Wales again, he thought, and with a shock, he realized that he had enjoyed Wales. Not enjoyed it, exactly, but he had felt alive there in a way he had never felt since. Until now.

He wondered if he was crazy for feeling that way when a figure appeared on the path ahead of him. Three figures.

It was Ediva and Blackie, and with them was the Viking.

Chapter 51

The ragged column stumbled to a halt at this unexpected encounter. A number of the men drew their weapons and started forward. Toli was in the lead, axe in hand, with Matthew and some others behind him.

Miles held them back with an outstretched arm. "Wait."

Miles hesitated because the Viking seemed to be on easy terms with Blackie and Ediva. Blackie grinned at Miles and indicated his new companion. "Meet our new friend, Fromont."

Fromont wore a hooded cloak in the storm, and was only recognizable by his blond beard. Beneath his brown hood could be seen a thick bandage over his left ear. He said, "You are Miles?"

"I am," Miles said. "So your real name is Fromont. We know you as—"

"The Viking." Fromont smiled. "Yes."

Miles went on. "I recognize your accent. You're Flemish, aren't you?"

"That's right. From a village called Tenhoute. Don't worry if you've never heard of it. No one else has, either."

The air was tense, angry men crowding forward on the narrow track. Blackie gestured for them to back up. "He's all right," Blackie said.

Ediva stood next to Fromont, looking unconcerned. She had lost as much to the outlaws as any of them, but her child's instincts obviously led her to trust this man.

Fromont patted her shoulder. "I encountered *Mademoiselle* Ediva some distance back," he told Miles. "I am afraid I must have scared her at first. The young lady is very brave to be out by herself."

"She is that," Miles said, and his eyes narrowed. "Given your reputation, I'd have expected you to kill her or take her back to your camp."

"I am a thief, not a killer. Unlike some, I do not make war on children."

"When you say, 'some,' you mean . . .?"

"I mean Ernoul. He killed the boy Hugh."

There was a buzz of anger. Hugh's father, Matthew, gasped, and tears filled his eyes.

"What about the people of Fairleigh?" Toli shouted. "You didn't have any trouble making war on them."

"It was not my idea to raze Fairleigh," Fromont said. "In fact, I argued against it. It made no sense."

"What are you telling us?" Toil sneered. "That you and your bunch got some kind of code you follow?"

"I'm telling you that we're practical. When people have nothing left to lose, they are at their most dangerous. Give them hope, and they are docile—they can accept the occasional theft of their property. No hope, and they fight, like cornered animals. My men and I are not angels. We kill when we have to, but we do not kill for the sake of killing. For sport. But I am no longer in charge of the Brotherhood. Ernoul is."

Miles said, "And Lady Blanche. Do you approve of Aimerie kidnapping her?"

"I do not approve of any violence against women. Aimerie is stirring up trouble when he does not have to. Your presence here is proof of that."

While Miles and the others digested what they'd heard, Fromont went on. "I asked young Ediva what she was doing out in this weather, and she said she was scouting for you. She said you were not coming to attack my camp, and I believed her. Then *Monsieur* Blackie appeared, and he said the same thing. We had a talk, and here we are."

"And what brings *you* out in this weather?" Miles asked him.

Fromont shrugged. "Looking for travelers. There are people foolish enough to brave the elements, and it would be remiss of me not to relieve them of their valuables for their folly. None of my men wanted to come with me, so I went by myself."

"Thought you'd be at Aimerie's wedding," Miles said.

A corner of Fromont's mouth lifted in wry amusement. "I am the last person Aimerie wants at his wedding. I'm only good for doing his dirty work." He regarded Miles steadily. "If you are not bringing your people to attack my village, there can only be one place you're headed."

The clearing grew as quiet as it could be with a storm raging.

"And?" Miles asked him.

Fromont spread his hands. "It is not my affair. Neither I nor any of my people will hinder you."

"For God's sake," Toli said to Miles, "don't believe this lying bastard."

"Aye," said Matthew. "String 'im up."

"Hang 'im!" shouted one of the Edsworth brothers.

The men surged forward again. "Who's got a rope?"

Ediva stepped in front of Fromont, shielding him. "Leave him alone!"

That stopped them. No one dared to lay hands on Ediva, even to move her aside, no matter how gently. Ediva had become a hero. More than a hero, she was a legend, almost a saint in their eyes. She could do no wrong. And Blackie's look made it plain that anyone who did lay hands on her would answer to him.

Miles motioned everyone to be calm. To Fromont, he said, "I thought you and Aimerie were allies."

"No longer. It might even be in my interest for you to succeed."

Miles gave him a questioning look.

Fromont went on. "There have been, shall we say, difficulties between myself and the baron's son. Not only am I no longer in charge of the Brotherhood, but Ernoul has abused my woman."

"Your woman?" Wada blurted. "You mean Hersent?"

Fromont lifted his brows in surprise. "You know Hersent?"

"I . . . I know who she is. She done me a good turn."

Fromont nodded. "She is a good woman, for all she tries to seem fierce."

Miles considered. "We have an awkward situation here, Fromont. I believe what you say, but some of these men do not. Will you pledge not to interfere with us or to warn Aimerie of our coming?"

"I will," Fromont said.

"Your word as a soldier?"

Fromont smiled, probably because Miles had deduced that, as a Fleming and landless in England, he must have come here as a mercenary. "My word as a soldier."

"No!" shouted Toli. "Kill him!" and a number of others cried assent.

"Stop it!" Ediva cried. "I believe him."

"So do I," said Blackie, who seemed to have formed a bond with Fromont.

"And I," added Wada. He stepped before the crowd. "I been in trouble with the law, and it's only by the grace of God I'm still here. When you live outside the law, you do what you can to survive. Any of us could find ourselves in Fromont's position. We could find ourselves in his Brotherhood, and happy to be there. That don't mean they're all bad people, or that they got no sense of honor."

"Well done, Wada," Miles told him. "That's the most I ever heard you say at one time." To the rest, he said, "Fromont has pledged not to interfere, and I trust him to honor that pledge."

Father Albinus rubbed his wooly jaw. "I don't know, Miles. You're asking—"

“His word as a soldier is enough for me,” Miles said.

“And for me,” said Blackie.

“Now let’s get moving,” Miles said. “We’re losing time.”

Ediva waved goodbye to the outlaw chief, then set off down the path, followed by Blackie. “Sorry about your ear,” Blackie told the outlaw. “I was the one what done it.”

Fromont smiled. “Fortunes of war, my friend. God be with you.”

The rest of the column gathered itself and started after. Miles looked back, but Fromont had already faded into the vastness of the forest.

Father Albinus looked back, as well. “Hope you know what you’re doing, Miles. Letting him go like that.”

“So do I,” Miles said.

Chapter 52

They gathered at the edge of the woods—wet, tired, and cold. The storm howled around them. Here and there, snow splotched the limbs and trunks of trees.

Brightwood Castle lay in the distance. Beyond it was the Upper Eal, raging in the storm. Despite the weather, a line of people and animals gathered at the bailey gate, guests for the wedding and the knighting ceremony, along with their entourages. Men and women who had already passed through the gate crossed the bailey and climbed the hill to the square keep, entering by the ramp that led to the main door.

Stands had been set up outside the gate, with vendors selling food and drink.

"Some people will do anything to make a penny," Matthew observed. "Even in this weather."

"Some people have to," Sewale said. "Starvation's not pretty. You know that."

"Aye," Toli lamented, "and starvation's only one bad harvest—or having your manor burned—from any of us."

Miles stood next to Toli. It was the closest he'd gotten to Toli's burned face—the pink, wrinkled skin on his left cheek and neck, the drooping eye, the shriveled ear.

"Go on, ask," Toli said. "Everybody does."

Miles started, guiltily.

Toli sighed, as if he'd told the story a hundred times before, which he probably had. "As I heard it, it happened when I was a babe—year, year-and-a-half old, maybe. Me mum was boiling water. The church was right across the street from our house. Mum heard the bell for Communion. She ran across to take Communion, and left me by meself. While she was gone, I somehow managed to pull the kettle onto meself."

Miles winced. "That must have been painful."

"Suppose it was, don't remember."

"Lucky you weren't blinded."

"Yeah, there's that." Toli fingered his scarred cheek. "Bit of a miracle, really."

"Look!" said Father Albinus.

By the gate, one of the stands blew over in a gust of wind, scattering its contents and the people manning it.

"Poor buggers," said Blackie.

Miles got back to business. "This storm may work to our advantage. I had planned to burn the palisade and attack through the smoke, but this might be better. They won't be expecting trouble in weather like this. With luck, we'll take them off guard."

He looked over the bedraggled group. "I'll go first, straight to the keep. I'll take Wada, the two brothers from

Edsworth, Ivor, and Sewale. We'll go through the main gate separately, mix with the servants till it's time to strike."

A blocky woman named Isabel said, "I'm coming with you. There must be something I can do."

"It'll be dangerous, Isabel," Father Albinus warned her.

"That's why I'm here," Isabel said. "Aimerie's men killed my husband and son, and I'll do anything to pay that bastard back. I don't care what happens to me."

Ediva piped up. "I'm going with you, too, Miles."

"Oh, no, you're not," Blackie told her.

She stuck out her tongue at him. "You can't stop me."

"Blackie's right," Miles told Ediva. "You could get hurt—killed, even. Your mother's ready to skin me as it is."

"*I'll* skin you if you don't let me go," Ediva said boldly.

"And I'll skin *you* if you get yourself killed out here," Blackie said. "Do you understand?"

"Yes," she said, but there was an impish smile on her face as she said it. Without warning, she turned from them and started toward the castle, skipping down the slope in the storm.

"Brat," said Blackie, but there was more than a hint of admiration in his voice.

Miles watched her go, shook his head, and went on. "The rest of you will attack in three groups. Blackie, Father Albinus, and Toli will lead. I don't like dividing the force, but this time it seems to make sense. Toli, you're first. Attack the bailey wall on this side. Create a diversion. I'll leave it to you to pick the spot you want to hit. Give us time to get into the keep before you start. Approach the wall calmly, spread out, no cheering, and you may get to the ditch before they notice you. You may even be able to cross it, if the guards are hunkered down. Make them think it's an all-out assault on the castle. With luck, they'll shift men to meet it."

"Wish we had that extra scaling ladder," Toli said.

"So do I, but there's nothing for it now. If you break through on the wall, come to the keep. Otherwise, hold the wall and make them send reinforcements after you."

Miles turned to Albinus and Blackie. "Father, you and your men infiltrate the gate. Once Toli's diversion is under way, head for the keep and help us there. Blackie, you'll work your way through the village, then attack the bailey from the river side."

"What about the villagers?" Blackie said.

"Shouldn't be many about in this weather, and they probably won't do anything to you if they see you, you being armed and all."

Blackie grinned.

Miles went on. "Let the other groups go first. If you're lucky, they'll have sent men from the river wall to reinforce against Toli's attack. Once you're over the wall, make for the bridge over the keep's ditch. Hold the bridge and keep any of Aimerie's reinforcements from getting to the keep."

Miles went on, addressing them all. "Don't worry about controlling the bailey. It's the keep we want. Wada and the others will hold the keep door until Father Albinus and his lot get there. That's the idea, anyway."

"What about you?" Albinus said.

"I have my own disruption planned."

Toli said, “And the Viking? Can we trust him not to warn Aimerie that we’re coming?”

“We’ll have to,” Miles said. “He could have killed Blackie and Ediva when they ran into him, but he didn’t.”

“We’re taking a big chance with him, Miles,” Albinus said. “We could be walking into a trap.”

“Too late to worry about that now,” Miles said.

“We should have killed him,” Toli told Miles. “He needs to pay for what he done.”

“I understand,” Miles said, “but let’s take one thing at a time. It was Aimerie that ordered your manor burned, not the Viking. Start with him and worry about Fromont later.”

Toli was visibly frustrated, but he said nothing.

Miles straightened. “All right. Father, give us your blessing, and then let’s get moving.”

“Better hurry,” Blackie added, “before Ediva takes the castle all by herself.”

Chapter 53

The storm pounded the castle. On the top floor, where Blanche was, the wind banged the wooden shutters that covered the windows. Water leaked in and puddled on the floor. Warmth came up the flue from the hearth below, but not enough, so a charcoal brazier had been lit in the room's center, with the rushes kept away from it to avoid sparks setting the room ablaze.

The lord's large, curtained bed was not far from the brazier. In one corner, a separate "room" had been fashioned out of screens to give Blanche privacy while she prepared for her marriage. She'd slept under guard in the old hall in the bailey since she'd been kidnapped, and she'd been dragged up here this morning. Food and drink were on a table, but she ignored them. She'd eaten nothing since she'd come from Redhill, and she'd drunk only enough watered wine to keep herself alive.

So much for her plan to stall marriage negotiations, she thought bitterly. She'd given Aimerie more credit for nobility than he was due. In reality, he was a brutal, backwoods lord who used force to take what he wanted. At first she couldn't believe what he'd done to her, but on reflection she believed it only too well. Barons in France and Normandy didn't hesitate to abduct noblewomen—for brides and for other purposes. Blanche had thought things were different in England, but apparently they weren't.

She racked her brain for a way out of her predicament, but came up with nothing. The king was a long way off; so was Lord Tutbury, the sheriff. Anyway, how would she get word to them? Her only hope was Miles, and God knew where he was. He might have reached Bradford Town and be bringing help; he might be hiding in the woods; or he might have been caught by Aimerie's men and hung. For all intents and purposes, Blanche was on her own.

A wooden bathtub occupied the center of Blanche's room. Three maids were filling it with hot water, hauling the buckets from the hall. Blanche assumed these were the maids who had attended Aimerie's first wife, Oudinette. There was no door to the room, just an angled passageway through the screens. Music floated up from the second-floor gallery, mingling with the hum of conversation as guests arrived for Ernoul's knighting, then the wedding, then the massive feast to follow.

One of the maids, the one who did most of the work, was big and strongly built, like a man. The second was fair and slender, with a noble mien. The third was older and prim, with a pinched face.

When the tub was full, the slender one came over, smiling. "The guests are arriving, my lady. It's time for you to bathe and get dressed. Get ready for your big day."

Blanche fixed the young woman with her dark eyes. "I'm not having a 'big day.' "

The prim one tisked. "Come now, Lady Blanche. You have to—"

"I don't have to do anything. I was brought here against my will, and I have no intention of marrying your master."

The big one shook her head. "Bad enough we lose Lady Oudinette. Now we have to put up with this whore's whining."

Blanche held her anger at being called a whore. "No, you don't have to put up with it," she told the big woman. "You're free to leave. Indeed, I prefer that you do so."

The prim one said, "See reason, my lady. We'll get in trouble if—"

"Leave!"

They did, the big one casting a baleful look back over her shoulder.

Blanche waited. Soon enough, footsteps were heard on the circular stairway, and Aimerie entered through the screens. He had bathed; his long hair was washed and brushed to a sheen, his beard trimmed. He wore a long red robe, bordered in gold thread, over a white shirt, and a blue cloak over his left shoulder against the cold. The cloak was fastened with a large brooch. A gold circlet adorned his hair, and he smelled of perfume—Blanche couldn't place the kind, but he wore too much of it for a man who had just bathed. He hobbled on a swollen ankle.

"You're limping," Blanche noted. "The first stage of leprosy, I hope?"

Aimerie ignored the jibe. “Therese says you refuse to dress for our nuptials.”

“Whichever of those clowns Therese is, she’s correct. And there aren’t going to be any nuptials.”

Aimerie smiled. “That’s where you’re wrong.”

“No, I’m not,” she told him. “I won’t take the marriage vow with you.”

“That’s of no matter. Father Richard will pronounce you my wife whether you take the vow or not. It will all be legal, the charters attested to.”

“Fine. Since you don’t seem to need me, I don’t have to take part in your sham ceremony.”

“You’ll take part in it if my men have to drag you into the hall and hold you there.”

Aimerie put a hand on Blanche’s left breast and kneaded it, playing with the nipple. She knocked his hand away, glaring at him.

“No matter,” he said. “I’ll see what’s under that robe soon enough, and you’ll see what’s under mine. I’m going to give you pleasure like you’ve never known before.”

“You mean you’ll fall over from apoplexy?” she said hopefully.

“I mean I’ll have you screaming with delight.”

“So you’ll fall over from apoplexy and die. Even better.”

He slapped her ear. She staggered, her head ringing.

“Make all the witty remarks you like, but by vespers, you’ll belong to me.” He leaned in close. “You know what that means, don’t you? I can lock you away, if you don’t please me. I can prevent you from ever seeing the light of day, from ever seeing another human. I can beat you. I can rape you. If I want to give you to my knights, I can do that. If I want to give you to the serving boys, I can do that, too. If I want to give you to Fromont and his outlaws, I can do that, as well. Why, I can give you to my dogs if it suits my fancy. I can do whatever I want to you."

This was the fate of many noblewomen, Blanche knew. They had no control over their lives, and they disappeared into marriage as surely as prisoners disappeared into the *oubliette*. Blanche faced Aimerie boldly, but inwardly she trembled, her ear still ringing. "What about Ernoul? Can you give me to him?"

"If it pleases me."

"Why didn't you let him have me to start with?"

"Because I love you. I've loved you from the moment I laid eyes on you."

"That's odd," Blanche said, "I felt just the opposite."

Aimerie went on. "Ernoul is rough with women. He'd come back from France, beat you, get you with child, and leave again. When you get older, he'd have you killed and replace you with someone new."

"The same way you killed your wife?" Blanche said.

Aimerie slapped her ear again, and she staggered. "Oudinette was drunk. She fell."

Blanche tried to act like the blow hadn't hurt. "Of a surety she did. Still, it worked out well for you, didn't it?"

"I've had enough of this," Aimerie said. "You have two choices. You can act like a spoilt child, and I can treat you in kind. *Or*." He paused dramatically. "Or I can treat you well, lavish you with gifts, give you a comfortable life. The life you deserve. You can be the wife of an earl once again; later, wife of a councilor to the king."

"My, my, ambitious, aren't we?" Blanche said.

"Yes, and you can share my ambitions."

Blanche said nothing.

Aimerie went on. "No one is coming to your rescue, Blanche, get that idea out of your head. Your *capuchins* have been destroyed. Lord Guillame is prepared to pledge fealty to me. Miles is being hunted by my men, and they'll hang him when they find him. You're mine now. So bathe and get dressed."

She glared at him.

"Must we force you? The result will be the same either way."

Again, she said nothing.

He snapped his fingers and the three maids came in. Blanche wouldn't lower herself to fight these serving women, a fight she couldn't win. She'd go along with this part, think of a way out of this marriage later. She hoped.

"Very well," she said.

Aimerie bowed politely to her and left.

Blanche held out her arms. Wordlessly, the young blonde maid drew the robe over her head, then the shift. Naked, Blanche stepped into the tub. She settled in the still-hot water, feeling its welcome warmth flow through her on this cold, stormy day, and for a moment she felt—

Her head was shoved under the water. Held there by a strong grip. She thrashed around, but was kept down. She thought they were going to drown her, wondered how they would explain that to Aimerie, then wondered if it was

Aimerie's idea, and wondered why he would do it. Her lungs screamed for air. Her vision blurred. Her thrashing grew weaker, and—

She was pulled from the water by her hair. She gasped wildly for air, and as she did, she was plunged under again. It must be the big one holding her down because she could do nothing against the pressure. She panicked, knew she was going to die. At last she could hold her breath no longer. She opened her mouth to inhale and—

She was dragged up again. Managed a deep breath before they pushed her under once more. She held her breath against the pressure this time, no longer thrashing, no longer wasting energy or air.

She was pulled up again, and this time they let her stay. "That was for Lady Oudinette," the big one said into her ear. "She was good to us, and we don't appreciate a whore like you taking her place."

Blanche said nothing. These women knew there would be no consequences for their action. Blanche would choose her own servants after the marriage, and these three would be out of work then. By rights, Blanche could have them whipped, or even killed, for what they had just done, but she suspected Aimerie would never allow that. He might even have told them to do it, a foretaste of what awaited her should she incur his displeasure.

She was too weakened by lack of breath to do anything but sit docilely while they bathed her and washed her long black hair.

The big one leaned close to her. "You can come here with your high and mighty airs, but you see that bed out there?

You'll get pounded to jelly in that bed this evening, and you better hope you perform to the baron's desires, or it'll go the worse for you. Now, get out."

Blanche obeyed, climbing from the tub. They dried and dressed her, braided her damp hair. Her ear still hurt where Aimerie had hit her. The blonde maid pulled a new linen shift, finely woven, over her head. That was followed by a green dress, trimmed in gold thread. A bliaut of white, also trimmed in gold. A linen headdress with a gold circlet. New shoes of white leather.

Joubert, Redhill's former steward, appeared. With a smirk on his toad-like face, he offered Blanche his arm. She didn't take it. Joubert shoved her through the entrance to her room. He grabbed her arm, pinching it hard, and led her roughly down the stairs to the castle hall.

Chapter 54

Miles made his way through the bailey's main gate. Others in his group mixed in with the crowd behind him. The guards were not expecting trouble, not with the bad weather and not with the Hoods eliminated, so they gave only perfunctory glances to those entering the compound.

Miles attached himself to a noble, his wife, and their servants, hanging close enough to the servants so it would look like he was one of them. Once through the gate, he left the noble's party. He passed the stone bake house and made his way to the kitchen, at the bailey's far end.

The kitchen was a large, three-sided building with brick ovens and a tiled roof. On the open side, under the roof, was a long table, where dishes were put on covered plates to be carried up to the keep. Aimerie had brought French cooks from Badford for the occasion, and these lorded it over their English counterparts. Servants lined up to take the dishes to the main hall, and Miles fell in at the rear of the line, keeping his head down on the off-chance that someone might recognize him. All the servants were wet from the storm, but

Miles was soaked through. He looked like he had been dragged out of the sea. Several times. More servants fell in behind him, then Wada. The others in his group would go directly up the hill to the keep and mingle with the crowd by the door.

Miles shuffled forward as servants left with dishes and jugs of wine. When he was within one place of the serving table, a voice said, "Here—you! I don't know you."

Miles looked over.

A bald-headed man spoke to him in Norman French. "Who are you? You're not part of my staff."

Miles shrugged. "Joubert told me to lend a hand here. If you don't like it, take it up with him. God knows, I'd rather be somewhere else."

"You look like a drowned cat," the man said disgustedly. "Oh, very well, keep on with what you're doing. And try not to drip water on the food."

The bald man turned to his younger companion, who was smiling. "Joubert's taking a lot on himself, telling everyone what to do. He's not the steward here, I am. He's got no official status at all, save as Aimerie's chief ass-licker."

His companion, a slightly built fellow with long hair, seemed unworried. "What difference does it make? Joubert goes back to Redhill tomorrow."

"Can't come soon enough for me," the steward said. "Please God he'll take that fairy Marcel with him."

The younger man laughed.

The steward saw Wada in the line and approached him. "I suppose Joubert told you to help out here, as well?"

Wada stared at him, uncomprehending.

Much to the amusement of his younger companion, the steward swore and repeated his question in broken English.

"Oh, aye, sir," Wada replied. "That he did, sir."

"Bah, these people can barely even speak," the steward said. "They're savages." He waved Wada forward. "Go on, go on."

Miles came to the head of the line, where he picked up a large serving dish. It was heavy, and Miles juggled it to get the balance right. "Be careful with that, you imbecile," snapped one of the cook's French assistants. "Hold it straight."

Miles left the kitchen and joined the crowd on the stairs to the top of the hill. He was grateful for the tarp that had been set up to cover the stairs, but the wind gusts were so strong that he thought the tarp might blow away. The wind blew cold rain and snow under the tarp and onto Miles's hands, numbing them and making it difficult to carry the heavy wooden dish. It didn't help that the people in front of him—two old women and an even older man—were moving slowly, having trouble on the stairs in the heavy weather.

At last he made it to the top. He didn't look back to check on Wada. He glimpsed Ivor the smith and one of the brothers from Edsworth, but he didn't want to make a show of looking around for the rest of his men. He would do nothing out of the ordinary.

He started up the temporary ramp to the keep's main door. The ramp had been covered by a raised tarp, as well, but it was still slippery from the weather. One of the younger guests stopped and helped the older man, who was having trouble again. Miles thanked God that the forebuilding that would guard the main door hadn't been started yet. He'd seen one before. It would be like a miniature castle, and he didn't think he and his men would have had a prayer of getting through it.

At the top of the ramp, he came to the thick main door, which was open for the occasion and guarded by armed men. He noted the Norman carving above the door's archway and wondered why the Normans couldn't seem to come up with anything to use besides that one stupid pattern. A guard waved him through the door.

Inside the door waited an under steward who lifted the cover on the dish that Miles was carrying. "Squab with perry sauce," he said. "About time that got here." He dipped a finger in the sauce, licked it with satisfaction, and pointed. "Put it on the center sideboard."

Miles nodded and entered a place he'd never been before—the great hall of a castle.

The room was not as large as he had expected. It was bisected by a massive arch. The head table was to the front of the arch, with a fireplace in the wall to the left side. Smaller arches in the walls formed alcoves, two to each wall, which led to windows, now shuttered against the storm. A gallery ran around the second floor, with arches and alcoves matching those on the first floor. People leaned over the gallery rails, watching the crowd below, chatting with, or calling to, other guests there. Among the people in the gallery, Miles recognized the girl with blue hair—Hersent. She seemed to be waiting—quietly, patiently.

"Stop yer gawping," said a servant in English. "Put down that tray and go get another."

"Sorry," Miles said.

He carried the tray to the sideboard opposite the head table, set it down, and removed the cover. Next to it on the table was a tray of spiced boiled eggs. Miles took one of the eggs and popped it in his mouth. *Not bad.*

As he reached for another egg, there were cheers and applause from the stairwell. Miles turned and Blanche came into the hall, accompanied by Joubert.

Chapter 55

Propelled by Joubert, Blanche entered the hall to applause from the guests, save for the few who knew the truth about how she came to be there.

The packed hall was stuffy. It smelled of wet wool and wet bodies. The guests looked Blanche over, curious about Aimerie's bride. They seemed to like what they saw. Joubert led her to the hall's northern side, where the head table was, in front of the arch that spanned the hall. Additional tables would be set up for the feast later. Sideboards with wine and cheese and sweetmeats lined the wall opposite the head table. On the hall's eastern side, the hearth blazed. Blanche guessed that the head table had originally been slated to go in front of the fire, but its occupants found their backs singed, so the location was moved. Smoke rose through a flue and was vented outside by holes, though a portion of it remained in the hall, hanging in the air and making Blanche's eyes sting.

In front of the table was an open space, with the crowd pressed around its sides, held back by heralds. Ernoul stood in the open space for his knighting ceremony. He was dressed in white, symbolizing purity. More people, along with the musicians, packed the second-floor gallery. Blanche saw the woman with the blue hair up there, wrapped in a heavy cloak.

Joubert's fingers dug painfully into Blanche's arm as he led her across the hall. "Promise you won't do anything stupid, and I'll let you go," he said.

"Sard yourself," she told him.

He released her anyway, because they had reached the head table. Feeling flowed back into her arm. She took her place behind the table, to the left of where Aimerie stood. To her left was some lord she didn't know. Aimerie leaned toward her. "You look lovely, my dear. Radiant. Your robes are beautiful. I can't wait to feast upon what lies beneath them."

Blanche said nothing. Her ear was still sore from where Aimerie had struck her earlier. There must be a way out of this, but for the life of her, she couldn't see what it was. The end of her freedom drew closer with each passing moment, and the moments seemed to be passing faster and faster.

The guest to Blanche's left said something to her, but she ignored him. Aimerie motioned to a young herald behind him, who sounded a horn.

The room fell quiet.

Aimerie smiled at the assemblage and raised his voice. "Greetings, my friends, and welcome. This is a momentous day, for on it, my son becomes a knight." He paused. "And I become a husband."

The crowd applauded. Aimerie indicated Ernoul. "Today is Ernoul's eighteenth birthday. He will go on to do great deeds and win fame, but he will never forget where it began—the day he became a knight."

More applause.

Aimerie held up his hands for quiet and went on. "As you know, I recently suffered a great personal tragedy, when my wife of many years, Oudinette, died in an accident." He paused and looked down, biting his lip. Then he looked up again. "My grief has been intense. However, it was alleviated when the lovely Blanche of Redhill consented to become my bride."

More applause, louder this time.

"Smile," Aimerie told Blanche in a low voice.

"Sard yourself," Blanche said.

Aimerie's hand twitched, as if he was going to hit her again. Then he recovered. He motioned Blanche to sit, and he did the same. He nodded to Father Richard. Father Richard advanced and stood before the table. His hair and beard were stylish, and his rich vestments had no doubt been paid for by Aimerie. He beckoned Ernoul. "Approach."

Ernoul moved forward, restraining his normal arrogant gait.

There was no formal ceremony for becoming a knight. Each lord made up his own, and many had no ceremony at all. Father Richard said, "You are Ernoul, squire, son of Aimerie, lord of Brightwood?"

"I am," Ernoul said.

"Kneel."

Ernoul did.

Father Richard took a chased silver pot from the table, removed the aspergillum from it and sprinkled Holy Water on Ernoul. "Do you, Ernoul, promise to uphold the laws of the Church, to protect women and the defenceless, and to conduct yourself as a Christian warrior?"

"I do," Ernoul swore.

Father Richard made the sign of the Cross. "In the name of the Father, the Son, and the Holy Spirit?"

"In the name of the Father, the Son, and the Holy Spirit," Ernoul affirmed, crossing himself.

"Hold out your hands."

Ernoul did, the hands palm up.

Father Richard returned the Holy Water to the table. Aimerie came round the table and lifted a sword from it. He placed the sword in Ernoul's hands. "Use this in the service of God."

"I shall," Ernoul said.

Father Richard said, "Arise, Ernoul of Brightwood, knight."

Ernoul stood, to applause and even some cheering. Blanche looked into the gallery and noted that the woman with blue hair was quiet.

Ernoul turned the sword over in his hands. It was newly forged, with a large ruby in its pommel, and from the eager look on Ernoul's face Blanche knew he could not wait to try it out on someone. He looked pleased with himself, as well he should. As a knight, Ernoul was nearly above the law. He was untouchable, save by others of his caste. He could kill a man with impunity, unless the man was another knight or a cleric of rank. He could steal, plunder, rape. He was a law unto himself.

His eyes touched Blanche's, and he smiled, and the smile chilled Blanche to the bone.

Chapter 56

Father Albinus, Hamo, and their men filtered from the woods, singly and in pairs, to join the rain-soaked throng at the bailey gate. The men had given any long weapons—spears, pitchforks, scythes—to Toli's and Blackie's parties. They carried axes and short swords concealed beneath their cloaks.

The numbers at the gate had begun to dwindle. Most of the invited nobles were already in the great hall. Those who were arriving now had been delayed by the weather, by washed-out roads or bridges. There was also the daily traffic of victuallers bringing supplies to the castle. A few men and women looted the vendor's stand that had blown over, much to the ire of the vendor, who tried to chase them away.

The plan was for Albinus's party to get through the gate, then head for the keep and attack the main door. This would give them the element of surprise. Toli's attack on the wall was to provide a diversion and draw guards from the gate, but for some reason it hadn't started yet. Albinus and his men—and the few women with them—were to avoid trouble and keep moving.

Albinus made it through the gate with no trouble, so did the men who came just after him. As Hamo went through, one of Joubert's bailiffs, who had been with him at Redhill, passed by.

"Well, well, look here," cried the bailiff. "It's Hamo, the so-called 'steward' of Redhill. Better enjoy that title while you have it, Hamo, because you won't have it long. Tomorrow Joubert will be back where he belongs, and you'll be a common peasant again." The bailiff frowned. "What are you doing here, anyway?"

Before Hamo could answer, the bailiff spied Hugh's father, Matthew, farther down the line of people waiting to get in the bailey. "And here's Matthew. Say, what's going on?"

One of the guards noticed what was happening. The bailiff's hand went to his dagger but before he could draw it, the blocky woman named Bertha leaped on him with her own dagger, jabbing the blade in and out of the bailiff's torso repeatedly until he collapsed.

The guard thrust his spear through Bertha's neck. Other guards rushed in. The crowd yelled and screamed and tried to get out of the way. Hamo dispatched the guard who had killed Bertha with an axe he drew from beneath his cloak, hitting him at the base of the neck and cleaving deep into his chest.

Where is Toli? Albinus thought.

A horn sounded. More guards appeared, and there was a fight at the gate. In the bailey, Albinus was faced with a dilemma. Go to the keep with the few men he had or stay here and help the others.

He headed for the keep. The keep was the prize.

Chapter 57

Toli's party approached the bailey's wooden wall.

They were strung out, heads down against the storm, walking casually, even the two men carrying the ladder, as though walking around with a scaling ladder was an everyday occurrence in this part of the world. Toli wished they hadn't lost that second ladder while crossing the stream.

Rain and snow lashed them; leaves blew wildly across the open ground. Toli had chosen a spot along the castle's southeastern wall halfway between that portion of the wall's two watchtowers. There was no sign of guards—they must be in the covered towers, hunkered against the wind and rain.

Toli's party consisted of the men from Fairleigh and Edsworth, along with two women from Redhill who would hold the scaling ladder. Toli was grateful to have been made Fairleigh's steward, though he wasn't happy about the circumstances under which it had occurred. Evrard had been a good friend of his.

Toli hoped to live up to Miles's trust in him. He was a hard worker—with his scarred face, he'd had to be. By virtue of that hard work, he had become prosperous and had gotten an attractive wife, with a good dowry, from a nearby village. Margery had been repulsed by him at first, but had come to love him. The people on his own manor had known him like this all his life, and most took no notice of his looks. Not now, anyway. He'd had to fight a lot as a boy. When he got better at fighting, the other boys left him alone. A lot of them became his friends. Some were with him now.

Incredibly, the party made it to the bailey ditch without being seen. Toli stopped at the edge of the ditch. "Shit," he muttered.

The ditch was filled with water from the storm.

Toli waved his men, and the two women, down the ditch's muddy side. *What the Devil are those guards doing up there? How have they not noticed us? Are they all asleep?*

Toli slid into the ditch. For the second time that day, he was immersed in icy water. The water was over the heads of the smaller men. One of them slipped and went under. Toli didn't see the man come back up, but he didn't have time to look for him. Two men floated the scaling ladder across. Two more assisted the women.

They climbed out the far side of the ditch, slipping in the mud and going back into the water. It seemed as though they might be trapped in the ditch; then Toli bent, made a stirrup with his hands, and hoisted one of the Fairleigh men to the top. Others followed his example, and the men on top pulled up those still in the water.

"*Qu`est-ce que c`est—?*" came a French voice from above.

They'd been seen.

No need for silence now. "Quick, lads!" Toli cried. "Get to the wall and get that ladder up!"

"What are you men doing?" cried the voice from above. He yelled in the direction of the watch tower. "Pierre!"

"Hurry!" Toli said.

"*Alarme! Alarme!*" cried the guard.

Toli heard a horn from the direction of the gate. Albinus and his men must have been discovered. Toli and his party should have taken this part of the wall by now to keep that from happening. Their diversion was late.

Two men raised the ladder, and the women held it in place while the rest lined up to climb.

Something flew by. An arrow. Another arrow stuck in the ground near the ladder.

A fierce gust of wind blew the ladder away from the wall. It wavered and toppled to the ground.

"Hold it still!" Toli ordered.

He helped the women raise the ladder and hold it in place. Even so, the ladder's top was waving wildly in the wind.

"Up! Up!" Toli cried to his men. "Hurry!"

The first man went up. He was hit by an arrow from the wall's walkway. He held on for a moment, then dropped off. The next man started up, but a guard at the top, with the aid of the wind, pushed the ladder away from the wall again. One side of the ladder cracked when it fell.

More arrows. One of the women was grazed in the arm.

This wasn't going to work. Not without a ladder. "Maybe we could use a rope?" someone suggested.

Horns sounded from above. Cries.

Toli made a decision. "Come on!" he yelled. "We'll join the fight at the gate."

Chapter 58

There was a break between the knighting ceremony and the wedding. The musicians played. Guests refreshed themselves with food and drink from the sideboards. Lines formed at the curtained garderobes located in each corner of the gallery, the longest lines at the two reserved for women. Blanche didn't see Hersent anymore; she seemed to have disappeared into the crowd.

A guard made his way into the hall and crossed to the head table. "There's some kind of disturbance at the main gate, my lord," he told Aimerie in a low voice.

Aimerie seemed unworried. He motioned to one of his knights. "Blaise, deal with it."

Dressed in his finest, the blond knight called Blaise bowed and left the hall. He looked unhappy—he was probably afraid he was going to miss the meal.

Normally, a Mass was said both for a knighting ceremony and for a wedding, but because the two ceremonies were being held at the same time, and also because Father Richard was only permitted to say one Mass a day, the service had been postponed until after the wedding.

Two horns in the gallery sounded a flourish. The guests hurried back to their places, and the priest once more stepped into the empty space before the head table. He held out his arms. "The bride and groom will please step forward."

Aimerie rose and went around the table, taking his time, everyone watching him. Blanche sat with her arms crossed, her almond eyes daring Aimerie to try something.

Aimerie could have had Blanche forcibly removed from her chair and dragged across the room to join him, but he didn't. "The bride is not here," he told Father Richard in an amiable tone, as if she wasn't sitting ten feet away. "Let's get on with it."

There was a shocked murmur from the crowd. Blanche's stomach curdled. This was it. She fought rising panic.

Father Richard said, "Do you, Aimerie, baron of Brightwood, take Blanche of Redhill as your wife?"

"I do," Aimerie said.

Father Richard turned to the audience. "In the bride's absence, I will speak for her."

There was another, louder, murmur, and Blanche jumped to her feet. "I'm not absent, I'm right here. And I refuse to marry this—"

The priest ignored her and kept talking. He intoned, "I, Blanche . . ."

A commotion from the audience.

One of the servants by the sideboards pushed through the crowd. Blanche almost fell over because the servant was Miles.

Aimerie recognized Miles, as well. “Get that man,” he snapped.

But before the surprised guards could do anything, Miles ran across the hall and nimbly bounded onto the head table. He was wetter than a just-caught fish, his shoes torn to shreds. Where had he come from?

Miles raised his hands for silence, smiling as he spoke. “My apologies for the intrusion, my lords and ladies, but this marriage cannot proceed.”

Aimerie stared.

“Why not?” Father Richard demanded.

Still smiling, Miles extended an arm toward Blanche. “Because the lady is already married.”

That set off an uproar in the hall. Now it was Blanche’s turn to stare.

“Married to whom?” Aimerie fumed.

Miles’s smile broadened. “Why, to me, of course.”

That caused an even bigger commotion. “You?” Aimerie scoffed. “You’re a peasant.”

Miles said, “We were married secretly by Father Albinus of Redhill some weeks prior to this.”

Aimerie had recovered from the surprise of seeing Miles here. He shrugged. “No matter. We’ll kill you, and she’ll be a widow again.”

Miles was unfazed by Aimerie’s threat. “That will do you no good, my lord. She is pregnant.”

An uneasy hush fell over the hall. Guests looked from Aimerie to Blanche. Blanche's jaw fell open. She knew she should speak, but she could think of nothing to say.

Miles went on, still smiling. "You *can* kill me, Lord Aimerie, but then you'll have to raise my child as your own. Or you can kill the baby when it's born, but even you might think twice about doing that."

That caused an even greater uproar, people shouting at Miles.

Ernoul snarled and drew his new sword. "Time to try this out, I think."

He started toward the table.

There was a *thunk* and Ernoul stopped.

There was an arrow in his back.

In the gallery, blue-haired Hersent stood with her bow, her cloak thrown back over her shoulders.

Ernoul staggered, the arrow not fatal to his bull-like frame, and he started for the table again.

Ernoul's wounding gave Miles just enough time. He ran down the table, scattering cups, and jumped from the end, Ernoul in pursuit. Miles grabbed a spear from a stunned guard and turned. Ernoul was right behind him, sword raised. Before Ernoul could strike, Miles thrust the spear through Ernoul's mouth and out the back of his head.

He let the spear go and Ernoul fell, brains and blood on the floor. All round were shrieks and cries, and at that moment, there came the sound of fighting from the keep's ground-floor entrance.

Chapter 59

Sewale sidled up to Wada. "I'm freezin'. When do we start?"

"We'll know when, that's what Miles said," Wada replied.

"This waitin' gets to me. I like to get things done."

"Shouldn't be long now."

Wada and his men lagged about the keep's entrance door. It helped that the entrance, and the porch around it, was crowded, not only with men and women going to and from the kitchen, but also with servants of the nobles and manor stewards inside, braving the storm and hoping to grab a share of the food and drink when the nobles were finished with them.

The commotion at the bailey gate had intensified, with horns blowing.

"Think it's our lot?" Sewale said.

"Has to be," Wada said.

"East wall's still quiet. Few horns blew over there a while back; now, nothing. What happened to Toli?"

"No idea," said Wada, who was wondering the same thing.

People around them looked toward the gate, some of them pointing, commenting. At that moment, a man came down the stairs from the hall. He was maybe thirty and hard bitten, with long blond hair—a knight, judging by his fine clothes and the sword at his belt. He yelled at the guards to be alert and made his way slowly down the ramp, which was still crowded with people coming up. Frustrated by his rate of progress, the knight vaulted the ramp's rail and dropped into the mud below. He picked himself up, angrily brushed mud from his clothes, and continued toward the stairs that led down the hill.

Wada didn't have time to observe more because from the hall came a huge shout of surprise mingled with anger.

"There's our signal!" Wada yelled. "Now!"

Nearby, Ivor reached beneath his wet cloak and dragged his hammer from his belt. He turned and struck the nearest guard in the head with the hammer, and the man dropped like a felled ox.

Wada drew his scramasax and jammed it into the neck of another guard. Blood squirted. The guard yelled and tried to fight back, but he was stabbed in the chest by Sewale. The Edsworth brothers, Aelfhere and Aelfgard, leaped on another guard, dragging him to the ground and killing him with axes.

All around, people were yelling, trying to get out of the way. More shouting from the hall.

"Get inside!" Wada shouted to his men. Wada was supposed to be joined by Father Albinus and his group.

Along with Miles, they would capture the keep and take Aimerie and Ernoul prisoner. Or kill them. Either way, that should end the fight. Albinus wasn't here, though. Neither was Blackie, whose men were supposed to guard the bridge to the keep.

A guard thrust at Wada with a spear, which missed and pierced the side of a servant who was caught up in the press of men and women. Wada used his superior strength to wrest the spear from the guard. He tripped the man and, as they fell to the porch, Wada slammed his fist several times into the man's face, rendering him unconscious.

Wada rose, found his short sword, and made his way to the heavy, iron-studded door. The two surviving guards hastily attempted to shut the door. Ivor smashed one with his hammer. Aelfhere hacked the other one down with his axe.

"Inside!" Wada yelled. Just then, Father Albinus pounded up the ramp, pushing people aside, followed by four men.

Wada was surprised. "Where's the rest of your men?" he asked Albinus.

The priest jerked a thumb. "Back at the gate. They got caught—that's what the fight's about. We'll have to make do with what we have."

"Look," said Sewale, pointing.

In the bailey, armed men were pouring from the quarters. A lot of them. Wada said, "What the . . .?"

The knight who had left the hall formed the men into two lines. One line he sent to the gate. The other, he led toward the keep.

“Where did all those men come from?” Sewale said.

“Where the Devil is Blackie?” said Albinus.

“I don’t know, but let’s get into the hall while we still can,” Wada told them.

Chapter 60

Aimerie let out a cry of rage and grief. "My son! You've killed him!" Then he yelled, "Somebody give me a sword."

Before anyone could comply, Miles picked up Ernoul's sword, ran at Aimerie and swung the sword at him. The blow was blocked by a quick-thinking guard's spear. The guard went to thrust the spear at Miles when he was struck in the neck by an arrow from the gallery. The blue-haired woman, Miles guessed; there was no time to look.

One of Aimerie's knights tossed Aimerie a sword. Miles was no swordsman. He barely parried Aimerie's first slash, then he rolled over the table to the other side, as Aimerie's second blow thudded into the table's wood behind him.

Miles landed at Blanche's left side. He was aware of someone approaching to his own left. It was a mail-shirted guard, spear leveled. Miles recognized the man's rat-like face even as he knew he had no time to parry the man's thrust.

"Macaire!" Blanche cried. "Remember me?"

Macaire stopped. He looked at Blanche and stunned recognition flashed across his face. A heartbeat later a thrown dagger entered his left eye. He staggered and fell to the floor, screaming.

Miles looked to Blanche, who had thrown the dagger. "Got it right this time," she said.

People scrambled to get out of the hall. There was no screaming; these people had seen violence before. Some had seen a lot of it. Only Aimerie's knights had swords, the rest of the nobles were unarmed. The half-dozen remaining guards wore hauberks and helmets and carried shields. Some of the nobles loyal to Aimerie drew daggers. They formed a semi-circle around the head table, the only sound the scrabbling of Macaire's feet and his agonized cries of pain.

One of the guards used his shield to block Aimerie from another of the blue-haired woman's arrows. An arrow hit the guard in the side and he staggered.

"Get that damned woman!" Aimerie ordered.

A knight and two guards headed for the stairs to the gallery.

Miles and Blanche had the heavy oak table as a barrier between themselves and Aimerie's men, but the barrier wasn't impenetrable, because Aimerie's men could go around the table and attack from the sides.

Miles was ready with Ernoul's new sword; Blanche had picked up a carving knife. "Thank you for coming to rescue me," she told Miles.

"Glad to be of service," Miles said.

"I have one favor to ask. Next time, can you try to think of a plan that actually works?"

"I'll do my best," Miles said.

Aimerie, his three knights, and the loyal nobles took a place across the table from Miles and Blanche. The remaining guards circled the table and came at Miles and Blanche from the sides.

Aimerie's rage had cooled. "Take them alive," he ordered the guards. "I want him to put on a show before he dies, and I want her to watch."

The guards advanced. Miles readied the sword. "Get behind me," he told Blanche.

"And spoil my wedding day?" she said. "Not likely."

There was a scuffle at the entrance way. Father Albinus pushed into the hall, followed by Wada and Sewale and the others. The guards who had been advancing on Miles and Blanche turned to meet this new threat. So did the knights. Aimerie fell back, swearing.

Swinging his axe, Albinus bulled his way to the table while the others took on Aimerie's men. "Where's the rest of your men?" Miles asked.

"This is all there is," Father Albinus said. "And there's the Devil of a lot of Aimerie's men right behind us."

Miles swore, then he grabbed Blanche's hand. "Quick! To the gallery!"

Chapter 61

Blackie's men had left the woods before the other groups did. They had more ground to cover.

Blackie kept his bow beneath his sodden cloak for what little protection that might provide it from the storm. He hadn't strung the bow yet—in this weather, the tension on the string wouldn't hold long. He was glad he'd brought extra strings with him.

They went the long way round, passing behind the village, not wanting to attract notice from the guards on the watchtowers by the gate. The few villagers who were about were suspicious of these men, and two women, crossing their land.

A middle-aged man who was probably the reeve accosted them. "Who are you?"

A crowd gathered, not a friendly one. "Be you robbers?" the reeve went on with narrowed eyes.

Blackie held up his hands peaceably. "We're not robbers. We're just passing through."

"Ha!" said an old woman "In this storm? With ladders like that? Likely story. Make sure you stay out of our fields."

"And leave our animals alone," another man added, "or it'll go the worse for you."

"We're watching you," the old woman warned.

Blackie's group tightened their formation and went on. A horn sounded from the direction of the bailey gate, followed by shouting.

"Father Albinus and his crowd must have been discovered," Blackie said.

"They were supposed to get through without that happening," said Edwine, Will's older brother.

"That's war," said Blackie. "Nothing ever goes the way it's supposed to."

Blackie found himself worrying about Ediva. He hoped she was all right. He wished she hadn't gone off with Miles; he wished she hadn't come with this expedition at all. Despite what had happened to her friend Hugh, the girl thought herself invincible. Blackie felt responsible for her somehow, maybe because he didn't have any kids of his own—none that he knew about, anyway. It was past time for him to take a wife and settle down, yet he always resisted—resisted responsibility, the loss of freedom. Was that selfish of him, or a by-product of his having been a soldier? There was no one in his sight to marry—all the girls he'd known from his younger days were taken—but that didn't bother him. Women were where you found them, and he was popular with the whores. Still . . .

Edwine's voice: "Blackie."

Blackie looked up to see a group of men blocking their path. The men carried axes and knives and short swords, along with pitchforks, scythes, and bills. There were hedges on both sides of the path here, so there was no chance of going around. More armed men from the village had come up and blocked the party's rear.

They had walked into a trap.

"Friendly lookin', ain't they?" said Edwine. "Maybe they come to invite us to dinner."

"If they did, looks like they'll be serving something sharp," Blackie said.

The leader of the men blocking the path was burly—huge, even—with a bushy blond beard, the kind of man who looked like he enjoyed a good fight. Probably because he always won. He wore a leather coif under his hood. Rain dripped from his face. "What's with them ladders?" the man asked Blackie in a good-natured voice. "You boys building a house? Good day for it."

The others laughed, and the leader went on, his tone sharper. "You ain't from around here. What're you up to?"

The men from behind closed in. Blackie's men fingered their weapons.

The leader took a step forward. "Better talk," he warned Blackie.

There was no choice but tell the truth. "We're going to attack the castle," Blackie said.

"Don't fuck with me," the leader warned.

"It's the truth," Blackie said.

"Bullshit. You swear?"

"I swear. We're from Redhill."

A second man said, "Wait a bit, you some of them Hoods?"

"We're what's left of 'em," Blackie said.

The leader's hard face softened. "Well, bless me, whyn't you say so in the first place? Always admired you boys. Wish we could've helped you, but there's no chance of that while you're working for Aimerie. Hated to see you boys get beat." He thought. "Hell, if you're goin' to attack the castle, maybe we'll join you."

"Aye," the man beside him said, "We hate that bastard Aimerie. Hate his whelp Ernoul even more. We have to put up with those fuckers every day. You can't imagine what that's like."

The leader inclined his head in the direction of the castle. "Sounds like fighting at the gate already. Friends of yours?"

"Aye," Blackie said.

The leader smiled and extended a paw. "Name's Ordgard."

Blackie took his hand. "Glad to have you with us. I'm Ulf, but everybody calls me Blackie."

"Why're you attacking the castle now?" Ordgard asked.

"We come to save Lady Blanche," Blackie said.

"Save 'er from what?"

"From Aimerie. He kidnapped her."

The villagers looked at each other. "That ain't the story he puts out," said one.

Another added, "Aye, Aimerie put it about that she asked him to marry her. Begged him, so he says."

"Aimerie lied," Blackie said. "He took her from Redhill by force."

"Bastard," Ordgard said. "I don't hold with kidnappin' women, even if they are French." He turned, "Edhere, take a couple men and block the miller's house. If he gets wind of what's up, he'll warn Aimerie, sure as shit."

The man called Edhere and two others set off down the storm-swept lane. "You in charge?" Ordgard asked Blackie.

Blackie shrugged. "Ex-soldier. Near eight years' service."

"Fair enough," Ordgard said. "Lead on, then."

The two groups from Brightwood merged, and the party, now at more than double its original strength, went on. The sound of fighting from the gate grew louder, more horns blaring the alarm. Toli's bunch should have started their diversion by now, but that side of the bailey was quiet. Everything seemed to be going wrong.

Blackie and his party came parallel to the bailey wall. There was a large open space, used for exercising horses, between the lane and the wall. The men formed up at the edge of the field, and Blackie divided them into sections of five, each with a leader. For the benefit of the newcomers, and to refresh the memories of his own men, he said, "The plan is for us to go to the bridge to the keep, cover it, and prevent Aimerie's men from using it to reinforce the keep. Father Albinus and his lot will attack the keep itself."

"Sounds like this Albinus might be stuck at the gate," Ordgard pointed out.

"We'll worry about that when we get to the bridge," Blackie said. With luck, the guards on this part of the wall, or most of them, had been pulled away to join the fight at the gate.

Blackie bent his bow and strung it. Edwine did the same. So did a couple of the men from Brightwood. "Ready?" Blackie asked the men. "Let's go."

They crossed the churned-up open space. It was hard going, fighting the wind and rain. Several men lost shoes in the deep mud. Blackie and his men were tired from the march here and half frozen, as well. On the wall, there was no sign of guards. So far, the plan had worked.

Blackie was not surprised to find the ditch full of water, not in this weather. "In you go, lads," he said. He grinned at the two women. "You, too, ladies."

"Bugger yourself," said the younger one, a pretty thing named Hild, but she smiled at him as she said it.

The party went into the ditch and made their way across. Blackie held his bow and quiver over his head. He slipped in the ditch's uneven bottom, but managed to keep the bow and quiver from going under. Some of the foul water sloshed into his mouth, and he spit it out in disgust,

On the far side, they climbed out, helping each other on the slippery bank. Blackie pulled Hild up, and she acknowledged his help with another smile. The ladders were carried to the wall and raised. Blackie raised his hand. "Up!"

Blackie went first, bow in one hand, climbing as quickly as he dared. As he went higher, the rickety ladder swayed dangerously in the wind. At the top, he grabbed the pointed end of one of the logs that made up the wall, held onto it, and edged through the gap between two logs onto the walkway.

He turned to see a guard in the nearby watchtower staring at him in amazement, too surprised, it seemed, to sound the alarm. Blackie nocked an arrow and shot the man in the chest. He dropped from sight.

"Good shot," said Ordgard, who was first up the other ladder.

The rest of the men poured up the ladders. Hild and the other woman came last. The men steadied the ladders at the top for the women, then hauled the ladders up, in case they were needed later. Blackie and Edwine nocked arrows, but no more guards appeared in the tower.

"Check that guard I shot," Blackie told a man. "Make sure he's dead."

Below them, around the gate, a confused fight raged, its noise muted by the storm. Impossible to tell who was getting the better of it.

To Edwine and Ordgard, Blackie said, "You thinkin' what I'm thinkin'?"

"Take 'em from behind?" Ordgard said.

Blackie nodded.

"Those ain't our orders," Edwine said.

Blackie knew a soldier should obey orders. It was a principle he lived by. But a soldier should also show initiative and adapt to changed circumstances. "We're supposed to guard the bridge while Albinus takes the keep, but Albinus can't get to the keep if he's bottled up at the gate, so us bein' at the bridge won't help anybody," he told Edwine.

Ordgard nodded agreement to that.

Blackie raised his voice so that everyone could hear. “The plan has changed. We’re going to go down and hit those bastards in the yard. Ordgard and Edwine, take your sections and capture the watchtowers. Ordgard, take your archers with you. The rest of us will go down and pile into the fight from behind. Then it’s on to the keep. Everybody got it?”

Nods all around.

“Let’s go, then.”

Chapter 62

Blackie and his men clambered down the stairs from the bailey wall. Ordgard and his section attacked the watch tower on this side of the gate, climbing the ladder to its entrance and taking its occupants by surprise, while Edwine's men crossed the yard and captured the tower on the gate's far side.

The fighting at the gate was confused. Men pushing and shoving, yelling, horns blowing. The gate and bridge were narrow, so the defenders were able to hold on with fewer men than those they faced. The guards were easy to distinguish—leather jacks, mail shirts some of them, along with spears or swords and helmets. Blackie nocked an arrow and loosed. Missed—the target moved. Another arrow. Hit a guard in the back of the thigh. The guard reached back and grabbed his leg, and as he did, the man he was fighting rammed a short sword into his throat.

Blackie slung his bow. He might need the arrows later. He drew his axe and joined his men charging into the rear of the gate's defenders, stabbing with knives and swords and pitchforks, slashing with bills and scythes. Aimerie's surprised men turned and tried to fight back, but it was useless. Arrows rained down on them from the captured watch towers. Beyond the gate, in the group fighting to get in, Blackie made out Toli and the reeve, Hamo. Toli must have abandoned his original plan of attack for some reason. There was no sign of Father Albinus.

Aimerie's men were surrendering, running, a few still fighting. Then came a bellow from the watch tower. "Blackie!"

It was Ordgard, pointing.

Blackie looked over his shoulder, and through the driving rain and snow he saw a line of armed men crossing the bailey yard. They carried round shields and spears and wore helmets—soldiers. Led by a big blond fellow, a group of similarly equipped men double-timed up the hill to the castle's keep, crossing the unguarded bridge that Blackie was supposed to be defending.

"Where did they come from?" Blackie swore. Joining the fight at the gate had seemed like a good idea, but it might have been a death sentence for Miles and his group in the keep. Blackie had fucked this up, no error. Whatever happened to Miles was Blackie's fault.

"Turn around! Turn around!" Blackie yelled to his men, physically grabbing them by collars and hoods and turning them.

He was faced with a fight on both sides, as the remnants of Aimerie's guards were inspired to battle on. Arrows flew from the watch towers at these new men, but there were not enough archers, and most of the arrows were deflected by shields. The towers were abandoned before they became death traps.

"There's too many," said Ordgard, coming up. "We can't fight them." Toli was there, too, and grizzled Hamo.

Some of Blackie's men were already running away from the gate, back to the woods. Others remounted the wall and used the ladders to escape, or held on to the pointed logs and dropped into the water-filled ditch, hoping for the best.

"We can't stay here," Toli said.

"If we retreat, we'll abandon Miles," Blackie said. He waved an arm. "Get around that line and join Miles at the keep!"

His men—those who hadn't fled—tried to run around the disciplined line that approached them, and many were successful since these new men had no archers and their line did not extend across the entire bailey. Not all of them made it, though. Hamo went down with a thrown spear in the back, and he was not the only one.

At an order, the soldiers broke their ranks and started after Blackie's men. Blackie stopped, to cover the rear. Ordgard joined him with an axe. Blackie unslung his bow, shot an arrow, dropped one of the soldiers. Another. Edwine joined them.

"Go on!" Blackie yelled at the rest of his men. "Go!"

Hild hesitated, as though she wanted to stay with Blackie. He waved her toward the keep. "Go! Go!"

The first soldiers were on them. Blackie threw down his bow and drew the axe from his belt. He knew his only chance was to get inside the reach of the soldiers' spears. He and Ordgard ran forward, while Edwine let go a last arrow.

Blackie banged into a shield. Swung his axe over the top of it. Chopped through a hard layer, then something soft. Heard a sigh and the man fell. Turned to the next man. As he did, something sliced through his side, cold at first, then burning hot. His legs got wobbly, then he lost the use of them altogether. He felt dizzy. Dropped to his knees.

There was a roar from the wall. Armed men were pouring over it, led by a man with a blond beard and topknot, his bare chest covered with inked designs.

Chapter 63

Miles and his party fought their way to the stairs, Miles shielding Blanche and Ediva. He swung Ernoul's sword at Joubert, missed, but forced Joubert back and opened the stairs to the others. Isabel drove a shoulder into a guard who was about to spear Miles. Another guard hit her in the head with the haft of his spear, and she fell unconscious.

The knight opposite Miles advanced with his sword, but before he could strike, Ivor bashed him between the shoulder blades with his blacksmith's hammer, crushing the man's upper spine. Wada bulled some of the newly entered soldiers aside, while Albinus and Aelfgar struck at them with axes. Sewale kicked a knight in the genitals, and as the knight bent over, Aelfhere stabbed him. Aimerie, in turn, struck at Aelfhere, gashing his thigh.

They started up the stairs to the gallery, Father Albinus and Wada leading. Aelfgar helped his brother, Aelfhere, who grimaced, blood flowing from the wound to his leg. Still holding the carving knife, Blanche gathered Ediva. "Come." They were followed by Sewale and Ivor.

Miles covered the rear, slashing at Aimerie, who was right behind him. The stairs curved to the left, so Miles had free use of his sword arm, while Aimerie had his field of motion constricted by the wall on his right, and that was the only thing that saved Miles's life.

Aimerie's face was constricted by rage and frustration. "You'll pay for what you did to Ernoul."

A knight and two guards had gone up the stairs before them, chasing the blue-haired woman. At the top of the stairs, the blue-haired woman shot the knight with an arrow as he came round the last curve to the landing. He fell and tumbled back, knocking the two guards off balance. They were attacked from behind by Albinus and Wada. Albinus dispatched one with his axe; Wada stabbed the other with his short sword.

Followed closely by Aimerie and his soldiers, Miles ran up the last stairs to the gallery, stepping over the bodies of the knight and the two guards. The blue-haired woman covered him as he reached the landing. Aimerie and the other pursuers were wary of her bow and hung back.

The gallery ran around the second floor of the hall. It was packed with guests and the musicians. Men and women backed against the stone walls or cowered in the alcoves, some of them begging not to be killed.

"Get them out of here," Miles ordered. "Hurry! They'll block the stairs and buy us some time. Make sure no one's hiding in those latrines, too."

Albinus and the others alternately threatened and pushed the people in the gallery toward the stairs. Most were only too happy to go, and they jammed the narrow stairway, preventing Aimerie and his men from coming up.

Tables lined the gallery walls. "Bring those tables over," Miles shouted. "Barricade the top of the stairs. Leave a gap for us to attack through."

Blanche helped Miles turn over one of the tables and push it toward the barricade. "How did you know I was pregnant?" she asked him.

Miles stopped, and his jaw fell. "What?" After a second, he went on, "I . . . I made that up. Why didn't you tell me?"

"I was only certain of it myself yesterday."

Miles continued to stare, and she added, "You must have known it was going to happen eventually."

When the table was in place, Blanche crossed the gallery to the blue-haired woman, who watched what was going on below. "How many arrows do you have left?" Blanche said.

"Not enough," the woman replied.

"Thank you for what you did," Blanche told her.

"I didn't do it for you, or for Miles," the blue-haired woman said. "I planned to kill Ernoul all along, that's why I brought my bow. Ernoul raped me. More than once."

Blanche pursed her lips in sympathy. "Your name is Hersent, is it not?"

"Yes," said the woman.

"Pretty name," said Wada, grinning at her as he helped Aelfgar drag one of the tables past.

Hersent rewarded Wada with a smile. "Remember it for my headstone."

Below, more soldiers crowded into the hall. They, along with Aimerie, tried to get the people coming down from the gallery out of the way, pushing them and swearing at them. Archers joined the soldiers. A flight of arrows came over the gallery railing and through the thick arches. Most rattled off the stone walls, but one hit Sewale in the hip while he was pushing a table, and he fell, swearing mightily.

Miles chanced a look around one of the gallery arches. As he did, an arrow bounced off the stone near his head. Aimiably, he called down to the hall. "Where did all your new men come from, Aimerie?"

Down below, Aimerie regarded Miles with loathing, but he couldn't hide his own self-admiration. Joubert stood beside him with a smug look on his face. "I brought them in secretly," Aimerie said. "I intend to spend Christmas at Bradford Castle. No one will expect an attack at Christmas."

Miles was surprised. "Big gamble, isn't it? Earl Galon won't like that."

"It's called a *fait accompli*, Miles. I'll take Badford Castle and make myself earl. Galon is in France. The king won't allow him to start a war against me in this country, and the king won't commit the resources to drive me out of Trentshire himself. There will be a lot of negotiation, but in the end I will be allowed to keep Trentshire, in return for paying the king and Galon a tidy fortune. That money will come from Galon's estates here—and from yours—so I don't mind."

"Very clever," Miles acknowledged.

"Thank you," said Aimerie, inclining his head. "After that, things get very interesting. Pity you won't be alive to see any of it. And I'll trouble you to remove your peasant hands from my son's sword."

"I plan to," Miles said. "Right after I drive this sword through your heart."

Aimerie laughed derisively. Another arrow flew by Miles's head, just missing him. Hersent raised her bow to reply, but Miles stopped her. "Save your arrows for when they rush us."

The crowd was finally off the stairway. Soldiers clattered up the stairs. The first man around the head of the stairs was shot with an arrow by Hersent. He fell, and as the others tried to step over the body, Miles, Wada, Ivor, and Father Albinus burst through the gap in the barricade of tables and attacked them. Wada had gotten rid of the short sword and was using his iron bar again. The soldiers were at a disadvantage, fighting from below. Two were killed, another had his arm shattered by Wada's iron bar, and the rest fell back. The bodies at the head of the stairs became another obstacle for the soldiers to overcome.

Another rush. Again, Hersent shot the first man and the rest were attacked by Miles and his companions. Archers fired into the gallery from below. Aelfgar went down, struck just below the eye. Ediva ran through the gallery, picking up the spent arrows and giving them to Hersent.

"Stop," Aimerie ordered his archers. "You're giving that bitch more arrows to use against us."

Another rush. Another. Each time, the first man went down while those following were attacked by Miles and his men. Father Albinus reeled back up the steps, bleeding from a wound in the side. "God damn it to Hell!"

Ediva chided him. "You're using bad words, Father."

Albinus grimaced, and in a kindlier tone he said, "Yes, child, I'm using bad words. The Church permits it when you've been stabbed."

Blanche tended the injured as best she could, cleaning their wounds, bandaging them, and giving them watered wine. Ediva tossed empty wine jugs on the soldiers and guards below, hitting a couple of them on the head and driving them back with yells of pain. When there were no more wine jugs, she threw the musicians' instruments—a viol, a tabor, a pipe. Blaise, the knight who had brought the reinforcements, threw a spear that struck the already wounded Aelfhere in the chest. There was another rush at the stairs, and Wada was slashed down the left arm.

Hersent shot her last arrow. The pile of dead and wounded at the head of the stairs had become considerable, and Aimerie's men started dragging them away. At first they were hesitant, afraid of Hersent's bow, but when they realized she wouldn't—or couldn't—shoot, they grew bolder. They cleared the stairs almost all the way to the tables, behind which Miles, Wada, and Ivor crouched.

Below them, Aimerie prepared his men for the final rush.

"Well, we tried," Miles told his companions.

Wada's arm had been wrapped by Blanche, but it was already wet with blood. "I've no regrets," he said. "Please God we all meet in the hereafter."

"Hope there's a tavern up there," said Ivor, who was flush faced from his exertions. " 'Tis quite the thirst I've worked up."

Blanche joined the three men, ducking behind a table. She had left the carving knife and now carried Wada's short sword.

"Get out of here," Miles told her. "Take Ediva and get to the far corner."

"No," she said, "I'll stay beside you."

"But—"

"Don't question me," she ordered, dark eyes blazing. "You forget that I am your lord."

"What about the baby?" Miles said.

"Do you think Aimerie will let it live?"

Miles knew the answer to that, and he hardened himself for what was to come.

Aimerie marshaled his men and led them slowly up the stairs. "Miles is mine," he told the men. "Keep Blanche alive, if you can."

There was a commotion from the hall.

Aimerie stopped, looking back. Miles, Blanche, and Wada left the barricade and peered through one of the gallery arches.

More men had entered the hall, led by Fromont, bare chested as always. Some of Miles's men were with them, including Simon and Toli. "Fromont!" cried Joubert in welcome. Then he saw Simon and Toli, "Why are those rebels with you?"

"They're not with me," Fromont said. "I'm with them." He drove his axe into Joubert's head.

This was followed by shouts and renewed fighting.

While everyone was distracted, Aimerie ran forward and slashed Ivor with his sword. He darted through the gap in the barricade and made his way up the stairs to the roof.

Miles charged after him, Ernoul's sword in his hand. He heard Aimerie's feet pounding the steps ahead of him, so he didn't have to search the third-floor living quarters, or be wary of an ambush on the curving stairs. Above him, the door to the roof opened, and cold air rushed down the stairway. The door didn't close.

Miles moved warily now, sword ready. He came to the roof landing, saw Aimerie waiting on the walkway, sword in hand.

Miles stepped onto the slippery walkway. Into the wind and rain and snow. Into the freezing cold. His wet hair whipping around his head in the wind.

Below, the fighting in the bailey yard and around the keep slowed, then stopped, as men saw what was happening on the battlements.

Miles approached Aimerie slowly, thinking of the best way to fight him, the best way to kill him. Aimerie was a skilled swordsman, and Miles realized that he had been tricked. There was no way he could beat Aimerie. He had been lured up here to his doom.

There was nothing he could do about it, though. He had to see it through. He gripped Ernoul's sword tightly.

At that moment, Aimerie reversed his sword and laid the blade across his left arm, hilt pointed toward Miles. "I surrender," he said.

Chapter 64

Miles stopped. "What?"

"You heard me," Aimerie said, "I surrender. I give up. I quit. I won't surrender to a peasant, of course. I'm surrendering to your mistress, through you."

Miles felt cheated. In anger, he raised his sword.

"There are witnesses," Aimerie warned him, inclining his head toward the battlement.

Miles glanced over the battlement, saw upturned faces, watching.

"Why?" he asked Aimerie. "You'll be beheaded for what you've done."

"Don't be so dramatic, Miles. I'm a noble. The only thing that can get me beheaded is treason, which I've not committed. Not yet, anyway. If I'm guilty of anything, it's ambition, which makes me no different from any other member of my class. The king will strip me of all my possessions, of course, but he's done that before. After that, he'll send me back to Normandy, and I'll begin again."

Miles knew this was true. That was how the system worked. He thought of all the dead and wounded, of all the blood spilled, the lives ruined. Had it all been for nothing? Had it all been some kind of game? A game played for people with the right blood?

Aimerie smiled, still holding out the sword.

Miles sighed with resignation and moved forward to accept it. Then he rushed Aimerie, picked him up, and heaved him over the battlement.

* * *

Blackie lay curled on his side in the cold, wet mud.

The pain in his side was terrific, but lying curled up like this eased it a bit. They said sleep was the best treatment for injuries, so maybe he should try to sleep. He closed his eyes . . .

He was an infant again, in a walker his father had built for him, with little wheels at the corners and a rail around it to keep him standing upright. It was a beautiful autumn day, and his mother was there, picking apples. "Blackie," she said.

But his mother never called him Blackie. For some reason, the voice was Ediva's and she was crying. "Blackie . . ."

He smiled. The pain was going away.

Sleep came.

EPILOGUE

Brightwood Castle

December 1106 A.D.

"Damned mess," Lord Tutbury grumbled. "Shocking. We could have lost the kingdom."

Tutbury, the king's justice and now sheriff for Trentshire, held court in the castle's hot, crowded hall. Miles's messenger had gotten through to him, and he had come forthwith, with as many soldiers as he could raise on short notice, alarmed by news of a possible rebellion in western Trentshire. He had been told of Aimerie's plot to depose King Henry in favor of William Clito, with Aimerie as lord protector.

Most of the local nobles were present, along with the stewards of nobles who were in France. Near them were their former enemies, Fromont and his outlaws, as well as Hersent, who had let her hair go back to its natural red, and some of the outlaw women. Also present was Guillame of Edsworth, looking wan and thin, accompanied by Blanche's maid, Millicent. Guillame had hovered at the edge of death for a month, but Milli nursed him back to life. They had fallen in love and were to be married in the spring. The leading men from Redhill, Fairleigh, and Edsworth—Wada, Simon, and Toli—were there, as well. Wada was puffed up because he could finally wear his wolf-fur cloak again. Almost as important, Miles had appointed him steward of Redhill. The only member of Aimerie's entourage who was present was the knight Blaise, who had repented his deeds and taken service with Tutbury. No one was armed save for the soldiers who surrounded the hall.

Miles thought of those who weren't present, of Blackie and Ivor, who had died from the wound given to him by Aimerie. Of Hamo, Evrard, Aelfhere, Will, Ailwyn, and the rest. Sewale had lived, but he walked with a limp from his wound and was in constant pain. Isabel suffered headaches from when she'd been struck by the spear haft. Ediva had been broken up about Blackie, to whom she had become quite attached, and she had vowed to be a normal farm girl from here on out. She and Hild had become good friends.

The hearth burned brightly, and Tutbury warmed himself near it, coughing from the smoke. The blood and wreckage of fighting had been cleaned up. Soon the hall would be decorated with ivy. Miles wondered if they'd be able to get a Yule log up here, or if—being French—they would even try. Outside, several inches of snow covered the ground.

Tutbury looked as well fed as ever. He still wore the embroidered yellow robe, and he still had a young woman with him, though not the same woman Miles had seen him with last summer. This one was dark and sultry, and she sat at the head table, admiring her nails.

Tutbiry's gilded chair of justice was placed in front of the head table. At a small table to one side of the chair sat a boyish clerk, with a stack of quills, a pot of ink, and sheets of parchment.

Tutbury moved away from the fire and assumed a spot in front of his chair. He looked round the hall. "Nice place, I'll give Aimerie credit. Wish it were mine. This weather keeps up, I may have to spend Christmas here."

"What about your wife, my lord?" his clerk asked.

Tutbury glanced back at his young woman. "Yes, well, I'm sure Mathilde will understand if I have to stay. Duty and all."

The clerk said nothing. When Tutbury wasn't looking, he winked at the young woman.

Blanche stood beside Miles. Her pregnancy was barely showing, but her face had a . . . a glow. Miles knew that's what they always called it, but he couldn't think of a better word. She looked more beautiful than ever now that she was with child, and Miles was amazed that God in His wisdom had thought to make women that way.

"To business," Tutbury said. He held out a hand in the direction of the head table. "Wine."

A servant scurried over with a chased goblet. Tutbury sipped and lifted his thick grey brows in surprise. "This is excellent."

Blanche inclined her head. "The wine comes from Redhill, my lord."

Tutbury's brows rose higher. "You have a winery, Lady Blanche?"

"We do."

"In England? Will wonders never cease." Tutbury took another sip and began. "First. As you are aware, we have dodged a great threat to the king, and to the kingdom. It is unthinkable that Lord Aimerie's plot should have been allowed to progress so far. Those of you who pledged fealty to Aimerie have been forgiven by King Henry, since the plot was apparently kept secret from you. However, you will be subject to fines by your liege lords, as they see fit."

Murmurs and groans of resignation sounded through the hall. Lords didn't appreciate disloyalty, and some of these fines were liable to be heavy. A number of the stewards who had supported Aimerie would likely lose their posts.

Tutbury continued. "Second. In the matter of this castle, which was constructed illegally. On the advice of the royal surveyors, King Henry has decided not to tear it down. Instead, he will make it a royal castle. A castellan will be appointed and take possession by summer. As for the manor of Brightwood, there seem to be no heirs, Aimerie having killed them all. Therefore, the king grants said manor to Blanche of Redhill, with the rents unchanged but with the imposition of one additional knight's fee."

More murmuring around the hall. Blanche and Miles shared a glance.

Tutbury went on. "Lady Blanche. You claim to be married to the Englishman Miles?"

Blanche stepped forward, head high. "I do, my lord. Father Albinus, of our parish, married us on the feast of St. Cecilia. As soon as he was well enough to do so."

Albinus beamed from the crowd. He was still bandaged and couldn't perform heavy labor, but he was healing well from his wound.

Tutbury frowned at Blanche. "That was not part of the arrangement you made with the king. You were not to marry without his permission."

Blanche attempted to sound contrite. "I know, my lord. But things . . . happened."

Tutbury harrumphed. "You have rendered the king good service in this affair. More than good service, you may have saved his crown. Therefore, he is willing to overlook your transgression. Your marriage will be permitted to stand, in return for a . . ."

"For a fee?" Blanche finished for him.

"A fee, just so."

Blanche smiled. "I expected no less."

"Howbeit, the king cannot have you married to a peasant. That would never do for the widow of an earl, and a great landowner in her own right. Consequently, Miles will have to be made a knight."

There was a buzz from the crowd, some applause from the English, enraged grumbling from the French. This meant that Miles the Englishman would be lord of three manors. This meant that Miles the Englishman would be an important man in this part of the world.

Miles was taken aback. "I—I don't know what to say, my lord. I . . ."

His voice drifted off. He hadn't expected this, and he wasn't sure he was happy about it. He had rejected the path of knighthood years before, when it was offered to him by Earl Thibault of Trent, but this time he had no choice. He'd have to socialize with the French nobles now, and he didn't like that—or them. More importantly, his children by Blanche would be nobles. That meant his sons would be knights, soldiers. Miles had seen war, and he didn't like it. He'd have preferred his sons to be tillers of the soil, as was right and proper. Still, the reality was that nobility was the life Miles had been born into, the life he would have had if the battle at Sand Lake had gone differently.

Tutbury turned to his clerk. "Damned lot of English knights we've got of a sudden—eh, Samson?"

The clerk had been gazing at the sultry young woman. Hastily he turned back. "There are, my lord."

"Let's see. There's Galon's man, Stigand, and now Miles. That's two, and that's just in Trentshire. We're setting a dangerous precedent here."

Samson lifted dark brows. "Indeed, my lord."

"Still, it can't be helped, not in this case anyway. Don't want to make a habit of it, though."

"I should think not, my lord."

Tutbury beckoned for more wine and sipped. "Next, we have the so-called 'Brotherhood.' "

He shifted his gaze to Fromont and his followers. After meeting Miles and Blackie in the forest, Fromont, who never forgave Ernoul for what he had done to Hersent—and Aimerie, for having allowed it—had persuaded his men to join the attack on the castle. Many had refused to join in, but enough had accompanied Fromont to turn the tide of battle long enough for Miles to kill Aimerie. After Aimerie's death, his mercenaries and guards had lost heart, and the fighting had stopped. And the outlaws had discreetly looted what they could.

Tutbury said, "You men have been a plague to this area for too long. You are all hereby sentenced to death."

There was a shocked uproar from the outlaws. The armed soldiers around the hall braced themselves for trouble.

Tutbury raised a hand and shouted, "However!"

The hall quieted.

Tutbury went on. "However, because you men aided Lady Blanche, King Henry has offered to suspend your sentences and transport you and your dependents to Normandy, where he and his nobles are in need of experienced soldiers."

Relief among the outlaws. Smiles. A few cheers.

Tutbury went on. "Those who do not wish to go to Normandy will be offered lands to replace the men killed in the recent unpleasantness. Alton Forest is to be cleared out, and any outlaws found living there past the feast of St. Benedict will be killed."

Fromont beamed with satisfaction and turned. "Hersent?"

"I'm not going to France," Hersent informed him.

"Why?"

"For one thing, it's full o' Frenchies, and I ain't forgot what they done to my family." She went on. "Think I might take Lord T. up on his offer. Stay here, settle down, maybe start a family. I've always fancied that." A smile played about her lips, and her eyes rested on Wada's, who grinned at her.

Fromont didn't seem surprised. He accepted his rejection with good grace. "I thought you might. I'd like to settle down, as well, but not yet. I have a yen to do some real soldiering again. Who knows, maybe this time I'll capture an important lord, ransom him, and get rich."

Tutbury had more wine, waited for the outlaws to stop talking among themselves, or at least to quiet down a bit. "Lastly, we must consider the question of Baron Aimerie's death. We have witnesses to that unfortunate event—most of them reluctant, I might add. It seems that Aimerie surrendered and that, you, Miles, threw him from the battlements of this castle."

The audience stirred.

Tutbury was grave. "Are these the facts?"

Miles straightened. He couldn't lie about it. "They are, my lord."

"Aimerie went against the crown, it is true, but the fact remains that you are English, and a peasant. An English peasant is not allowed to touch a Norman noble, much less hurl one from the roof of a castle."

More stirring from the crowd, the French among them hoping that the upstart Miles had been led into a trap.

Blanche stepped forward. "Miles is my steward. He was acting on my orders."

Tutbury stared at her for a long moment. "You ordered him to throw Aimerie from the roof?"

"I told him to kill Aimerie. I didn't specify how he was to do it."

"And you will swear an oath to that effect?"

"I will," Blanche said.

Tutbury turned to the clerk. "That should suffice, eh, Samson?"

The clerk almost got caught looking at Tutbury's young woman again. "It should, my lord. Besides, this Miles is to be made a noble. If you like, we can back date his knighting to before Aimerie was killed, just to make everything legal and above board. There can't be any questions about what he did, then."

Tutbury nodded agreement. "Very well." He turned. "Miles, you have done the king—and me—great service this year. I speak for the king when I say that we are grateful, but that we desire your good deeds to cease. I do not want to hear your name spoken in my court again."

Miles grinned. "You won't, my lord."

Blanche hooked her arm through Miles's. "That's right, my lord. From now on, we're going to spend our lives in peace and quiet."

About the Author

Robert Broomall is the author of a number of published novels, including the popular *Death's Head (Roger of Huntley)* trilogy. Besides writing, his chief interests are travel and history, especially military history, the Old West, and the Middle Ages. He also likes to cook, much to the dismay of those who have to eat what he prepares.

Amazon author page:
https://www.amazon.com/author/robertbroomall

Facebook:
https://www.facebook.com/RobertBroomall.author

Connect with Bob:
robertbroomall@gmail.com

Made in the USA
Columbia, SC
15 September 2023